JILL SORENSON

BACKWOODS

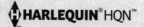

PLEASE RECYCLE · THIS PRODUCT IS RECYCLABLE

Recycling programs for this product may not exist in your area.

ISBN-13: 978-0-373-77872-0

BACKWOODS

Copyright © 2014 by Jill Sorenson

HARLEQUIN®

™ www.Harlequin.com

Printed in U.S.A.

CHAPTER ONE

ABBY'S ANXIETY INCREASED with every mile she drove away from the main road.

She tightened her hands around the steering wheel, trying to ignore the sinking feeling in the pit of her stomach. Only twenty minutes had passed since she'd exited the freeway, but it seemed like longer. Her daughter, Brooke, was sitting in the passenger seat. She yawned into her hand, unfazed by the increasing remoteness and looming trees. At dusk, the branches took on menacing shapes, forming an oppressive canopy overhead.

"You didn't have to come," Brooke said.

Abby rolled her neck to relieve tension. "I wanted to."

"Mom."

Abby studied her daughter's pretty face. It was hard to believe Brooke was almost nineteen. She was a young woman now, strong and confident. Abby's heart ached to look at her. "What?"

"You don't like hiking."

"I love hiking."

"Backwoods hiking?"

Abby made a noncommittal sound. She didn't like

backwoods *camping* because it meant being cut off from modern amenities, but she'd travel to the ends of the earth for Brooke. "I'll stay in the cabin. We can go on a few day hikes."

"You'll be bored."

"Never," Abby said, lifting her chin. She'd brought plenty of reading material, only half of which was work-related.

"Just don't try to coordinate activities, okay?"

Abby was the wellness director at Seaside Retirement Center in San Diego. She planned exercise classes, therapy sessions and outdoor excursions for the residents. It was a challenging job that required close attention to detail. Brooke had often complained of Abby's tendency toward scheduling every moment. OCD, she called it.

"You won't even know I'm there," Abby promised.

Brooke sighed, shaking her head.

They didn't discuss the main reason Abby had tagged along. She didn't trust her ex-husband to show up. He'd canceled last year's trip at the last minute. Ray Dwyer was a successful plastic surgeon, always running late or flaking out. He showered Brooke with expensive gifts instead of giving her his full attention.

Ray was supposed to arrive tonight with Lydia, his current wife, and Leo, her son from a previous marriage. Leo was about Brooke's age. The combined families would spend a week at the cabin, hanging out and exploring the wilderness. Brooke got along well with Lydia and Leo. She was an easygoing, well-adjusted child of divorce.

Abby wasn't so well-adjusted. She'd been co-parenting with Ray for seven years, and they were civil. Under normal circumstances, Abby wouldn't impose on their vacation. She didn't try to limit his visits or interfere in his relationship with Brooke. He'd taken her to Hawaii two summers ago. Ray was a good father—when he made the effort.

But if something went wrong and Ray changed his plans, which happened all too often, Brooke would be on her own. Abby didn't want her daughter traveling through the High Sierras by herself or hanging out alone at the cabin. It was easy to get lost in this area, by vehicle or on foot, and there were innumerable dangers. Last fall, a young couple had disappeared while camping in these woods. The boyfriend had turned up in a shallow grave. The girl's body was never found.

Abby shivered to think of what might have happened to her. A lost child was a mother's worst nightmare. Abby had been separated from Brooke for several days after the San Diego earthquake. The agony of not knowing if her daughter was dead or alive still haunted her. She continued to struggle with anxiety and overprotectiveness.

Abby had missed Brooke terribly since she'd gone off to college. They were still going through an adjustment period. Abby had been looking forward to reconnecting with her over the summer. Instead, Brooke had been traveling with friends and jumping from one activity to the next. Abby wanted to sit her down and hold her close, but Brooke seemed determined to maintain her newfound independence. Maybe she thought keeping her distance would make it easier to leave again.

Abby smothered the urge to ask Brooke how things were going at school again. Every time she reached out, Brooke retreated a little more.

"Where is this cabin, at the edge of nowhere?" she asked.

"Practically," Brooke said with a smile. "It's tucked right up against the mountains, close to the trailhead."

Brooke lived for adventure. She had the temperament of an extreme athlete, always pushing herself physically, game for any challenge. She was a track star at Berkeley. Whenever Brooke wasn't making Abby proud, she was driving Abby crazy with worry.

The cabin at the end of the road was no rustic shack, thankfully. It was an impressive getaway, sturdy and sprawling. Abby knew it boasted a full kitchen, three bedrooms and two bathrooms. There was a fireplace and a stocked fridge. Ray might not be reliable, but he didn't skimp on luxuries.

She parked next to a beat-up motorcycle in the driveway. "Whose is that?"

"It must be Leo's," Brooke said, her eyes bright with excitement. Not bothering to bring in her bags, she hopped out of the car and bounded to the front door.

Abby followed Brooke up the walk, pocketing the car keys. She was relieved that Ray and Lydia hadn't arrived yet. It had been a long drive. She needed a few minutes to collect herself, to take deep breaths and smooth her hair.

When Leo answered the door, Brooke tackled him with an exuberant hug. He stumbled backward, laughing in surprise. Although she was tall for a girl, almost his height, he didn't drop her or fall down. She clung to him for a few seconds and let go, squeezing his shoulder for good measure. "Is that your motorcycle?"

His lips curved into a smile. "Yeah."

"Take me for a ride."

Abby had never met Leo before, and he wasn't quite what she'd expected. He had a mop of jet-black hair, in dire need of cutting, and ragged clothes. His Green Day T-shirt, torn jeans and high-top sneakers gave him sort of a punk-rock edge. Although he didn't look like a jock, his physique appeared strong and lean.

Instead of agreeing to mount Brooke on his death machine, he cleared his throat and glanced at Abby.

"You must be Leo," she said, stepping forward. "You look exactly like your mother."

He didn't seem embarrassed by the comparison, as some boys might have been. But then, his mother was beautiful. "Thanks," he said easily.

"I think he looks like his father," Brooke said.

Leo frowned at this comment. Abby had only seen Leo's father in photographs, and in the infamous video clip that Leo had uploaded to YouTube. The pro baseball player had been falling-down drunk in the footage. It hadn't cast him in a very flattering light.

"Your dad is seriously hot," Brooke added.

He grimaced in distaste.

"Will your bike hold both of us?"

"Sure."

Abby studied the motorcycle with trepidation. Brooke was an adult now, so she couldn't forbid this activity. "There's only one helmet?"

"She can wear it," Leo said.

Brooke let out a squeal and ran toward the motorcycle, hair flying.

Abby rubbed her temples, trying not to visualize deadly accidents. Maybe she shouldn't have come on this trip. It was bound to be one anxiety attack after another. "Brooke, you should put on real shoes. Flip-flops aren't safe."

"She's right," Leo said.

Sticking her tongue out at Leo, Brooke opened the car door and grabbed her hiking boots. She sat down in the driveway to put them on quickly. Her jeans offered minimal protection against injury, but her tank top left her arms bare.

"And a jacket," Abby said.

"Oh my God, Mom. We're not going on the freeway."

Leo sided with Brooke this time. He was a teenage boy with a motorcycle, so his judgment was questionable. "I'll keep it under fifty, Miss…"

"Abby," she murmured, waving her permission.

He climbed aboard the bike and released the kickstand, passing the helmet to Brooke. She tugged it on and settled in behind him, curving her arms around his trim waist. With a loud pop, he started the engine. Seconds later, they were off.

Abby stood in the driveway for a long time, listening for the sound of screeching tires. Dark crept into the corners of the balmy evening, bringing a chill that only Abby could feel. Brooke and Leo, with their superior circulation and raging hormones, would be warm enough. She'd never considered the possibility that the stepsiblings might have romantic feelings for each other. Not that Brooke's overzealous embrace indicated as much. She was friendly with everyone, and often seemed unaware of her effect on men.

Abby unloaded her bags from the vehicle and went inside the cabin, sighing. The interior was beautiful, with high ceilings and exposed wood beams. A bouquet of purple wildflowers rested on a glass-topped coffee table in front of a leather couch. Abby found a room with a worn duffel bag on the bed, obviously Leo's. Bypassing that and the master suite, she retreated to the opposite end of the cabin to stake her claim.

In the bathroom, she washed up and scrutinized her appearance. She was healthy. She ran five miles on the treadmill every other day. Her figure was still good.

Since the divorce, work and motherhood had taken up most of her energy. She'd dated a physical therapist for several years, but their relationship had fizzled in recent months. Her daughter's absence had made her realize that something *else* was missing in her life. She'd rather be alone than settle for the wrong person.

It was a little embarrassing to be the fifth wheel at Ray's cabin, single and unattached. His betrayal with Lydia had devastated her. Maybe the missing piece was inside Abby, and she'd never be able to give herself completely to a man again.

Sighing, she reached for her favorite distraction: her cell phone. She'd found that redirecting her thoughts often helped her stay calm. Daily exercise, relaxation techniques and steady breathing worked, also.

Abby called her favorite person: Ella.

Her sister answered the phone with a throaty giggle. Abby could hear Ella's boyfriend, Paul, in the background. Ella had met Paul at California's Channel Islands last summer, on a previous ill-fated family adventure trip. After Ray canceled, Ella and Abby had stepped in to accompany Brooke. Paul had been their handsome kayak guide. Ella had ended up stranded for a night with him on remote, uninhabited San Miguel. They'd been inseparable ever since.

"We just got here," Abby said.

"How is it?"

She glanced around the bedroom. "It's nice. Ray and Lydia aren't here yet. Brooke went on a motorcycle ride with Leo."

Ella didn't have to ask how that made Abby feel. "I'm sure they'll be fine."

"Has Brooke ever talked to you about him?"

"Um…"

"How old is he now?"

"Nineteen, I think."

"Where does he go to school?"

"Humboldt."

Not far from Berkeley. But not that close. Abby paced the room, nibbling her lower lip. Ella was ten years younger than Abby, and more like a sister than an aunt to Brooke. Sometimes Brooke confided in her, rather than Abby.

"I have to tell you something," Ella said.

"What?"

She made a breathy sound. "We're getting married."

Abby almost dropped the phone. "What?"

"He asked me last night. Can you believe it?"

Her sister went on to tell the story of Paul proposing at Rose Valley Falls. They were both outdoor nuts, like Brooke. He'd gone with a nontraditional ring and a rare gemstone that sent Ella into raptures. She was a geophysicist.

"Oh, Ella," Abby said, her chest tight. "I'm so happy for you."

Ella couldn't wait to show her the ring, so she sent Abby the photos via text message. The first was of the happy couple at the falls. In the second, a slim platinum band with a sparkling gray stone graced her sister's slender finger.

Gorgeous, Abby texted back. Love you.

She put the phone in her purse, torn between joy and melancholy. Her baby sister was getting married to a great guy who adored her. The ring was unique and beautiful. Abby should be dancing on a table. Instead she felt like curling up in a corner. To her dismay, tears gathered behind her eyes. She'd been engaged once. She'd shown off her big, traditional diamond and held her head high.

Their situations were different, of course. Ella was twenty-six, with an established career. Abby had gotten married right after high school. She'd been a mother at eighteen. Years later, she'd pursued a degree in nursing and gone to work at Ray's cosmetic surgery office. Her entire life had revolved around him.

Ella and Paul were on equal footing. Ella knew what she was doing. And Paul wasn't the cheating type…was he?

Abby sat down on the edge of the bed, plucking at a loose thread on the comforter. The question always niggled at the back of her mind, infecting her chances of having a committed relationship. In her experience, marriages didn't last. Partners strayed.

Love was ephemeral.

The doorbell rang, startling her. It was probably Ray and Lydia. As she rose to answer it, an X-rated image of the couple popped into her mind.

Abby had learned of the affair by walking in on them in flagrante delicto. It was after regular business hours, so the front office was deserted. Ray had a back room with a leather couch for napping between surgeries. Abby had found him there with his pants around his ankles. Lydia had been bent over the couch, her breasts exposed and her skirt raked up. Their expressions had been priceless. Eyes wide. Bodies frozen, midstroke.

Pushing that unpleasant mental picture aside,

Abby continued forward. It seemed odd for Ray to announce his presence by knocking, considering that he'd rented the cabin. She glanced through the window blinds to make sure it was him. A stranger was standing there in the dark. He was taller than Ray, his shoulders broader.

"Who is it?" she asked, raising her voice.

"It's Nathan," he replied. "Nathan Strom."

Nathan Strom. Leo's father. Lydia's ex-husband. The world-famous baseball player whose career had gone up in flames.

"Is this the wrong cabin?" he asked.

Abby opened the door warily, giving him a closer study. She recognized him from the YouTube video, though he looked different. A little older, more weathered and clear-eyed. In person, he did resemble Leo. They had the same square jaw and handsome features. Nathan's hair was brown, rather than black, and expertly cut. His clothes were elegant. An expensive watch glittered on his wrist.

Brooke had described him as "seriously hot." That was right on the money.

Abby didn't know how to welcome him. This was the man Lydia had been married to when she started seeing Ray. Lydia had cheated on Nathan with Abby's husband. Ray had cheated on Abby with Nathan's wife.

His appearance here was unexpected, to say the least.

Maybe Ray had invited him. Ray was so arrogant and oblivious that he might not anticipate any tension between them. And now they were supposed

CHAPTER TWO

IT TOOK NATHAN a moment to place her.

He'd been anticipating a confrontation with his son, not a blank stare from a pretty stranger. Had Lydia given him the right address? She'd mentioned that Ray's daughter, Brooke, would be here. Nathan knew at a glance that this woman wasn't her. She had to be at least thirty, with honey-blond hair and lovely blue eyes. Her clothes were casual, but stylish and feminine. She wore a body-hugging tunic and cropped leggings. Her leather sandals had a studded strap around the ankle.

The speech he'd planned for Leo faded into the background as he dragged his gaze up her slender body, lingering for a second too long on her breasts. Then his brain kicked into gear. "You're Abby."

"Yes."

He was knocked for a loop. She didn't look old enough to have a daughter in college. And…she was hot. Not flashy, in-your-face hot, like Lydia, but too damned beautiful to be Ray's ex-wife.

"Leo took Brooke on a motorcycle ride," she said.

Nathan glanced at the deserted road, hoping his son was sober.

"I'm sure they'll be back soon."

"Can I come in?"

A pulse fluttered at the base of her pale throat. She must have seen the YouTube video. She didn't want to let him in.

"I'll wait outside," he said, ignoring the blow to his pride. Not so long ago, women had tripped all over themselves to talk to him. Fans clamored for his autograph. He'd been cheered in public and treated like a rock star.

Now people recognized him as the guy who'd thrown away his career. He'd been videotaped in a state of extreme intoxication by his own son. The clip of him stumbling out of a taxicab and falling down on his front lawn had gone viral. He'd lost visitation rights with Leo. Their relationship had been strained ever since.

Nathan didn't make excuses for the mistakes he'd made in the past. He'd gone to rehab and cleaned up his act. He was no longer a famous baseball player, and he might always be remembered for personal lows, rather than professional highs, but he'd come out okay. He'd gotten his life back on track. Most addicts weren't so lucky.

Instead of getting defensive about his bad reputation, he'd learned to shrug off criticism and roll with the punches. Although he'd stopped caring about the opinions of strangers, he didn't want Abby to be afraid of him. Maybe because of their tenuous, broken-family connection. Maybe because he found her attractive.

Her cheeks flushed pink. She was embarrassed by her hesitation to let him in. "Is Leo expecting you?"

"No."

"What are you doing here?"

She was direct. He liked that. "Lydia sprained her ankle this afternoon. She can't hike or even walk."

Her lips parted with disbelief. "What about Ray?"

"He's staying with her. They asked me to come instead."

"Son of a bitch," she muttered, propping a hand on her hip. "He does this every time!"

"I'm sorry."

"It's not your fault."

"I'm sure your daughter will be disappointed."

"Yes."

Leo would also be disappointed. His son had made it clear that he didn't want to see him, but Nathan hadn't given up on reconciling.

Abby stepped aside. "Come on in."

"Thanks," he said, passing by her.

After she closed the door, they stood there, staring at each other. She was tall and poised. With her careful makeup and chic clothes, she didn't strike him as an outdoor explorer. He couldn't picture her hiking into the wilderness. But he couldn't see Lydia doing it, either. His ex-wife was more of a yoga-and-latte type.

"I was wondering if Ray had invited you," she said. "I imagined the four of us around the breakfast table, plus Leo and Brooke."

Was she joking? He'd rather eat with wolves.

She cocked her head to one side. "Do you get along with Ray?"

"No."

"Why not?"

"Why do you think?"

She smiled wryly, crossing her arms over her chest.

Nathan had forgiven Lydia ages ago, and he no longer wanted to beat Ray to a pulp. He could say hello and be polite, but he'd never be friends with the man who'd fucked his wife while they were still married. He wasn't that evolved.

"Have a seat," she said.

"I'll stand."

With a shrug, she retreated into the kitchen, which was separated from the living room by an island with a speckled granite surface. "I was going to make a drink. Do you want something?"

The hair on his nape prickled. "Is this a test?"

She took a mug off the shelf and held up a square package. Not a glass tumbler or a bottle of hard alcohol. Instant cocoa.

"Sorry," he said, rubbing a hand over his mouth. It was an old gesture, back to haunt him. "I'm nervous."

"Why?"

"You must not know Leo."

"We just met."

"He doesn't like me very much."

She filled her mug with water from the tap, not commenting on his parenting failure. Her daughter was a shining star at Berkeley. She'd been a straight-A student in high school. According to Lydia, the girl excelled in athletics, as well. Brooke was everything Nathan wished Leo would be.

"Is he a good driver?" she asked.

Nathan doubted it. The only activity Leo put effort into was getting stoned. "He's never been in an accident."

"You don't want cocoa, I take it."

"No."

"Club soda?"

"All right."

She put her mug in the microwave and filled a pale green cup with ice, pouring the clear soda on top.

"Thank you," he said, giving her another once-over as she stirred the cocoa. Her legs were shapely, with smooth, suntanned calves. The leather straps around her ankles resembled Roman slave cuffs. Surely they weren't meant to inspire bondage fantasies. He tore his gaze away, sipping his club soda.

Looking at her like that was a bad idea. If he wasn't careful, he'd start entertaining thoughts about wife-swapping and poetic justice. Not that Lydia cared who he slept with nowadays. Nathan felt no particular urge to try to make her jealous, either. Hooking up with Abby wouldn't close the circle of betrayal or right any wrongs. He felt dirty for considering it, which of course made the notion all the more appealing.

"Do you still drink?" she asked.

"No. I've been sober three years now."

"Congratulations."

He acknowledged her with a curt nod.

Silence stretched between them. "My sister just

got engaged," she said, showing him a photo on her cell phone.

He glanced at the image to be polite. "Is that a gray diamond?"

"Musgravite," she said. "It's very rare. She's a geophysicist."

That was impressive. "Are you a scientist, as well?"

"I'm a wellness director at a nursing home."

"What does that mean?"

"I plan activities and interact with the residents."

"Do you play pinochle?"

Her lips twitched at the question. "We play strip poker."

The comment sounded suggestive, like an invitation to picture her naked. Somehow he resisted the urge. "You must see a lot of sock suspenders."

She laughed, shaking her head. "What do you do?"

"You don't know?"

"I know you used to play baseball."

"I manage a college team now."

"Is that like coaching?"

"Sort of. I handle recruiting and business decisions."

"Where at?"

"San Diego State."

The season had just ended and Nathan was happy with their performance. The Toros had done well in the play-offs. Maybe next summer they'd go all the way. He felt good about their future prospects—and his own.

Professionally, he had few complaints. Managing a

talented young team was lucrative and rewarding. His love life was nonexistent and his son refused to speak to him. But hey, nobody said sobriety would be easy.

The sound of a motorcycle engine made his heart jump into his throat.

"That's them," Abby said.

Nathan set his cup on the countertop and proceeded outside with her. Leo parked what appeared to be a vintage dirt bike on the sidewalk by the driveway. It was an old Honda with a single headlight. The seat didn't appear large enough for two, but they'd managed. Brooke clung to Leo like a second skin, her slender arms wrapped around his midsection. She was wearing a black helmet, obviously his.

She hopped off the bike and removed the helmet, pale blond hair spilling down her shoulders. She was tall and leggy, like her mother. Her jeans and tank top were tight enough to rev up any teenage boy's hormones.

Leo grinned at her as he stomped down the kickstand and cut the engine. He took the helmet she offered, seeming a little dazed by her beauty.

Nathan could relate to the feeling.

Leo didn't notice Nathan's car in the driveway or even see him standing there. Nathan stepped forward, clearing his throat. Leo startled at the sound. His smile faded and all of the joy drained from his face.

"Is that thing street legal?" Nathan asked.

Leo ignored his question. "What the fuck are you doing here?"

Brooke gaped at his rudeness. She probably never spoke that way to her parents.

"This is Leo's dad," Abby said, putting her arm around Brooke's shoulders.

The girl recovered from her shock and greeted him politely. "I'm Brooke."

"Nathan," he said, shaking her hand. "Pleased to meet you."

Abby guided her inside, aware that Nathan and Leo needed some privacy.

Nathan didn't know where to begin. He hadn't talked to Leo since Christmas. Now that Leo was an adult, Nathan couldn't force him to accept his calls or allow visits. Ray and Lydia supported him financially.

Nathan had no say in his life. No rights. No relationship.

He'd lost his son in the divorce, as well as his wife. Although he took responsibility for the problems he'd created, he still resented being out of the parental loop. Lydia never consulted with him about important issues, like vehicle ownership and college enrollment. Ray gave Leo free rein to fuck up and footed all the bills.

Leo had grown several inches since last summer, when Nathan had stopped by to see him after a game at UCLA. Between semesters, he lived with Ray and Lydia in Beverly Hills. They'd converted the pool house into a small studio apartment where he could jam loud music and hang out with his hoodlum friends.

His hair was longer. His shoulders were a little

broader. Though he refused to play sports, he was a natural athlete. He had quick reflexes and a quick mind—when he wasn't under the influence. Someday his dissolute lifestyle would catch up with him. For now he was lean and strong and brimming with health.

"You need a haircut," Nathan said.

Leo lodged his helmet under one arm, feigning boredom. "What do you want?"

"Your mom and Ray couldn't make it."

He swore at them both under his breath, which set Nathan's nerves further on edge. Leo didn't appreciate the easy life he'd been given.

"Don't disrespect your mother," Nathan said.

"Only you can?"

Nathan hadn't badmouthed Lydia since he quit drinking, but he'd called her some unflattering names over the years. They'd argued and exchanged scathing insults. Once, Leo had gotten between them, shoving and kicking. Tears streaming down his face, he'd yelled at Nathan to leave his mother alone.

"She called me from the E.R.," Nathan said.

Leo tensed at the news. Still protective. "What happened?"

"She sprained her ankle. She can't walk, so she asked me to fill in. She thought we could go hiking together."

"I hate hiking."

"Then why did you come?"

Leo fell silent, glowering into the dark shadows beyond the cabin. Nathan already knew the answer.

Leo was driving an old motorcycle for a reason. Ray had taken away his car after finding a joint in the ashtray. Lydia was planning to confront him about his drug use this week. His attendance wasn't optional.

Maybe Lydia's injury was real and maybe it wasn't. Nathan wondered if she'd delegated this responsibility because she couldn't deal with it. She had a certain sense of fatalism, a belief that people followed a set course in life. No one could change their destiny and everything was meant to be.

The upside was that she had a loving, accepting personality. The downside was that she gave Leo very little guidance. He needed boundaries and discipline—tough love. Ray wasn't a pushover, but he served his own interests and avoided conflict. It was up to Nathan to reach Leo. Nathan hoped he could get through to him before it was too late.

"Your mother wants us to spend time together," he said, his throat tight. "*I* want us to spend time together."

With a scowl, Leo fished his cell phone out of his pocket and stepped away from Nathan to call Lydia. They began a rapid conversation in Portuguese. She was from Brazil, so she'd taught Leo her native tongue and a fair amount of Spanish. Leo could tell Nathan to fuck off in three different languages.

Nathan was proud of that. Sort of.

Apparently Lydia held her ground. She wasn't going to give his car back unless he stayed at the cabin with Nathan. Leo mumbled goodbye and pocketed his phone.

"Are we clear?" Nathan asked.

Leo strode toward the front door, not bothering to respond. Nathan followed him inside. Brooke was sitting on the couch, her eyes wet with tears. Either she'd spoken to Ray or her mother had broken the bad news. Nathan felt sorry for her. Brooke exchanged a glance with Leo, who glared at Nathan as if *he'd* made her cry.

Lydia had told him that this trip had been Brooke's idea. Brooke was the intrepid explorer who loved communing with nature. Abby handed her daughter a mug of cocoa. Brooke sipped the drink, studying Nathan.

"Would you like some cocoa?" Abby asked Leo.

He sat down on the couch next to Brooke. "No, thanks."

Abby leaned her hip against the side of the couch. She reached out, as if to smooth her daughter's hair. But instead of following through on the motion, she drew back a curled fist. "We can still go hiking."

Brooke shrugged, wiping the tears from her cheeks.

Abby's presence at the cabin was both a relief and a complication. With her here, Nathan didn't have to look after Brooke. He'd figured that she would stay with him and Leo or go home. The idea of hiking as a foursome hadn't occurred to him.

Until now.

"Where were you planning to hike?" Nathan asked.

Brooke had a map open on the surface of the coffee table. "There are a bunch of cool places around here," she said, sniffling. "I wanted to go to Echo Lake." She pointed to a round blue spot on the map. "The trail splits off from there. It's a steep climb to Miracle Hot Springs or a gentle slope to Lupine Meadow."

Nathan settled into a nearby armchair.

"My dad and Lydia would have picked the easier route," Brooke said.

That was all Nathan needed to hear. He'd endured grueling training sessions throughout his baseball career, and he still exercised every day. Physically, Ray was no match for him. Not that they were in competition or anything. "Then let's take the hard way."

Brooke met his gaze. "Really?"

"Sure. There's no reason to cancel your plans."

Her face lit up with excitement. "Can we, Mom?"

"We don't want to impose," Abby said.

"Not at all," Nathan said. "If anyone's imposing, it's me."

"You got that right," Leo muttered.

Brooke slapped his shoulder. "Leo!"

"What?"

"Be nice to your dad."

Abby went into the kitchen and grabbed a bottle of water from the fridge. She came back, passing it to Leo. Although he hadn't asked for it, he untwisted the cap and took a drink. "Brooke and I can hike on our own," Abby said.

"That's no fun," Brooke said, as if hanging out with Abby was a chore.

Leo smirked at her plaintive response. He wasn't keen on camping with his old man, either, but he might enjoy following Brooke up a mountain. Leo would probably be on his best behavior around her. He also couldn't take off on his motorcycle if he got angry with Nathan, which was bound to happen.

This was perfect.

"Hiking as a group is safer, especially in remote wilderness areas," Nathan said. "Lydia told me there was a murder just a few miles from here last summer. They found a guy with an arrow in his chest."

"I read about that," Abby said. "It was a couple. The girl is still missing."

"Maybe she killed him," Leo said.

"Ooh," Brooke said with approval. "Spooky."

Nathan caught Abby's exasperated look. *Kids.*

"How many days will we be gone?" Abby asked.

"Four or five at the most," Brooke said. "But we'll be near water the whole time. You don't have to worry about being dirty."

Abby made a noncommittal sound.

"She's kind of a neat freak," Brooke explained to Nathan and Leo.

"I'm a fan of regular showers, myself," Leo said.

Brooke wrinkled her nose at Leo's lame joke and they both laughed. Nathan wasn't sure what to think of them. He hardly remembered being a teenager. When he was Leo's age, he'd been a professional baseball player, married with a kid on the way. These two weren't children, but he couldn't see them as adults.

"Is it settled?" Nathan asked Abby.

"My dad had all of the supplies delivered," Brooke

said, leaping to her feet. "If we pack up our gear to-night, we can get an early start tomorrow."

Leo groaned at her enthusiasm, but Brooke couldn't be dissuaded. Denying her was like trying to stop the sunrise.

"What do you say?" she asked, arms spread wide.

"Okay," Abby said, giving in.

CHAPTER THREE

ABBY WOKE BEFORE DAWN.

She reached for her cell phone and noted the time. Her alarm would ring in ten minutes. Turning it off, she scooted away from Brooke and climbed out of bed. Nathan and Leo had taken the other two bedrooms, so she and Brooke had shared.

Last night, Brooke had organized all of the supplies they needed. Two small tents, four sleeping bags, four mats. Miscellaneous food items and dried meal packages. A bear canister, water filter, flashlight, first-aid kit. Toiletries and cooking utensils.

Brooke was a ruthless minimalist. She wouldn't allow Abby to bring any makeup or unnecessary clothes, claiming she'd regret every extra ounce. As a result, the packs weighed less than ten pounds each.

Abby put on the clothes she'd laid out the night before. They'd be stopping at the lake before they reached camp, so she started with her swimsuit, a sporty blue two-piece. Over that, she pulled on basic running shorts and a gray tank top. Her anklet socks and black hiking shoes completed the look.

After brushing her teeth and pulling her hair into a ponytail, she studied her appearance. Devoid of makeup, her face looked plain and bare. She saw smudges under her eyes, pale lips, freckles and crow's feet.

Tiptoeing toward her beauty case, she unfastened the latch.

"Don't even think about it," Brooke mumbled.

"What?"

She rolled over in bed and squinted at Abby. "Your makeup will wash off when you swim."

"I'll keep my head above water."

"What about tomorrow? I'm not carrying that stuff for you."

Abby would give up a couple of meals for her MAC case. Just a little mascara, some lip gloss, a bit of concealer...

"You don't need it."

That was easy for Brooke to say; *she* didn't need any. She had a smooth, even complexion. Her skin tanned easily. Although her hair was blond, like Abby's, her brows and lashes were dark.

Brooke propped her head on her hand. "What do you think of Leo's dad?"

"He's very nice."

"Nice?"

Abby glanced at the closed door, hoping Nathan couldn't hear them. They hadn't talked about this last night. Brooke had stayed up late playing video games with Leo. She'd fallen asleep as soon as she crawled into bed.

"Leo says he's single," Brooke added in a low voice.

"How would he know? They don't get along."

"Lydia knows."

"Don't embarrass me."

With a smile, Brooke threw back the comforter and rose from the bed in her underwear. She was lithe and lean, pantherlike. Sometimes Abby couldn't believe this fully grown woman had come out of her body.

Not so long ago, her daughter had been gap-toothed and giggling, wearing a party hat. She'd been a newborn who refused to latch on for the first two weeks, and then a toddler who'd refused to stop when Abby tried to wean her. She'd always been stubborn, prone to outbursts, quick to laugh and full of energy.

Brooke flipped open the makeup case and rifled through its contents. "Here," she said, choosing a single item. She tucked the rose-tinted lip moisturizer into Abby's palm and closed her fingers around it, as if bestowing a precious gift.

Abby turned to the mirror and applied it, her throat tight.

Brooke came up behind her. "Do you think I need boobs?" she asked, covering her small breasts with her hands.

"Absolutely not," Abby said, appalled. Brooke had a runner's figure, strong and sleek. "You're perfect."

"I look like a boy."

"Who told you that?"

"No one important."

"Good, because it's ridiculous."

"Were you flat, before?"

"You don't remember?"

Brooke shook her head.

Brooke had been twelve when Abby had her breasts done. Too young to notice the flaws Abby had seen so clearly. "I wasn't flat...I was asymmetrical."

"Like, one big boob and one small?" She adjusted her hands over her chest to demonstrate.

"Yes." It wasn't the only reason for her augmentation; Abby's self-confidence had taken a hit during the divorce. If she hadn't been such an emotional wreck, she might not have gone under the knife, but she was happy with the results. "You have a lovely figure, very proportional. Besides, large breasts are a pain for sports."

"True."

"They also seem to attract jerks," Abby pointed out.

"Why is that?"

"I don't know."

Although her implants weren't that obvious, Abby worried about the example she'd set for Brooke. Until now, Brooke had never complained about her shape or acted self-conscious. She certainly wasn't shy about wearing revealing clothes. Abby wondered what had prompted this conversation. "What are the boys like at Berkeley?"

Brooke stopped posing in front of the mirror and dropped her hands. She'd steered clear of serious relationships in high school, preferring to concentrate on sports and academics. "They're hot, rich and smart."

It was a succinct summary, delivered with more

cynicism than a girl her age should have. Maybe Brooke had some trust issues of her own.

Thanks, Ray.

Brooke scooped up a pile of clothes and escaped into the bathroom. Abby hoped her daughter would come to her if she needed someone to talk to. She also wished Brooke had a better male role model. Too often, her father wasn't there for her.

With a frown, Abby left the bedroom and headed for the kitchen. The soles of her shoes made no sound on the lush carpet. When she exited the hallway, she saw Nathan and almost jumped out of her skin.

"You scared me," he said, removing the carafe from the coffeemaker.

It took her a few seconds to realize he was joking. "I didn't know you were up."

"I was trying to be quiet."

He went to the sink and filled the carafe with water, whistling. After transferring the water to the reservoir, he plugged in the machine and turned it on.

Abby studied him as they waited for the coffee to brew. He was wearing a faded blue Toros T-shirt with tan cargo shorts and brown hiking boots. The clothes fit well on his body, which appeared to be in fantastic shape. She figured he had to be close to forty, but only his face showed his age. He had thick brown hair, broad shoulders and a trim waist. An outdoor setting would only accentuate his rugged features.

It wasn't fair.

Abby didn't want to "rough it" with a man this attractive. She was going to be sweaty and anxious and unkempt. The idea of trekking through the woods and leaving civilization behind intimidated her. She didn't like feeling out of her element, out of control.

"You must have been a child bride," he said.

She'd heard that one before. It was an odd sort of compliment, but she saw no censure in his expression. "And you were twelve when you fathered Leo, right?"

He laughed, shaking his head. "I was nineteen. The same age he is now."

"Were you more mature than he is?"

"Maybe, but not by much."

She fell silent for a moment, pondering her own teen marriage. At eighteen, she'd thought she was ready to be a wife and mother. She'd wanted her own family more than anything. Ray had been five years older, and on a fast track to a promising career in medicine. They'd skipped the courtship and gone straight to playing house.

"Was the pregnancy unplanned?" she asked, tentative.

His brows rose at the personal question. "It's hard to say that, considering how careless we were with protection. The real surprise was that it didn't happen sooner."

"Did you want to get married?"

"I did, actually. I had to talk *her* into it. She had reservations about the amount of time I spent traveling with the team."

Abby couldn't blame her. She imagined a young, beautiful Lydia, taking care of a baby by herself while Nathan "the Storm" Strom hit home runs in front of a roaring crowd. Lydia had gotten the short end of that stick.

When the coffee was finished brewing, Nathan grabbed a cup and handed it to her.

"Thanks," she said, disconcerted by his proximity.

"Isn't this cozy," Brooke said as she walked in. She was wearing a red tank top, frayed denim short-shorts and sturdy hiking boots. Her long hair was braided under a baseball cap. "You two should get revenge on Lydia and Dad by hooking up."

Abby stepped back from Nathan too quickly and spilled coffee over the rim of her mug. "Brooke!"

"What?"

Nathan coughed into his fist, as if covering a laugh. He found another mug on the shelf and busied himself with the coffeemaker. Abby set her cup aside and wiped the floor with a paper towel, her cheeks hot.

"Coffee?" Nathan offered Brooke.

"No, thanks."

He must have preferred it black, because he left without adding any cream or sugar. "Ladies," he said, winking at Abby.

Brooke gave her a triumphant smile.

Abby opened the refrigerator, half hoping she could crawl inside and die. "I can't believe you said that."

"Relax. He thought I was joking."

Abby took out a carton of soy milk and a jar of orange juice. "Should I make breakfast?"

"Definitely. Be domestic."

Abby rifled through the utensil drawer for a spatula. "You can scramble eggs," she said, pointing it at Brooke.

They cooked almost a dozen eggs, along with turkey bacon and wheat toast. Nathan came back for a plate. Leo also roused from his slumber. He was dressed casually in basketball shorts and a T-shirt that said High Life across the front. Nathan's gaze darkened with irritation when he saw the marijuana logo.

Abby could cut through the tension between them with a knife. Nathan had said that Leo didn't like him. It appeared to be true. He was polite to her and Brooke, seemingly indifferent toward his father.

After breakfast, Leo helped Brooke with the dishes while Nathan walked outside to make business calls on his cell phone. Abby perused the local newspaper, which must have been delivered with the groceries. She found a disturbing story about Echo Lake. A few years ago, a group of teenagers had hiked there for an afternoon swim. When it was time to leave, one of the girls hadn't returned to shore. Divers searched a portion of the lake but were unable to recover the body. She was presumed drowned.

Abby read the article out loud to Brooke and Leo. "You'll have to be careful swimming. There are obstacles in the water. Sunken logs."

"We'll use the buddy system," Leo said.

Brooke handed him a plate to dry. "Stop reading that stuff, Mom. You're going to get all worked up."

Abby flipped through the pages with a sigh. Near the back, there was a photo of a smiling young woman hugging a terrier mix. Both were missing. She was last seen at a pet store, buying a leash for the dog.

Maybe she'd gone hiking.

Pulse racing, Abby returned to the Echo Lake article and noted the victim's name. Then she picked up her cell phone and did a quick search for the drowning victim's name plus the missing girl's name. They were connected, but only as former residents of Monarch. Both were young, blonde and pretty.

Curious, Abby looked for more information about missing girls and women in the area. There were dozens of articles about the college student who'd been murdered on the Pacific Crest Trail. He'd been shot in the chest with an arrow from a crossbow. His girlfriend—young, blonde and pretty—had never been found.

If Abby hadn't seen the first two women in the same newspaper, she might not have noticed the similarities. She skimmed the other articles for evidence that law enforcement officials were investigating a link between them. They weren't even trying to find the drowning victim. The woman and the dog could have gone anywhere. Forest rangers and volunteers had combed the woods for the college student's girlfriend, to no avail.

What if all three women had fallen prey to a killer?

Abby didn't voice this concern out loud. It was far-fetched, she supposed, and Brooke would accuse her of obsessing over nothing, which Abby did often. She continued to browse for clues, mapping the distances between the pet store, hiking trail and lake. They were located within a twenty-mile radius.

When Brooke clapped her hands for attention, Abby glanced up, startled. Brooke and Leo had finished with the dishes. Nathan had just come back inside with his cell phone. Leo was sitting on the couch, disentangling the cord to his earbuds.

"I'm calling a family meeting," Brooke said.

Leo snorted at the announcement. "We're not a family."

"For the next four days, we are," she said, gesturing for Abby to join them. "Bring it in, Mom."

Nathan sat down on the couch next to Leo. Abby took the space beside Nathan. Brooke's assertion that they were a family, if only for a few days, made Abby's chest tighten with an unknown feeling. It was a warm sort of discomfort, like…longing.

She hazarded a glance at Nathan, whose throat worked as he swallowed. He wasn't immune to the lure of togetherness, either. He seemed to want to repair his relationship with Leo. Abby understood that desire; her life would be empty without Brooke.

"Say goodbye to your cell phones," Brooke said. "They aren't going to work in the backcountry, anyway."

"What about emergencies?" Abby asked.

"I have one with GPS, just in case. But I'll keep it turned off to save batteries."

Nathan set his phone on the coffee table. "Fine."

"I need my music," Leo said.

"Don't you have another player?"

"Not with me."

Abby didn't want to give up her phone, either. She was ten times as attached to it as her makeup case. Her cell phone was her crutch, her comfort, her only connection to civilization. The last time she'd left it behind, she'd become physically ill. Abby still wasn't sure if she'd been seasick from kayaking or if crossing open water had triggered an anxiety attack.

"I'll sing you songs by the campfire," Brooke said, fluttering her lashes.

"Right," Leo scoffed, but he couldn't resist her flirty smile. Shaking his head, he placed his phone on the table.

Abby had no choice but to follow suit. Nathan was studying her with interest. Stomach churning, she surrendered her cell phone to Brooke. She felt like a police officer being divested of her badge and weapon.

"Okay," Brooke said, clasping her hands together. "I want everyone to wear a hat and drink lots of water during the hike. It's going to be hot out there. I know we're all at different fitness levels so I'll try not to go too fast. Don't be afraid to ask for a break, Mom. Tomorrow will be more difficult if you overexert yourself today."

Leo squinted as if her sunny enthusiasm hurt his eyes.

"Any questions?" Brooke asked.

"I have one," Leo said. "How much coffee did you drink this morning?"

"None, smart-ass. I stay away from mood-altering substances."

"You should try that," Nathan said to Leo.

Although Leo and Brooke had been joking around, Nathan's comment was dead serious. And it didn't go over well.

"Fuck you," Leo said, rising from the couch. "Don't tell me what to do."

Nathan rubbed a hand over his mouth, not responding to the provocation. He seemed perplexed by Leo's attitude. Maybe it hadn't occurred to Nathan that criticizing his son in front of Abby and Brooke would embarrass him.

Abby felt bad for both of them. Nathan obviously had no idea how to deal with Leo, and she couldn't blame Leo for acting out. He was a troubled kid from a broken home. His father was a recovering alcoholic, his stepfather was a jerk and his mother had probably faked a sprained ankle to avoid conflict.

"Chill out, Leo," Brooke said. "At least your dad is here, making an effort. Mine didn't even bother to show up."

Abby watched a mixture of emotions cross over Leo's face. He didn't want to spend time with Nathan. She suspected that he was being forced to by his mother. Otherwise, he'd leave. Brooke was the only highlight of the trip, but he didn't have a chance with her because of their family connection.

At least, Abby *hoped* he didn't have a chance. She assumed Brooke was too smart to get involved with her stepbrother.

Leo's gaze moved from Brooke to Abby. "Excuse my language," he mumbled.

"Don't worry about it," Abby said, standing.

"She says *fuck* all the time," Brooke added.

Leo looked impressed. "She does?"

Abby glanced at Nathan, feeling her cheeks heat. His lips quirked with amusement. Again, she noted how handsome he was. She admired his concern for Leo, and she liked what she saw in his dark eyes.

"Oh sure," Brooke lied. "It's her favorite word. Right, Mom?"

"Right."

Nathan studied Abby's mouth for several seconds, his interest clear. She bit her tongue to keep from giggling, aware that Brooke and Leo were watching them. Brooke appeared pleased. Leo's brow furrowed, as if he couldn't fathom his father's appeal to women even while witnessing him in action.

"Are we ready?" Abby asked.

They picked up their backpacks and headed out the door. The trailhead was only a short walk from the cabin. It was cool and overcast now, but the sky would clear and the clouds would give way to relentless sunshine soon enough. A fine mist coated her face, lending truth to Brooke's claim that hiking and makeup didn't mix. The Pacific Crest Trail, which ran from the Mexican border all the way to Canada, was marked with a triangle-shaped sign depicting a green pine tree and white mountains.

"Hang on," Brooke said. "I want to take a picture."

Abby, Leo and Nathan stood in front of the signpost while Brooke propped her cell phone on a nearby boulder. She set the timer and hurried to join them. Instead of posing by Abby, she put her arm around Leo.

After the red light flashed, Brooke retrieved her phone from the rock. Abby studied the photo, which had turned out okay even though Brooke was the only one smiling. They looked like a family. The dark forest in the background added a hint of intrigue, as if they were about to embark on a great adventure.

CHAPTER FOUR

NATHAN SPENT THE NEXT few hours enjoying the climb.

Brooke took the lead and insisted on a certain hiking order. She passed Leo the map, appointing him as navigator. Abby followed in third place and Nathan brought up the rear, which gave him a fantastic view of her ass. He wasn't sure if Brooke had considered this benefit beforehand, but Nathan had no complaints.

He liked Abby. She cut to the chase and asked frank questions. He enjoyed watching her expressions as she spoke, and even when she was quiet. He liked the way she was put together, from her long legs to her freckled shoulders and everything in between.

He took a drink of cool water from his pack, trying to clear his head. This trip was about reconnecting with his son, not checking out Abby. Making progress with Leo might score him some points with her, but Nathan didn't need the incentive. He cared too much about Leo to throw away this opportunity to make amends. His game with women was rusty anyway, and Leo had made it clear that he resented the intrusion. Leo didn't want Nathan here, ingratiating himself with Abby and Brooke.

This was Leo's territory.

Leo couldn't have Brooke. He certainly wasn't going to sit by while Nathan put the moves on her mother.

Fine. Nathan could control himself. He'd been celibate for most of the past three years, so he was no stranger to going without sex. Keeping his distance from Abby shouldn't be difficult. Maybe she could give him some parenting advice. She'd hit a home run with Brooke.

Abby had been kind to Leo, as well. Nathan had noticed that, and he was glad Leo had been polite in return. Lydia had raised their son to respect women. Nathan couldn't take any credit for that aspect of Leo's upbringing, unless Nathan's poor treatment of Lydia had encouraged Leo to be a better man.

As a father, Nathan had made a lot of mistakes. He'd been gone most of the time. The first few years had been tough. They'd traveled to many of his away games as a family, but Lydia had hated being on the road with a baby. By the time Leo was in elementary school, Nathan had become a top-ranked major league player. He was in high demand for endorsement deals and charity events. His relationship with Lydia had been solid. She didn't love his career focus, but she enjoyed the perks of being a successful athlete's wife.

Then he got injured, and everything fell apart. Although his shoulder had healed quickly, he didn't have the same snap to his release or power in his swing. He worked out like crazy, pushing himself harder than ever, but it was no use. His body had too much wear and tear. He was washed up at age thirty.

Around the same time, Lydia had suffered a miscarriage. She'd become depressed and withdrawn. He didn't know how to fix things between them, so he'd focused on saving his failing career. The team he'd helped take to the World Series let him go. Lydia refused to uproot Leo by following Nathan to Detroit, and then to Cincinnati. He couldn't sleep at night. He'd started mixing his pain pills with alcohol.

It was difficult to pinpoint the exact moment his drinking had gotten out of hand. The third trade, maybe. The strikeout that killed their play-off hopes. The infield error in the last inning of his last game.

At twenty-eight, he'd been one of the most celebrated baseball players in the league. He had more money than he could spend. Five years later, it was over. He had no hope of getting another lucrative contract. To say he went on a drinking binge was an understatement. He'd pretty much just stayed drunk.

He hadn't known who he was, outside of baseball. He'd been drafted at eighteen. He'd never gone to college. His self-worth was all tied up in the game. After more than ten years of people telling him he was a superhero, he'd believed it. And when his fans thought he was shit, he internalized that, too.

A commotion ahead startled him out of his reverie. Brooke and Leo had hiked around a bend, past a group of tall pine trees. Nathan heard the deep voice of a stranger, along with Brooke's friendly hello.

Abby hurried to catch up. Nathan followed close behind, more curious than concerned.

There were two men blocking a fork in the trail. Leo stood silent next to Brooke, his shoulders square. Her body language was more relaxed; she didn't consider these men a threat, even if Leo did.

Both strangers were scruffy and unkempt. Their long hair was incongruent with the military-style fatigues they wore. The man in front of Brooke had grimy hands and a thick beard. His companion was younger, with the sparse mustache of a teenager. They were hunters, judging by their camouflage gear and backpacks.

Nathan found their appearances strange, but he was probably biased against hippie backpackers. What really disturbed him was the avaricious gleam in the older man's gaze, which faded as soon as he saw Nathan.

"Is it this way to Echo Lake?" Brooke asked, pointing to the left.

The stranger nodded. "Good day for a swim."

Brooke inquired about drinking water sources and they had a short discussion about filtering. When Abby joined them, the older man gave her breasts a quick study before glancing at Nathan once again. Sizing him up as an opponent.

"Where are you headed tomorrow?" the man asked Brooke.

"Lupine Meadow," Nathan said.

Brooke opened her mouth, as if to dispute him, but she went quiet when Abby gripped her elbow.

"That's a nice area," the man said.

Abby murmured goodbye and continued down the path with Brooke and Leo. Nathan stayed behind. It was part protectiveness, part male posturing. His instincts told him to stand his ground instead of scurrying along. The men had a strange, earthy smell. Not marijuana or stale sweat, but something else, like wet fur.

"Any luck hunting?" Nathan asked.

"Caught a few quail," the man said, his eyes twinkling.

"With what?"

"Traps."

Maybe that was the odor he'd detected: fresh game. Nathan didn't care if they were poaching, growing pot or playing Jesus. The boy looked scared and guilty. As long as Grizzly Adams didn't mess with his women, Nathan had no beef with him.

"Have a good one," Nathan said, nodding goodbye.

The older man stared at him for a few seconds, not moving. Nathan was reluctant to turn his back on him. The grungy teenager broke the spell by starting down trail. Nathan and the other hunter left the scene in unison.

Freaks.

Abby was waiting for him nearby, her mouth tight. She didn't ask any questions. Sound carried in the forest. Nathan walked beside her, glancing over his shoulder at regular intervals. They caught up with Leo and Brooke as the trail narrowed into a steep incline.

"Are we really going to Lupine Meadow?" Brooke asked.

"No," Nathan said.

"Why did you lie?"

Leo seemed surprised by her naïveté. "Because that guy was looking at you like he wanted to eat you."

Brooke turned to her mother for confirmation. The fact that she hadn't picked up on the stranger's demeanor raised a number of red flags for Nathan. Thank God he had a son instead of a daughter who seemed unaware of her own beauty. When Abby didn't say anything, Brooke flushed and continued hiking.

For the next hour, they ascended a series of switchbacks that made conversation difficult. It was a tough climb, even for Nathan. His shirt grew damp and his pack felt heavy on his back. Leo kept up with Brooke better than Nathan figured. Abby was also a trouper.

They reached the top of the first mountain and paused to take in the view of Echo Lake, nestled in the valley below. It was a gorgeous blue oval, surrounded by white granite rock formations and tall pine trees.

"Let's have lunch here," Brooke said.

It was a good place to stop. Nathan could keep an eye on the trail, though he doubted the strange duo had followed. They shrugged out of their backpacks and sat in the shade of a sturdy oak tree. Nathan was sweating like crazy. So was Leo. Abby looked hot and bothered in an attractive, post-orgasmic way. Brooke didn't even appear winded. She passed out a lunch of mixed nuts and oranges.

"This is our only fresh fruit for the trip, so enjoy it."

They did. Nathan was ravenous. He tried not to notice Abby's ample chest or her hollow cheeks as she sucked on an orange slice. She'd be stripping down to her bathing suit soon, so he needed to get a grip. Think about something else.

"Lydia tells me you're a runner," Nathan said to Brooke.

She took a sip of water, nodding.

"Long-distance or sprint?"

"I do the 800 meter, which is considered medium-distance. Also the 100-meter dash."

"What's your time for the 100?"

"11.7."

"No shit?"

"No shit."

That was fast. Half of the boys on his roster couldn't beat her, and some of them were major-league bound. "Did you get an athletic scholarship?"

"It was part athletic, part merit."

Nathan arched a brow at Leo, who was on academic probation at Humboldt State University. Leo had maintained a 3.0 GPA in high school without exerting much effort, so Nathan knew he could do better.

"You don't pay my tuition," Leo said, defensive.

That was true. Ray and Lydia were funding Leo's

studies. "I'm impressed by the achievement, not the cost savings."

Abby touched Nathan's elbow. It was the same gesture she'd used to keep Brooke quiet. "Do you play any sports?" she asked Leo.

"He surfs," Brooke said.

This was news to Nathan. "Really?"

"We stopped by Mavericks after Christmas," Brooke said.

Nathan felt the blood drain from his face. He'd never been to Mavericks Beach, but he'd heard the waves were huge. Not for amateurs.

Abby let go of his elbow. "You didn't."

"We did," Brooke said, smiling. "Leo gave me a ride to Berkeley, and I wanted to check out the waves. I stayed on the beach while he went surfing."

When Nathan pictured Leo paddling out into a raging sea, pressure built in his chest. "Why would you take such a stupid risk? What if you'd gotten held under, and Brooke drowned trying to save you?"

"She wouldn't have come in after me," Leo said, rolling his eyes. "The waves were only ten or fifteen feet high that day, and there were other surfers in the water. It wasn't that dangerous. I didn't even catch anything."

Nathan wiped his hand over his mouth. Sometimes he could still taste the cool bite of a gin and tonic. He recognized cravings for what they were now. He was better at identifying stress and other triggers.

His emotions always ran high with Leo. There was no one he cared about more, no one who could make him as scared or angry. Nathan had to learn how to communicate with his son, and he was terrified of failing.

He took a deep breath, thinking back. His interactions with Brooke had been effortless. Why couldn't he talk to Leo that way?

"I can't wait to go swimming," Brooke said. "I'm melting in this heat."

Nathan used the hem of his shirt to blot his face. It was too hot to yell at Leo. He didn't like feeling this way, tense and unhappy, but he couldn't flip a switch to change the past. He couldn't make his son love him again.

They hiked the short distance from the top of the mountain to the shore. The lake was even more beautiful up close, crystal blue and fresh-looking. The entire area had been carved by glaciers, which had left giant pools in the granite. There was a sandy beach on one side near an island of towering boulders.

"I bet I can climb those rocks and dive off," Brooke said, shrugging out of her backpack and placing it on the sand.

"Don't you dare," Abby said.

"The water's really deep, Mom."

"We should test it first," Leo said. "Depth can be deceiving."

Brooke listened to Leo, rather than her mother. "Okay."

The four of them sat down to unlace their hiking boots. Brooke tugged off her shorts and tank top, revealing a striped bikini. "Hurry up," she said to Leo, who seemed to have forgotten what he was doing.

Leo fumbled to remove his high-tops and lame T-shirt.

Nathan resisted the urge to glance at Abby as she undressed. It would be rude to stare, hoping for a wardrobe malfunction. He imagined her breasts jiggling as she pulled her shirt over her head. Not looking also seemed weird—he wasn't a horny teenager, incapable of acting cool. So he waited until he thought it was safe and…

Gulp.

Her suit wasn't as skimpy at Brooke's, but her body made it sexier. Or maybe he just didn't see Brooke the same way because of her age and relationship to Leo. Abby was a mature woman, fair game for ogling. Her simple blue bikini accentuated her figure. She had pale skin and mouthwatering curves.

"Ever heard of manscaping?" Leo asked.

The question interrupted Nathan's perusal. It took him a second to realize Leo was referring to the hair on his chest, which narrowed to a strip over his abdomen. Nathan had never heard any complaints from women about it. He glanced at Leo, noting that he had the smooth, sculpted torso of a male model. "You wax your chest?"

"No. I don't have to."

"But you're saying I should?"

"Totally. Body hair is disgusting."

"My mom likes it," Brooke said.

Abby jerked her gaze from Nathan's stomach. "Brooke!"

"What? You do." She waded into the lake. "I think it's kind of sexy, too. On guys." Smiling at Leo, she dived into the water and swam away.

Nathan figured Brooke was being outrageous to tease Leo, who frowned at her retreating form. Abby escaped the awkward situation by submerging herself in the lake. It was cold, judging by her little shriek.

Nathan didn't know what to say to his son, as usual. Although Brooke's provocative comment had put him in his place, Nathan couldn't just let it go. Leo had been combative and disrespectful too often. His bad attitude sparked an equally negative reaction in Nathan, prompting him to needle Leo further. Hooking his arm around Leo's neck, he said, "Just keep shaving your balls, pretty boy. They'll drop soon enough."

Leo shoved him backward. "Fuck off!"

Nathan stumbled into the shallow water, his heart pounding. He wanted to duke this out, physically and emotionally. Wrestling wasn't a good way to communicate, but it felt better than doing nothing. So he threw his arms around Leo in a maneuver that was half tackle, half hug. Leo rewarded him with another hard push. Then they were both in the lake, splashing and grappling. The cold shock invigorated him.

Nathan tried to gain the upper hand, but Leo was a slippery sucker. His son elbowed him in the stomach and kicked him in the thigh. Nathan grunted in pain, scrambling for a better hold. His foot scraped against a sharp rock as they waded into deeper water. Leo broke free and retaliated with a swift punch in the mouth.

Nathan's head rocked to the side. He fell into the waist-high water and let himself sink. The urge to fight left his body. It was a well-placed hit, but probably not full strength, and nowhere near a knockout.

Good one.

Nathan didn't plan to stay under for more than a few seconds. He just wanted to avoid a second blow. To his astonishment, Leo came after him. He put his arms around Nathan and hauled him upright.

"Dad!"

Nathan found his footing and turned to gape at Leo, who'd clearly been worried. About *him*. His throat got tight and tears flooded his eyes. Nathan swiped a hand down his face, laughing suddenly.

"You were faking," Leo accused.

"No," he said, tasting blood. "You laid me flat."

"What the fuck is so funny?"

"You thought I was drowning."

Nathan didn't know *why* that was funny, but it was. Maybe because he'd been horrified by the thought of Leo drowning at Mavericks. Maybe because they were both fools, and it felt good to act stupid with his son.

"You're an asshole," Leo said, but he was smiling.

Still chuckling, Nathan swam into the deeper water. Leo followed, dunking him for good measure. Nathan returned the favor. He knew the issues between them couldn't be solved by an afternoon of horseplay. But for now, at least they weren't angry.

When he caught his breath, he noted that Abby and Brooke were watching from a distance. Although the altercation had ended on a friendly note, it hadn't started that way, and women tended not to approve of such shenanigans. Nathan didn't, either. He'd removed players from his team for brawling.

"She thinks you're an idiot," Leo said, following his gaze.

"What does Brooke think of you?"

"The same."

Nathan dunked him again, not caring at all.

CHAPTER FIVE

ABBY HELD HER BREATH as Brooke dove off a twenty-foot boulder.

She hit the water with a gentle splash and stayed under for several long seconds. Abby watched, her heart racing, until Brooke resurfaced next to Leo, who'd been waiting for her. Grinning, he gave her a high five.

They were both daredevils, egging each other on. Leo had gauged the depth of the lake and deemed it safe, with one exception. There was a large rock about six feet underneath the surface on the left side. Leo treaded water above it while Brooke jumped, and vice versa. They were using the buddy system, as promised.

That didn't mean Abby could relax. She tensed every time Brooke was airborne, imagining worst-case scenarios. She knew Brooke well enough to anticipate increasingly dangerous feats. Leo had started with short leaps and cannonballs from a smaller boulder. Now Brooke was high-diving. Backflips would be next.

Sure enough, Leo scrambled to the top and attempted a forward somersault. He didn't quite get his legs straight before he hit the water, which concerned Abby. But he came up to the surface quickly. Brooke twined her arms around his neck in a manner that would invite a kiss from any interested, available boy. Leo did something underneath the water that made her squeal and swim away.

Abby glanced at Nathan, who was lounging on the narrow beach beside her. He hadn't blinked an eye at their reckless jumps or flirty touching. Then again, he'd also laughed when his son punched him in the face.

"She has no sense of caution," Abby said, feeling obligated to explain Brooke's behavior. "That's why she was surprised you lied to those men. She notices attention and creepy looks on occasion. But she doesn't anticipate danger, and she only sees the good in people."

He rested his forearm on a bent knee. "That's a nice quality to have."

"It terrifies me."

"I don't blame you."

Abby appreciated the acknowledgment. Ray had always denied there was a problem. "She got knocked out during the San Diego earthquake. I've always wondered if the head trauma changed her. Ever since then, she's been more adventurous, more ambitious."

He studied Leo and Brooke for a moment, his brow furrowed. She got the impression that he found his son lacking in comparison. Maybe, as a former pro athlete, he had higher expectations than the average parent. "Should I talk to Leo?"

"He's done nothing wrong."

"To be fair, neither has she."

Abby was glad he didn't think badly of Brooke. Her daughter seemed determined to be a matchmaker. Abby's cheeks heated at the memory of the body hair remark. Although Abby had no particular preference either way, his chest *was* delicious. He looked strong and fit, with hard muscles and a flat stomach. He didn't have that much hair, just a lightly furred area on his pecs and an intriguing trail down his belly.

"I hope those hikers didn't follow us," she said, tearing her gaze away.

"I kept glancing over my shoulder, and I didn't see them."

Abby wished she had her cell phone. She could have taken an incognito picture of them and done an internet search. This lake was the site of the drowning. Her fingers itched to scroll for information about local runaways and hunting accidents.

Brooke climbed the boulder and prepared to dive again. Abby stifled a gasp as Brooke took a running leap off the edge and spread out like a flying squirrel. About halfway down, she tucked into a smooth somersault and plummeted into the lake. Abby didn't unclench her fists until Brooke broke through the surface.

"You know what you should do," Nathan said.

"What?"

"Try it."

"Jumping off?"

The corner of his mouth turned up. "There's only one cure for fear of the unknown."

Her pulse pounded at the thought of taking that plunge, sinking into the deep. So far, the trip had been full of triggers. Strange men in the woods, physical altercations, extreme stunts. Everything made her uneasy, from the thick forest to the wide expanse of open water before her. "Is it that obvious?"

"Your discomfort, you mean?"

She nodded.

"Not really. Ballplayers learn to read body language and facial expressions. We have to anticipate a player's next move."

"Does it work with Leo?"

He touched the sore spot on his lip, rueful. "Apparently not."

Nathan appeared to have instigated the fight. Despite this brief lapse in maturity, she still liked him. At least he hadn't traded punches with Leo. Somehow, the macho shoving match had broken the ice between them.

Men.

Abby frowned on Nathan's methods, but she could relate to what he was going through. She understood how it felt to be torn apart. He also seemed aware of his own failings and desperate to improve. That was appealing to her. The fact that he was handsome, well-built and observant didn't hurt, either. He might not have a clue about communicating with his son, but he knew how to please a woman. Shivery intuition told her that.

She inhaled a sharp breath, drawing his attention to her chest. Her nipples pebbled against the wet fabric of her bikini top.

He returned his attention to the lake. "I need to get back in the water."

It *was* hot. Sweat trickled between her breasts.

"Come on," he said. "I'll jump with you."

"That sounds more dangerous."

"Okay, I'll go first, and you can jump to me. I'll be right there."

The granite island loomed in the close distance, taunting her. She could climb up with Nathan and brave the unknown. Or she could sit on the sand, wallowing in heat and anxiety. "You really think it will help?"

"Sure. Most fears are based on inexperience and unfamiliarity. Our imaginations conjure all sorts of scary, but unlikely, scenarios. As soon as you jump, you'll realize it's not that bad. Then you can relax."

She smiled at his pep talk. "So this will be a quick, natural tension reliever?"

His eyes darkened. "I can think of a better one."

So could she. He looked interested enough to pounce on her at the slightest provocation, but they couldn't just wander off into the woods for a quickie. Even if she'd been willing to engage in a naughty fling, their kids were here, and encouraging a man like him would only lead to trouble. He was too charming, too sexy.

Too risky.

Brooke and Leo headed toward the rocks for another turn, spurring her into action. "Okay," Abby said. "I'll try it."

"The jump?"

"Yes, the jump."

He seemed surprised by her agreement. Cliff-diving was a sport for wild teenagers like Leo and Brooke, not women her age, with skittish temperaments. Maybe she was avoiding the greater danger—Nathan himself.

She stood, brushing the sand off her bottom. His lean physique made her feel self-conscious about her figure. He was extremely fit, without an ounce of spare flesh. Although she was on the slim side, she wasn't young and perky anymore. Her stomach and hips were softer. Her thighs had more jiggle.

He watched her wade into the lake, his neck flushed. "Splash me."

"Why?"

"For luck."

She'd never heard of such a thing, but she splashed him. The water hit his face and shoulders, trickling down his chest.

He shook it off like a dog and lumbered to his feet. Vanity had her wondering if he'd been overheated—aroused, even—because of her. She couldn't remember the last time she'd given a man an inappropriate erection.

Hiding a smile, she ducked under the icy water and swam to the cluster of boulders. Brooke and Leo were already jumping from the opposite side. Abby hauled herself onto the lowest boulder, with some difficulty. The path to the top was wet. She used the same handholds and footholds that Brooke and Leo had used, her mouth pursed in concentration. It was an undignified climb in a bathing suit, with Nathan right behind her. If she'd known a hot guy would be staring at her butt in broad daylight, she might have gone tanning or had her cellulite zapped.

She reached the plateau, breathless. "I didn't enjoy that."

"I did."

Abby laughed, accepting his help to stand up. A wave of dizziness struck her as she peered over the edge. "Oh God."

"What are you doing?" Brooke yelled from below.

Nathan kept a firm grip on Abby's hand. "What does it look like? We're jumping."

Leo put two fingers in his mouth and whistled to cheer them on.

Brooke was less than thrilled. "Be careful," she said with a frown, as if uncomfortable with the role reversal.

"I'll try not to break a hip," Abby said.

Nathan smiled at the joke, squeezing her hand.

He'd been wrong about the power of her imagination. Reality was worse. It looked so much higher from up here. The distance to the water made her stomach flip. She felt like she was standing on the roof of a skyscraper.

"I can't do it," Abby said.

"Sure you can. I'll go first. When I call out to you, jump. If you wait too long, you'll overthink it."

Brooke swam to the underwater obstacle with Leo and gazed up at them.

"Don't push me," Abby said.

He let go of her hand.

"I can't feel my face."

"As long as you jump away from the boulder, you'll be fine," he said. "Keep your arms and legs straight."

She was about to tell him not to leave her when he did it. He just leaped off the edge like it was nothing. His body hit the water, arrow-straight. When he resurfaced a few seconds later, he was grinning.

"Come on," he said, swimming backward to give her some room. "You can do it."

Abby didn't want to. She pictured herself fainting and dashing her head against the rock. "I have to sit down."

"Don't sit down. Jump!"

She looked for a way out, her shoulders shaking. The path they'd climbed would be difficult to descend. More dangerous than jumping. Leo gave her a thumbs-up signal. Brooke clapped a hand over her eyes. Nathan wagged his fingertips forward.

Abby jumped.

She was only airborne for a few seconds. Then she hit the water with a hard splash. It penetrated her eyelids and rushed in her nostrils. Panic bubbles emerged from her throat. After sinking deep, she clawed her way to the surface, gasping as she broke through.

Brooke swam to her side, excited. "Mom! You did it!"

She had done it. And she never wanted to do anything like it again.

"How was it?" Nathan asked.

"Horrible."

His smile faded. "You didn't think it was fun?"

"No."

The three of them seemed baffled by Abby's response. Tears stung her eyes. She turned and swam to the narrow beach, collapsing on the sand.

Nathan joined her. "I'm sorry," he said, chagrined. "I thought you'd enjoy it."

She put a towel around her shoulders, still shaking. "I feel like a jerk."

Abby didn't blame him for trying to help her. Maybe she was beyond hope. She practiced her steady breathing and positive visualization techniques. The sun warmed her wet hair. After a few moments, she calmed.

And she noticed a change.

The next time Brooke dived off the edge, Abby didn't freeze up as much. She knew the drop wasn't deadly. She'd survived it.

"To be honest, I'm surprised you even climbed up there, let alone jumped," Nathan said. "It was pretty scary."

She wiped the tears from her cheeks. "It was."

"You've got balls, lady."

"I feel better."

"You do?"

She nodded. "I didn't like it, but I'm glad I did it."

He studied her with a quiet sort of admiration, as

if seeing her in a new light. His regard for her went deeper, slipping below the surface. He was attracted to her for reasons other than the way her breasts looked in a bikini. She thought about his offer to relieve her tension the old-fashioned way and realized then that it would never happen. They couldn't have a no-strings sexual affair. The strings were already there.

A scream rang out across the lake, startling her. Abby scrambled to her feet. Her damp towel fell off her shoulders.

Nathan rose with her. "What was that?"

Leo and Brooke were treading water near the boulders, so the cry hadn't come from either of them. It sounded like a woman.

Another shriek followed, high-pitched with terror.

"Someone needs help," Brooke said. She started swimming toward a thatch of trees on the opposite side of the lake.

Abby covered her mouth with one hand. Her first instinct was to tell Brooke to stop, and the reaction shamed her. She'd always taught her daughter to help others, especially other girls. She went out of her way to do the same. But this was different. It was a threatening sort of unknown. An icy fear gripped Abby's heart and wouldn't let go.

Leo accompanied Brooke with no hesitation whatsoever. Nathan waded into the water, cursing under his breath. He swam toward them, his strokes sure and swift. Abby couldn't just stand there, frozen and helpless.

She dove in and started swimming.

Although Brooke had an early lead, Leo was the strongest swimmer. He caught up with her near the middle of the lake and pulled ahead. Nathan showed his athletic prowess by passing Brooke and continuing after his son. They were all scared. The race to the other side was no friendly competition, no fun adventure.

Leo climbed out of the water first, his chest heaving. Nathan was right there with him. Brooke arrived shortly after.

Abby concentrated on steady strokes, trying not to panic. By the time she stumbled onto the shore, Nathan and Leo were arguing about what to do. They stood in front of the thick copse of pine trees, faces tense.

Panting from exertion, Abby walked toward Brooke.

"Stay here," Nathan ordered Leo.

"Fuck, no," Leo said. "I'm going with you."

Nathan reached down and picked up a heavy stick. Holding it like a baseball bat, he entered the forest. Leo found a fist-sized rock and went with him, ready to strike. Neither of them appeared to consider bringing along Abby or Brooke.

Abby rested her palms on her knees, winded. She didn't approve of them creeping into the forest like white knights, armed with blunt objects. They had no idea what was going on. A woman in pain or danger would respond better to other women.

"Did you try calling out to her?" she asked Brooke.

"No one answered," Brooke said.

They waited at the edge of the trees, dripping wet. This side of the lake was cloaked in shadow, and it made all the difference. The temperature was ten degrees cooler. Abby shivered in the cool air, her skin and hair damp.

"How many screams did you hear?" Abby asked.

"Two. I'm not sure where they came from." Brooke wrapped her arms around her body, glancing over her shoulder.

Abby studied their surroundings. It was called Echo Lake for a reason. The granite rock formations caused sound to bounce off in all directions. She could have sworn the cries rang out from here, but she wasn't sure. "Could an animal make that noise?"

"Maybe a mountain lion."

"It sounded like a woman."

"Or a girl," Brooke said quietly.

Abby remembered the drowning victim's age: seventeen. The missing hiker was twenty-five, the lost girlfriend twenty-one.

Brooke wasn't the type to sit on the sidelines. She searched the branches by the shore and picked up two hefty sticks. Passing one to Abby, she tilted her head toward the woods. Abby debated the wisdom of following the men, but she couldn't stop Brooke from going, and she wanted to stay together.

Brooke tiptoed into the foliage, stealthy and silent. Abby crept close behind, wincing as her bare foot encountered a sharp rock. They inched forward, ears and eyes peeled. Abby saw no signs of humans or large animals. She heard no sounds, other than birds chirping and lizards rustling through the leaves.

Brooke continued through a small clearing. They were straying too far from the lakeshore, but Abby kept moving. She squinted at a strange shape in the trees ahead. Insects swarmed in a dark cloud. Her nostrils tickled with a muddy, metallic smell. She became aware of a stretching sound, like swaying rope.

"Ugh," Brooke said, wrinkling her nose.

Abby pushed past Brooke to see. Her stomach dropped as she examined the gory scene. A full-sized deer hung from the tree, eviscerated. Its entrails lay in a neat pile on the leaves. Blood dripped from the flayed belly, streaking the animal's dark fur.

Nathan and Leo entered the clearing a moment later. When Leo saw the hanging deer, his handsome face went gray. He stumbled away and retched in the bushes.

Nathan gave him a disgusted look. "Pull yourself together, Leo."

Abby couldn't believe he'd criticize his son for getting sick at a time like this. Brooke threw down her stick and went to see if Leo needed help. He shrugged off her attempts to rub his shoulder.

"It's fresh," Nathan said, inspecting the deer.

Abby stepped forward to investigate.

"They took the choice cuts and left the rest. That's illegal."

She noted the missing chunks at the animal's sides. "Those hikers, you think?"

"Maybe."

"What about the screams?" Brooke asked.

"We didn't see anyone," Nathan said.

"Neither did we," Abby said.

"A mountain lion can scream like that," Brooke said.

Nathan nodded. "They're drawn to the smell of blood."

Abby glanced around the woods, studying the dark shadows as if a big cat might spring from the depths at any moment. "Let's get out of here."

CHAPTER SIX

THE TRIP AROUND the lake took a lot longer than the swim across.

As the sun dipped lower on the horizon, the temperature dropped into the 70s. Comfortable for hiking, if they weren't wet, half-naked and barefoot. Nathan's shorts were soaked. He'd have suggested swimming back, but they were all cold, and Leo was still pale. Nathan didn't want him to throw up again.

The sight of the hanging deer brought back old memories. Nathan had hunted with his father in the woods of Wisconsin, where he'd grown up. He hadn't enjoyed the sport. He'd always felt a little queasy, pulling the trigger. Dressing the kill was no picnic, either. He'd never complained, of course. His dad would have cuffed him for whining or showing weakness.

He felt disloyal for remembering his father that way, as if being strict was a crime. Maybe it was, in California. Now Conrad Strom was dead and gone. Former military, he'd been tough as nails, unaffectionate and slow to praise. A parent from another era. But there was nothing wrong with a man wanting his son to be strong.

Was there?

Nathan owed a lot of his success in baseball to his stern Midwestern upbringing. If his dad hadn't pushed so hard, Nathan wouldn't have achieved half as much. He'd been drafted into the minor league right out of high school. His father had encouraged him to reach for the stars. Whenever Nathan tried to do the same for Leo, it backfired.

This whole situation was a mess. One minute he was palling around with Leo and getting cozy with Abby. The next, he was creeping through the woods with a club, searching for a screaming girl.

Maybe he'd needed an interruption. His comments to Abby had been too suggestive. After a few minutes in her company, he'd forgotten his vow to keep his distance. She was just so…beautiful. Her curves made his mouth water and his palms itch. In his defense, he hadn't gotten laid in a *really long time*.

It was more than that, though. They had great sexual chemistry, but he liked her personality. She had depth. If she'd been vapid or conceited or shrill, his urge to fuck her would have faded already. Instead, it kept growing with every smile he coaxed from her, every laugh that escaped her lips.

Damn.

She seemed interested, too. He assumed she was single. Her signals weren't so obvious that he knew he could score with her. With some women, he could tell right away. Others were more of a challenge. Abby was the type he'd have to work for.

But never mind that. He wasn't here to put the moves on Abby. His main priority was bonding with

Leo. He wanted to be a better father. When this trip was over and they were back in San Diego, he could call Abby. Unless he kept making a jerk of himself and ruining his chances, which was possible.

Anyway, he had other things to worry about. Law-breaking hunters and strange sounds and gutted animals. Nathan held the tree branch in a firm grip, just in case. He didn't want to tangle with a hungry mountain lion.

When they reached the other side of the lake, he drew in a sharp breath. Their backpacks had been tampered with. Zippers and pockets were gaping open. A few stray items were strewn across the sand.

"Son of a bitch," he said, tightening his grip on the club. They'd been robbed! "Check to see what's missing."

While Nathan stood watch, the others searched the packs.

"My cell phone's gone," Brooke reported.

Abby's eyes widened with dismay.

"At least it's my backup, so there's no information to hack."

"Why would they steal a phone they can't use?" Abby asked.

"They can wipe it and sell it," Leo said.

Nathan narrowed his gaze at the trees along the trail. Those long-haired creeps had drawn them away from their belongings to rob them. He didn't know who or what had made the screaming sound. This was some sneaky, sinister shit.

"My stuff is all here," Abby said. "I didn't bring any money."

"I did," Nathan said. "It was in the side pocket."

She reached into the zippered pouch of his pack and pulled out an empty clip. The wad of cash was gone.

"Fuck," he muttered, raking a hand through his hair.

"How much was it?" she asked.

"Three hundred."

Leo snorted at Nathan's stupidity. "There goes our fancy dinner at that four-star restaurant down the trail."

Nathan didn't bother to respond. He always carried cash for emergencies, and it was a trifling amount. When they were done looking for missing items, Brooke reorganized the backpacks and they put on their discarded clothes.

"What should we do?" Abby asked.

"We have to make camp," Brooke said. "It will be dark soon."

Abby studied the trail, her lips trembling. It went without saying that this situation freaked her out.

"They're gone," Nathan said.

"What if they come back?"

"They won't. We don't have anything left to steal."

This logic didn't appear to convince her.

Nathan tried again. "Fresh venison is worth more than my cash and Brooke's phone. In this weather, they have to get it to cold storage right away."

"How do you know?"

"I've hunted before. Meat has to be kept at forty degrees. The nightly lows have been in the fifties."

Abby exchanged a nervous glance with Brooke. "They might have a cooler."

"No. Ice is too heavy to hike in, and it won't last a day out here. The lake isn't cold enough, either."

She blinked a few times, close to tears. "I want to go to the cabin."

"Mom," Brooke said in warning tone.

Leo stayed silent, as if he had no opinion either way.

"Three young women have disappeared in this area," Abby said in a rush. "One right here at the lake."

"She drowned," Brooke said.

"They didn't find a body."

"You're overreacting! They're thieves, not serial killers."

Abby flinched at the accusation, crossing her arms over her chest. Her anxiety seemed like a direct response to Brooke's nonchalance. Abby had to be twice as careful to make up for her daughter's lack of fear.

Nathan fell somewhere in the middle. He doubted the hunters were a serious threat, but he'd been wrong before. "Whatever they are, they'll be on that trail. It's the quickest way back to Monarch. If they think we're following them, they might get defensive. Camping here is the safest option."

"I don't know," Abby said.

"My dad and I can take turns keeping watch tonight," Leo offered.

It was a good suggestion. Nathan agreed immediately.

Abby stepped away from Brooke and Leo, waving Nathan toward her for a private chat. "I have a bad feeling about this."

"What choice do we have?"

"I'm scared," she whispered.

"Don't be," he said, his chest puffing up a little. He liked the idea of protecting her. But he also felt conflicted, as if he shouldn't enjoy the ego boost. One day in the wilderness had turned him into a caveman. "I won't let anyone hurt you or Brooke."

"What about tomorrow?"

"We can look at the map and choose an alternative route back to the cabin."

"Not Lupine Meadow."

"No."

She exhaled a ragged breath. "Okay."

They put on their packs and prepared to leave. If they delayed much longer, they'd be pitching tents in the dark.

"Let's switch up the hiking order," Nathan said. "Leo should go first."

Leo didn't have to ask why. He found another good-sized rock to use as a bludgeon. Nathan had a buck knife in his pocket. He hadn't drawn it on the other side of the lake, and he didn't pull it out now, but he was glad to have a weapon. Before they walked away, Nathan noticed a small rectangular package on the sand.

Rolling papers.

Leo saw them at the same time. Guilt flashed across his features, replaced quickly by belligerence.

"Are those yours?" Nathan asked.

"Yeah. So?"

"Tell me you didn't bring pot with you."

"I didn't bring pot with me," he said in a flat voice.

He was lying. Nathan could read the truth all over his handsome, grown-up face.

"Take off your pack," Nathan said through clenched teeth, resisting the urge to shove Leo to the ground and rip it from his shoulders. When Leo didn't comply, Nathan whirled him around and unzipped the front pouch.

"Don't bother," Leo said, shrugging away from him. "They stole it."

"Goddamn it, Leo!"

Leo stepped back another few feet. He still had a rock clenched in his fist. He looked stubborn and rebellious and...scared.

He *should* be scared. Nathan couldn't remember being this angry with him before. Tenderness and concern were difficult emotions for him to express, but rage rose right up to the surface, spilling over. "What the fuck were you thinking? Were you going to light up after we went to sleep? Share a joint with Brooke?"

"Brooke doesn't smoke weed."

"I did once," she corrected.

"Who gave it to you?" Nathan asked.

Her nonresponse spoke volumes.

"I only brought it because I couldn't leave it at home or in the cabin," Leo said. "I wasn't going to 'peer pressure' Brooke." He made quotation marks in the air, as if he was talking about something that didn't exist.

"Ray could have you arrested if he found your stash," Nathan said.

Leo shrugged, playing hard-ass.

"I can't believe you'd be so stupid."

His eyes narrowed. "Okay, *boozehound*."

Nathan felt the insult like a punch in the gut. "You know I don't drink anymore."

"I know you're a hypocrite."

They stared each other down for a moment. Leo had put on at least twenty pounds of muscle in the past few years. He wasn't a kid anymore. Fine grains of stubble darkened his jaw. He'd started shaving. Nathan had missed his transition from boy to man.

He'd missed a lot of things.

Nathan glanced at Abby, who was watching from the sidelines. She looked sad and sorry and full of sympathy—for Leo. Maybe she thought Nathan was wrong for calling him out like this, but he didn't know what else to do. He couldn't ignore the problem and hope it went away. Leo needed help.

"Let's talk about this later," Abby said.

Nathan scrubbed a hand over his mouth, nodding. He remembered his first drink, given to him by his father on a hunting weekend the summer he'd turned twelve. He'd raided the camp for more beer and gotten tipsy as hell. His uncles had laughed as if Nathan was the funniest thing they'd ever seen.

He'd always considered that a good memory. Now it was sour, like the taste in his mouth when he was jonesing.

Nathan trudged forward until they reached the campsite. Although it was less than a mile from the lake, the uphill climb tired him out. They'd had a long day of emotional stress and physical activity. The campsite was located in a hilly area with a good view of the trail. It had a clearing for tents and primitive fire pits. There was a ramshackle outhouse about a hundred yards from the clearing.

Abby grimaced at the sight.

"This is great," Leo said with sarcasm, taking off his backpack. "And to think I wanted to go to the Bahamas."

"Were you expecting a hotel?" Brooke asked.

"No, I was expecting a bug-infested shit hole."

"This is a nice camp," she said. "There probably won't be many gnats or mosquitoes this far from the lake."

They set their backpacks down by a log in front of the fire pit. Abby stretched her arms over her head while Brooke removed a water filtration system from her pack. They'd passed a rushing creek on the way here.

"I have to get water," Brooke said.

"Why don't you go with her?" Nathan said to Leo.

"Why don't you?"

"Come on, Leo," Brooke said. "Let's try to make the best of it. I'd be happy if my dad was here."

"Yeah. Too bad he can't be bothered to spend time with you."

This cracked Brooke's sunny persona. Her brows slanted downward. "If it wasn't for your mom and her stupid ankle, he wouldn't have canceled."

"Leave her out of it."

"I don't think she wanted to come on the trip."

"For good reason."

"What?"

"They're getting a divorce," Leo said.

Nathan hadn't heard this news. He glanced at Abby, who appeared as shocked as he was. She sat down on a log in front of the fire pit and cupped a hand over her forehead. Nathan hated the way Lydia had left him, but he didn't wish another divorce on her. Abby didn't seem happy about it, either.

"Why?" Brooke asked.

"Ray's cheating on her with one of his nurses."

"Wow," she said, after a long pause. "Karma *is* a bitch."

"Brooke," Abby warned.

"What are you talking about?" Leo asked.

"Your mom cheated with him, too."

He shook his head in disbelief.

"My mom walked in on them in his office," Brooke said. "He had her bent over the couch with her skirt up."

Abby's eyes widened with horror. "How did you know that?"

"I heard you crying to Aunt Ella over the phone. I listened through the door."

"Oh my God," Abby groaned.

"My dad moved out the next day," Brooke said.

Leo looked to Nathan for a confirmation he couldn't give. He'd never mentioned Lydia's infidelity to Leo, and he hadn't been aware of the specific details of the affair. Lydia had told Nathan that she wanted a divorce because she was seeing someone else. When Nathan asked if she was sleeping with him, she'd said yes. It was probably the worst moment of his life, next to the YouTube debacle and his career implosion.

Brooke's bombshell brought back a rush of bad feelings. The image of Lydia in Ray's office stung, even after all these years.

"You're a fucking liar," Leo said.

"No, Leo. I'm not. And neither is my mom, so you better watch your mouth."

Abby rose to her feet and grabbed Brooke by the arm. "Apologize to Leo. You had no right to hurt him like that."

Brooke pulled her arm from Abby's grasp. She stared at Leo, seeming conflicted.

"She doesn't have to apologize," Nathan said. "Leo started it."

Leo turned to Nathan, his dark eyes gleaming. "Why didn't you tell me?"

Nathan wasn't sure what to say. Lydia hadn't wanted Leo to know she'd been unfaithful. She'd said he was too young to understand the complex-

ity. After mulling it over, Nathan had agreed with
her. They'd settled on a "mutual story," which was
that they just weren't happy together. It was true,
well before Ray came into the picture. Nathan had
cursed Lydia to hell and tossed out scathing insults
on multiple occasions—in Leo's earshot—but he'd
managed to stay quiet about the cheating.

Since Nathan had moved out, his relationship
with Leo had been difficult. They hadn't talked
about Lydia or the divorce. Nathan had been bitter
and angry, but not interested in dragging her name
through the mud. Lydia, in turn, hadn't taken him to
the cleaners. Leo had probably assumed that she'd
gotten fed up with Nathan's drinking. And that was
the bottom line. It was the reason she'd strayed.

"I'm sorry," he said, shifting his gaze from Brooke
to Leo. He *was* sorry they had to go through this
again. "You were only thirteen."

"I was old enough to hear the truth," Leo said.

"It was a mutual decision, Leo. We split up because
I was drunk all the time. I don't care what happened
between your mother and Ray. I care about what you
do. I don't want you to make the same mistakes I did."

Leo looked away, his mouth set in an angry line.
Instead of talking things out, he picked up the water
bag and strode away from camp with Brooke.

CHAPTER SEVEN

THIS WHOLE TRIP was fucking stupid.

Leo walked to the creek in front of Brooke, keeping an eye out for intruders. He was hungry and tired and annoyed with everything. He couldn't believe his dad hadn't told him his mom had cheated.

Leo didn't know what to think. Brooke never lied about anything important, and Abby seemed like the honest type. His mom, on the other hand, had been known to stretch the truth. He doubted she had a sprained ankle, for example.

"Shit," he said, kicking the dirt. For the past six years, he'd operated under the assumption that his mom had left his dad because he was a surly drunk. Now he found out that she'd only told Leo half the truth. He was furious with both of his parents for deceiving him. The reason they got divorced *was* important.

Leo resented being kept out of the loop. He resented Ray for taking his car away, and his mom for backing up Ray. Most of all, he resented his dad for trying to interfere in his life after making a mess of his own.

Leo's recreational drug use was nobody's damned

business. He was nineteen, not twelve. Pot was hardly even illegal. In a few years, it would be sold in every supermarket. Compared to alcohol and other drugs, it was healthy.

Leo wasn't a heroin addict. He didn't rob banks. He didn't drive drunk or disrespect girls or brawl in the streets. He was *fine,* and he didn't need his dad or anyone else getting in his face about smoking a little weed.

It made him happy. Why shouldn't he be happy? Adults wanted everyone to be boring and miserable, like them. He had to climb on the hamster wheel and become a "productive member of society."

Well, fuck that.

This wasn't even about him, it was about his dad. Mr. Bigshot Pro Baller had decided that drugs and alcohol were evil because he'd made a fool of himself on YouTube. Leo shouldn't have to get sober just because his dad couldn't handle his liquor.

It was stupid of Brooke to hint that she'd gotten high with him, too. Ray already thought Leo was a bad influence. If Ray learned that Leo had crossed the line with his daughter—in more ways than one—he'd go ape-shit. Ray had threatened to make Leo's life a living hell if he ever dared to touch Brooke. There were worse things than not having a car to drive. Leo could end up getting kicked out of the house or thrown in jail.

Leo knew he'd caused trouble between his mother and Ray. They fought over his bad grades and worse attitude. Was it any wonder that he wanted to escape? There was conflict everywhere he turned.

He glanced over his shoulder at Brooke. She followed him in silence, not chirping about the scenery or wildlife for once. He liked her more than a stepbrother should, but her high energy rankled when he was feeling down.

It was easy for her to be upbeat; she was perfect.

When they reached the creek, he handed her the water bag. "I'm sorry," he said, his stomach churning.

She threw her arms around his neck and hugged him tight. He was only an inch or two taller than her, so their bodies lined up in a pleasing way. "It's okay," she said, releasing him. "You were upset."

"Do you hate my mom?"

"No, I like her. I shouldn't have made that karma comment. It was mean."

He watched her nibble her lower lip, her blue eyes full of regret. Even Brooke said bitchy things in the heat of the moment.

"Do you really think they'll split up?" she asked.

"I don't know." It was going to suck either way. Ray was a jerk, but Leo's mom loved him.

"If they do, will you stay in touch with me?"

"Of course."

"Good," she said, smiling. "I don't want to lose my only brother."

Brother. Right.

She bent to fill up the water bag. It filtered inside the collapsible pouch and came out a tube at the bottom, ready to drink. He carried the heavy bag back to camp and hung it on the short tree branch Brooke pointed out. Then she fired up the camp stove and put a pot of water on to boil. Leo was starving, so he hoped the freeze-dried dinners were edible.

"Help me set up the tents," his dad said.

Leo rose with reluctance, not interested in another lecture. His dad was pretending to be a concerned parent for Abby's benefit, but he didn't really care. The Storm had always been more focused on sports and professional success.

Leo would never be good enough to suit him; he'd given up trying a long time ago.

His dad studied the instructions and started putting poles together, speaking to Leo only when necessary. The tents were compact and low to the ground, designed for maximum comfort in minimal space. Leo wasn't looking forward to sharing such tight quarters with someone who could barely tolerate him.

"Your mother didn't want to tell you," his dad said in a low voice. "She didn't think you'd understand."

"Did you cheat on her, too?"

"No," he said, his brows rising. "Never."

Leo wished they'd talked about this a long time ago. Maybe it wouldn't have made a difference. He'd never forgive his dad for treating him like a disappointment. But knowing this small truth changed Leo's feelings about him.

Once the tents were secure, his dad brought the gear inside and left Leo alone with his thoughts. Brooke wandered over to help him get situated. She showed him how to use the air valve to inflate the sleeping pads.

"Do you think they'll let us sleep together?" she asked.

He laid out his sleeping pad. "No."

"Why not?"

It was a silly question, so he started blowing into the valve.

"Then my mom could sleep with your dad."

Ugh. He didn't know which was worse, Brooke's lack of sexual self-awareness or her weird fascination with their parents hooking up.

"They'd make a cute couple. I like your dad."

"If you like him so much, why don't *you* sleep with him?"

She made a horrified face. "Ew, Leo! No."

He finished inflating his sleeping pad, smiling a little. Then he watched her blow into the valve on her sleeping pad with more interest than was appropriate.

Brooke tempted and teased him on a regular basis. She did it the same way she did everything, with unfiltered *joie de vivre*. Flirting was as natural as breathing to her. Maybe she toyed with him because he was safe. They were comfortable together. There was no possibility of a relationship. She meant no harm, but she wasn't so oblivious that she didn't notice his reactions to her. He'd gotten an erection once when she'd climbed on top of him. She'd been more amused than embarrassed, tickling him until it went away.

He knew she wasn't a virgin. She'd told him all

about her first time, and how her douchebag boyfriend hadn't bothered to be gentle. He assumed she'd had other, hopefully better, experiences since then. But it was clear that she was still innocent in many ways. She had no clue how much he wanted her. Sometimes that made him angry. Sometimes he wasn't in the mood for playful wrestling and blue balls.

He couldn't stay angry, though. Being mad at her for flirting was like being mad at her for being beautiful, or being mad at the sun for shining. If he needed space, he could put distance between them. But he never did. Because he enjoyed the attention. God help him, he liked her rubbing on him.

They'd never discussed what Leo had done at Mavericks. Leo wasn't sure she even remembered it. She'd been high as a kite, thanks to him.

They climbed out of the tent and pulled on jackets. The sun had disappeared on the horizon, bringing the chill of dusk. Abby and his dad were sitting on the log by the fire pit. While Brooke added boiling water to four meal packages, letting them steep for a few minutes, Leo cased the perimeter of the campsite.

He'd lied to his dad about the pot. It was still in his backpack.

Leo wasn't worried about the hunters coming after them. His dad had made a good point about the poached venison. Even so, the remoteness of their location left them vulnerable. As he stared into the dark recesses of the forest, he couldn't shake the feeling of being watched. Troubled, he returned to the others.

There was nowhere to sit except on the fallen log

in front of the empty fire pit. Leo took a space next to Abby. He didn't make eye contact with her. He was embarrassed by his contentious relationship with his father. Brooke's sordid tale about his mother and her father getting busy in the back office didn't help.

Brooke put another pot of water on to boil, humming a cheery tune. She was wearing a fluorescent yellow windbreaker and a blue knit beanie with her cutoff shorts and hiking boots. Her legs were about a mile long, smooth and tanned.

Leo hazarded a glance at Abby. She'd put on a gray fleece pullover to ward off the chill. She was pretty, and not that old. His friends would call her a "milf." He hated it when they said that about his mom.

"Brooke tells me you're a student at Humboldt," Abby said.

"Yeah," he said. "I like it there."

"Do you have a major?"

"International Studies."

"What happened to Music?" his dad asked.

Leo didn't know why his dad was frowning. He thought Music was for stoners. "I switched majors." He was interested in other cultures, so this seemed like a better fit. Being fluent in Portuguese and Spanish didn't hurt.

"Will you go abroad?" Abby asked.

"Next year," he said, nodding. "I'm thinking about Spain."

His dad made a sound of displeasure.

"You have a problem with Spain?" Leo asked him.

"No, I have a problem with your grades. I doubt

they let students on academic probation study abroad."

He was right, the judgmental bastard. "I have to get my GPA up first."

"I'd love to go to Spain," Abby said brightly. "I've always wanted to travel."

"Why didn't you?"

She shrugged, glancing at Brooke.

Leo figured that Abby had become a mother at a young age. His mom hadn't been able to travel much, either. His dad, however, had toured the world with his baseball team. He'd been to a dozen foreign countries while she stayed home with Leo. She must have been bored and unfulfilled. When he was in junior high, she'd lost a baby and cried all weekend. His dad had flown home to be with her, but only for a day.

Brooke served the freeze-dried dinners when they were ready. They ate the meat and carrots right out of the bag. She claimed they had to finish every morsel to comply with her "leave no trace" philosophy. Leo had no problem with that; he devoured his meal. For dessert, they drank vanilla mint chai from camp cups. It was a nice dinner.

Leo still felt uneasy about the thieves, and he wasn't proud of punching his dad or throwing up in the bushes. But he couldn't remember the last time he'd shared a comfortable evening with family. He also hadn't spent more than a few hours without his cell phone or gone to bed sober in weeks.

"Do you want me to take first watch?" he asked his dad.

"No. I'll do it."

"Okay," he said, stretching his arms over his head. "Wake me up at midnight or whenever you get tired."

"Don't worry about it."

"What do you mean?"

His dad just stared at him.

"You don't trust me to do it right?"

"Should I?"

Leo stiffened at the insult. He still had a bag of weed in his backpack and he wanted to smoke it. Even so, his dad's lack of confidence bothered him. It hurt to be treated like a loser who had nothing to contribute.

Clenching his hands into fists, he retreated to the tent and took off his shoes. Camping sucked. He couldn't escape. He didn't have any rolling papers. Hiking, swimming and exploring had sapped his strength.

Taking off his jacket, he bunched it up behind his head to use as a pillow. His shorts were dry and comfortable enough to sleep in, so he didn't bother to change before he slipped inside the sleeping bag.

A few minutes later, someone walked by with a flashlight and went inside the other tent. Leo straightened, looking through the mesh window. Less than ten feet of space separated the two tents. It was Brooke, judging by the outline of her body. She tugged her shirt over her head and removed her bikini top. He couldn't see anything, but his imagination supplied the details. After she wrestled into warmer clothing, he settled back down on the sleeping pad, wincing when it made a squeaky noise.

Instead of staying inside her tent, she crawled out and approached his. "Leo? Are you awake?"

"Yeah."

"Can I come in?"

"Sure."

She unzipped the front of the tent and climbed in with him. She was wearing a long-sleeved shirt and jogging pants. Her flashlight was really a headlamp, attached to her forehead as if she was going caving. She'd probably been caving. She was that kind of girl. She was also the kind of girl who said whatever popped into her mind, so he figured he'd have to listen to her opine on his relationship with his father. First, she got cozy in the available sleeping bag.

"He's doing the best he can," she said quietly.

"His best sucks."

"At least he's trying."

"Trying to do what, tear me down?"

"He wants to fix things between you."

"He wants to fix *me*. He thinks I'm a fuckup, and he can't stand weakness or failure. His mission in life is to criticize everything I do."

"Do you expect him to pat you on the back for smoking pot?"

"I expect him to mind his own business."

"Give him a break."

Brooke didn't understand the history between them. His dad had started drinking after his career hit the skids. He was even more critical of himself than he was of Leo. He'd been emotionally unavailable for years.

Now that he was sober and successful again, he thought he could just waltz back into the picture. It was almost as if Leo was a game and his dad had signed on for extra innings. His motivations were self-serving; he didn't like to lose.

"He asked me if I was gay once," Leo said.

Brooke adjusted the light on her forehead, smiling. "It's not an insult."

"Yes, it is."

"Why would he think that?"

"I was never good at competitive sports, but he kept making me try out. One of the kids on the soccer field called me a faggot because I was scared of the ball. He didn't say it very loud, but I heard it and so did my dad. After the game, he got really serious and sat me down. He said it was okay to be gay."

Brooke covered her face and dissolved in giggles. When she was done laughing, she said, "That's sweet, Leo."

"No. It's lame."

"He wanted you to know he'd love you either way."

"I think he was trying to pinpoint the reason for my lack of aggression. If I was gay, I had an excuse for not being good at sports."

"Gay people play sports."

"I know. I'm just saying that he thought I was girly. I could never be strong enough, tough enough or *man* enough for him."

She pondered that for a moment. "I get called a lesbian a lot."

"Why?"

"Because I'm an athlete, I guess. Because of my... body."

He sat up, frowning. "What do you mean?"

"I'm not curvy or womanly. I have muscles."

Leo had been staring at her body all day and had yet to find a flaw. She filled out her bikini to perfection. "You're smoking hot."

"Really?"

"Have you ever looked in a mirror?"

"Some guys are intimidated by my strength," she said, shrugging. "This jock at my high school told everyone I was a lesbian after I rejected him."

Leo stretched out on his back and tucked his hands behind his head. "Jocks are stupid."

"Hey."

"There's nothing wrong with you."

"What if I *am* a lesbian?"

His heart stalled in his chest. "Why would you say that?"

"I don't know. I'm not as boy-crazy as my friends."

"Well, you should definitely explore your options and sleep with a few girls. Then tell me all about it."

She punched him in the ribs. "Would you explore your options?"

"Don't need to. I'm 100 percent sure."

"Maybe I haven't been with the right person."

"Maybe you haven't," he agreed.

"You remember that guy I was dating?"

"Yeah." The jerk who hurt her.

"I didn't enjoy the…physical part of the relation-ship."

"Why not?"

"Well, I kept trying, but I never…"

"Came?"

"Exactly."

"Did he know that?"

"Yes. He said his last girlfriend came every time. He told me I needed to give up control and embrace my feminine side."

Leo rubbed his eyes, smiling wryly.

"What's so funny?"

"If you didn't come and he knew it, he wasn't doing it right."

She studied him with skepticism. "How many girls have you been with?"

"A few."

"What's a few?"

"Five."

"Did they all…"

"No. Jenna and I only did it once. With the others, I had a little more practice."

"Was it easy?"

He stared up at the ceiling of the tent, moistening his lips. The first time, he'd thought his jaw was going to lock up. He hadn't realized he could alternate be-tween fingers and tongue or work up to oral instead of diving right in. "It got easier."

She turned off her headlamp, casting them into darkness. When she snuggled closer, he turned onto his side, facing away from her. He didn't want her to feel his arousal. She curled up against his back and slid her arm around his midsection, her palm over his beating heart.

CHAPTER EIGHT

ABBY DUCKED INSIDE the empty tent to change.

Brooke had crawled into the other tent with Leo. Abby didn't protest the arrangement. She was too anxious to sleep, anyway. She'd rather stay up with Nathan than lie down and stress out over every little sound in the woods.

She took off her shorts and put on black leggings. She was already wearing a jacket over her bikini top and shirt, so she didn't bother to change the upper half. After slipping her shoes back on, she grabbed one of the sleeping bags and a sleeping pad. They didn't have to be cold and uncomfortable while they guarded the camp.

The temperature had dropped below sixty, which felt chilly. She wanted another layer between her butt and the ground. Her body was sore from hiking.

When she brought the gear toward him, Nathan rose to his feet, his eyes alight with approval. He'd pulled on a pair of sweatpants and a flannel shirt. She set the sleeping pad down in front of the fallen log before she spread out the sleeping bag. They sat down, using the log as a backrest and bringing the edges of the sleeping bag around them.

Cozy.

"This is much better," he said. "I think I'm getting too old to rough it."

"You don't look it."

"I feel it."

She scooted closer to him, sharing his warmth. He smelled delicious, like mint and cedar. A campfire would be nice, but she understood why he hadn't built one. Just in case.

"You don't have to stay up with me."

"I want to."

They were quiet for a few minutes. She felt fairly calm, considering the circumstances. This afternoon's adventures could have triggered a major panic attack. "Brooke is sleeping in the tent with Leo."

"Are you worried about it?"

"Not really." She might be worried if Brooke started dating Leo or fell in love with him. Snuggling was no big deal.

"I'm sorry for…causing a scene."

"You didn't cause a scene. Brooke was out of line."

"So was Leo."

She moistened her lips, reluctant to continue an unpleasant subject. "Did you know I'd walked in on Ray and Lydia?"

"No. Lydia never shared that story with me."

Her chest tightened with sympathy. It must have been difficult for him to hear.

"Is that how you found out?" he asked.

She nodded, picturing their guilty faces as she strolled through the door in a flirty red dress, carrying take-out bags. "I went there to surprise him with a romantic dinner. I thought he was doing paperwork."

"What did you tell Brooke?"

"We sat down with her together, but Ray did most of the talking. He said he'd fallen in love with someone else."

The corner of Nathan's mouth tipped up, as if he found Ray's positive spin ironic. Abby considered it a cop-out. He'd played a victim of circumstance, helpless to resist Lydia's charms. "How did Brooke take it?"

"Surprisingly well. Her best friend's parents had divorced amicably the year before. She wasn't worried about Ray moving out, since he was hardly ever home. He promised he'd never stop loving *her,* even though he'd stopped…you know."

Nathan studied her face for a moment. She hoped the dark hid her sorrow. Although she'd been over Ray for years, these memories still made her sad. The thing she'd wanted most in life—a stable family— had slipped from her grasp in one fell swoop, like the take-out boxes that had fallen to the ground. It was that loss she'd always mourn, not Ray.

"Lydia told Leo after I went to training camp, but we agreed on a 'mutual story.'"

Abby was familiar with the term. A mutual story prevented one spouse from demonizing the other and trying to alienate the children, in theory. "What was it?"

"We weren't happy together anymore."

This explanation brought tears to her eyes, when

the memory of breaking the news to her daughter hadn't. "He never asked your side?"

"No. He didn't want to talk about it, and I was a mess."

"Were you?"

"Completely wrecked."

"So was I," she whispered.

He didn't ask her to elaborate, but she felt this… need vibrating from him. It was more than curiosity. Their situations were so similar, their lives forever connected. Maybe talking about it would release them both in some way.

"You noticed my unease today," she said.

"Yeah, but that was just baseball intuition. You hide it well."

"It was ten times worse after the divorce. I'd built my life around Ray, as stupid as that sounds."

"It doesn't sound stupid."

"I went to nursing school so I could work in his office. I couldn't believe he had an affair with a client right under my nose." Lydia had been visiting Ray's practice for Botox injections and body sculpting, two treatments she hadn't really needed. "After we separated, I had to find a new job and start over. I'd been working at the retirement center for less than three months when the San Diego earthquake hit. I was on the freeway."

"Which one?"

"The 163, near the collapse."

He whistled at the close call.

"I was lucky to walk away. Very few of those who

were trapped in their cars, or under the rubble, made it out alive."

"Did you get hurt?"

"I fractured my elbow," she said, touching the scar. "My car was totaled."

"Leo and Lydia were in Palm Springs with Ray. I was at training camp in Cincinnati. Where was Brooke?"

"Home alone, close to the epicenter."

"You're kidding."

"No. It was spring break, and she was supposed to be with Ray. He dropped her off a day early to go to Palm Springs."

"Wow," he said, frowning. "I didn't know that."

"I think she got knocked out in the first quake, because she doesn't remember it. She said she woke up with a headache. She was afraid to leave the house because of the aftershocks. Then there were fires and gas leaks and other hazards. On the second day, she looked out the window and saw a cheetah in the street."

He shook his head in disbelief. "I heard that some animals escaped."

"Yeah. We lived about a mile from the zoo."

"So you were at the hospital with a broken arm while Brooke was battling a concussion and wild-cats."

"Pretty much. Phones weren't working, so...I didn't know she was alive."

"Jesus, Abby."

"I hoped she was, of course. But after the devastation I'd seen, I assumed the worst. Most of the survivors had been evacuated and accounted for. The roads were barricaded and only emergency service workers were allowed to go into the hard-hit areas. The recovery effort was methodical and thorough, but slow."

"How did she get out?"

"On the third day, she heard someone calling for help. One of our neighbors was trapped under a piece of machinery in his garage. Brooke helped him out and they left together. We were reunited that night."

"I can't imagine what the wait was like."

"Hell," Abby replied. "It was hell. I had nightmares and panic attacks for months. I still have them."

"What triggers you? Besides Brooke jumping off tall objects."

"I don't know," she said, staring at the dark shapes of trees in the distance. Night clouds drifted across the sky, filtering the moonlight. "Being away from my cell phone. Open spaces. Closed spaces. The unknown, like you said. Anything threatening."

"Open spaces, really?"

"Maybe just open water."

"Ah."

"But even big, empty fields can get to me. Views from a mountaintop. I used to look up at the sky when I was a kid and imagine myself way up there, like standing on top of a flagpole. It freaked me out."

"You're an intriguing woman," he said, arching a brow.

She laughed at this polite way of calling her strange.

"I mean that."

"I believe you."

"I can't help but feel responsible for all of this."

"The earthquake?"

"Our divorces. If I'd been a better husband, Lydia wouldn't have cheated with Ray, and your marriage wouldn't have broken up."

Although she didn't agree, she humored him. "How were you a bad husband?"

"I wasn't home enough. I drank too much."

"Did you cheat?"

"No."

"Were you tempted?"

"Of course. It gets lonely on the road, and the perks are unreal. Women throw themselves at professional baseball players."

"How did you say no?"

"Mostly by avoiding parties. Drinking alone."

She nodded her understanding. "I think you have to be open to cheating. There's an invisible wall that faithful people keep up, a distance we maintain. No one can get close unless we let them."

"That's a good theory."

"I like it."

"I'm sure it's harder to stay faithful to someone you're not in love with."

"Did you love Lydia?"

"Yes. Desperately."

Abby wasn't put off by his strong statement. If anything, it made him more appealing. She'd wanted her marriage to succeed. She knew Nathan understood how she felt. They had this hurt in common. "I loved Ray, too."

"Why did you get married?"

"Besides love?"

"You were young."

"It's kind of a long story."

He settled back against the log, tucking his hands behind his head. "I've got all night."

"My parents are divorced," she said, starting at the beginning. "My father didn't cheat, as far as I know, but he was controlling. They argued about her career a lot. She refused to quit her job to move across the country with him."

Nathan listened without commenting.

"After they split up, he started a new family. At that time, I was eight, and an only child. My mother remarried and had my sister, Ella."

"The one who just got engaged."

"Yes. Ella grew up in a stable home. My stepdad is a great guy. He's always treated me like his own daughter. I even took his last name."

"But?"

She moistened her lips, nervous. "Well, I was ten when my sister was born, and I noticed how much my stepdad adored her. He and my mom and Ella made this perfect little family. I felt left out. It was worse at my father's house. My stepmom was nice and I got along with my stepbrothers, but I didn't fit in."

"You wanted a family of your own," he guessed.

Nathan was intuitive; she'd give him that. "Yes. I met Ray right after graduation. He was twenty-three and ready to settle down. We got married two months later. Brooke came along in less than a year."

"Was it everything you hoped for?"

"No, but I enjoyed being a mother."

"Lydia hated staying home with Leo. She wanted to travel and 'have fun,' like me."

"Were you having fun?"

"Hell, no. In the minors I was playing a new city every night, sleeping on a bus."

"Do you think she had it easy?"

"I did at the time, yes. Looking back, I realize I was wrong. She felt left behind and restless."

"I started to feel the same way, after a while. Ray would ask me about my day, but he didn't seem to listen to my answer. He was obsessed with new surgery techniques. Nothing I did was as important as collagen injections and chin implants."

"So you got a nursing degree and went to work in his office."

"Yes."

"Did that make you more interesting to him?"

"Apparently not."

"His loss."

She fell silent for a moment, her pulse fluttering. "I've become a lot more interesting since the divorce."

"No doubt."

"What about you?" she asked. "What's your story?"

"We were just getting to the good part of yours."

"Come on."

"My story is on YouTube. Over a million hits."

"Was that your wake-up call?"

"No, I went downhill from there, if you can believe it. Even after I lost visitation rights and was released from my last baseball contract, I didn't get sober. I just drank alone in hotel rooms, where no one could videotape me."

"Why did you start drinking?"

"I drank socially before I got injured," he said, massaging his shoulder. "After, I drank because I was stressed out and performing badly. Then my marriage imploded. Near the end, I drank because I had to. I couldn't function without it."

"How did you stop?"

"The Reds needed a third-base coach. They offered me the job, and it's a pretty big deal. Not as big as playing, but lucrative and well-respected. It was the only way I could stay in the major leagues."

"Could you have gone back to the minors?"

"Sure, but the pay doesn't compare, and I was already pretty old, at thirty-four."

"Old at thirty-four?"

"The average retirement age in the majors is thirty-two. Anyway, I wanted the job, but there was a catch. I had to go to rehab for thirty days. I agreed to go, but my heart wasn't in it. The first time I only lasted twenty-four hours. John Christie, the Reds manager, found me and dragged me back. He said he'd keep coming after me. When I left again, he tracked me down in San Diego. The third stint stuck."

"He saved your life."

"I think so. I wish I could say I'd done it on my own, or I'd done it for Leo."

"Didn't you? The manager and the job requirement got you there, but you completed the program for other reasons."

"That's true. I ended up staying ninety days by choice, and moving into a sober living facility for ninety more. I also walked away from the coaching job. That was for Leo. I wanted to live closer to him."

"What did the manager say?"

"He was happy for me. I donated some money to one of the club charities to cover the rehab costs. We're still friends."

"You're lucky he didn't give up on you."

"Yes. He told me that someone had done the same favor for him. And he encouraged me to pay it forward."

A lightbulb went off inside her head. "You think you need to keep after Leo."

"I don't know what else to do. He's spending all of his pocket money on pot. Ray took his car away after he found a joint in the ashtray. It's been an ongoing issue with Leo. I'm afraid he's going to get arrested or have an accident."

"How are his grades?"

"Not great."

"Maybe that's why he changed majors."

"Maybe," he said, as if he didn't believe Leo was capable of making good decisions. "I guess any subject is better than Music."

Abby laughed, shifting to a more comfortable position.

"What do you think?"

The question caught her off guard. "About Music, or Leo?"

"Leo."

When she hesitated for the second time, he noticed. He was very perceptive when it came to everyone but his own son.

"Is it that bad?"

"You want my advice," she said, just to make sure.

"Yes, but now I'm afraid to hear it."

She smiled at his frank response, understanding. There was no faster way to put her on the defensive than a suggestion that she was doing wrong by her child. "Let's talk about something else then."

"Why?"

"You might get offended."

"So?"

"You're being too hard on him."

His reaction was just what she expected: disbelief and resistance. "Too hard? I haven't even started to get hard."

"Well, don't. It won't work."

"Ray and Lydia have been too easy on him. They let him get away with murder."

Abby disagreed, based on the information about the car. "I don't blame you for being concerned about his drug use. I would be, too. But he's not in a place to listen to you right now. You said something about trust earlier. He doesn't trust you."

Nathan seemed to recognize the truth in this. His attitude shifted into fix-it mode. "What can I do about that?"

"Stop criticizing him so much."

He shook his head. "I can't pretend everything is fine or let him disrespect me. I'm not the kind of parent who ignores problems. The 'give every kid a trophy and say they're all winners' type."

"You think I am?"

"I think Brooke would do well, no matter what."

She tried not to get annoyed and failed. Letting go of the sleeping bag, she turned toward him to look him in the eye. "I guess she didn't need me to drive her to track meets and swimming lessons and volleyball games. She didn't need me at practices three times a week and weekend tournaments, sitting in the stands in the rain."

His brows rose with surprise. "I only meant that she seems self-motivated, but I understand your point. Ray wasn't there for Brooke. I wasn't always there for Leo. That's why I'm here now. I'm trying to make it up to him."

She relaxed at those words. At least Nathan could acknowledge his mistakes. He understood that his absences had affected Leo. "I'm not saying you should never criticize him. But you scolded him for getting sick earlier."

He rubbed a hand over his mouth. "Yeah."

"Do you think he had control over that?"

"No."

"Then why were you upset by it?"

"I...don't know."

"You don't have to let him walk all over you. Just ease up a little. He wants your attention and your acceptance, even if he won't admit it. Give him a compliment."

"A compliment."

"You could also ask him about surfing, or his classes, but try to be positive. I see a lot of good qualities in him. He's kind to Brooke, even when she's annoyingly chipper. He's brave. He cares about you."

Nathan studied her for a long moment. A hint of anguish glinted in his dark eyes, as if he wanted that last part to be true, but feared it wasn't. "He doesn't show it."

"Do you?"

"Sure I do. You saw that big hug I gave him at the lake."

She laughed softly, aware that he was making fun of himself. She liked that. His lack of ego was refreshing for a celebrated athlete. "I'm not as anxious as I thought I'd be," she said, changing the subject.

"It's my calming influence."

She examined his rugged features in the moonlight, her stomach fluttering. If anything, he was a sexy distraction. He had a habit of touching his mouth, which drew her attention to it. The rough grain of stubble along his jaw would feel nice against her lips. He looked like a good kisser, the kind who took control and kept it. Physical contact had always comforted her. That was why she'd gotten involved with her coworker. Jeremy was handsome and eager, but bland. They'd had a passionless sexual relationship.

Sleeping with Nathan wouldn't be safe. It would be terrible or fantastic. Possibly both. He wasn't a man she could use and move on from, unaffected. But after a steady diet of bland, she longed for spice. She wanted something hot and messy and emotional. An ache to remind her that she could still feel.

She tore her gaze from his, her pulse racing. If she wasn't careful, she'd be leaning toward him. She couldn't afford the risk. Ray's betrayal had sent her into a tailspin for years. She'd fought hard to regain her equilibrium after the divorce, and she'd vowed to never let a man shake her up again.

Her heart couldn't take another hit.

CHAPTER NINE

NATHAN HAD TO put some distance between him and Abby before he did something he'd regret.

Like kissing her.

He didn't trust himself in her presence. He was supposed to be keeping watch, not staring at her mouth. His eyes were drawn to her fine features and the soft curves of her body. Even when he looked away, his memory supplied a detailed picture. His fingertips tingled with the desire to slip under her sweater and feel her warm, silky skin.

Smothering a groan, he rose to his feet. He filled a kettle with water and put it on the stove to boil. Brooke had left out the instant coffee for him, as well as cocoa and chai tea. The night air cooled his blood and cleared his head.

Maybe she was right about his interactions with Leo. He couldn't take the blame for all of his son's bad behavior, but he understood cause and effect. Every time Nathan made a critical remark, Leo responded in kind, and the gulf between them widened. This method of communication wasn't working.

Nathan considered himself an intelligent man. Doing the same thing and expecting a different result wasn't logical. On the other hand, strong-arm tactics had helped him get sober. His father had pushed him to improve in sports. Nathan owed it to Leo to keep trying. If he didn't, and Leo got in serious trouble, he'd never forgive himself.

"My dad was difficult to please," he said. "I think I got drafted early because he pushed me so hard."

"You wouldn't have done well no matter what?"

He smiled at his own words. "I don't know. Some kids succeed against all odds. Others fail despite enjoying every privilege."

"How did you succeed?"

"Like Brooke, I had the support of a dedicated parent. My father was the one who was there in the rain, yelling at umpires and cursing my take-out slide. At least half of my ambition came from fear of disappointing him."

"Maybe half of your addiction, too."

The theory was so plausible he couldn't believe it hadn't crossed his mind before. He'd talked about his dad's strong influence in therapy, but he hadn't made the same connection. Nathan felt disloyal for considering the possibility that his old-school upbringing had done more harm than good. "I'm responsible for my addiction."

"I didn't say he was responsible. I said your fear of disappointing him was a factor. It motivated you in positive and negative ways."

Nathan studied the dark clusters of trees in the distance, remembering one of his last conversations with his father. Although Conrad Strom didn't believe in namby-pamby things like rehab, he'd visited Nathan there on family day. Nathan's counselor had warned him not to let his sobriety hang on relationships. No matter what happened with his loved ones, he had to stay focused on himself. It was his only chance of survival. Once he had his addiction under control, he could work on rebuilding trust and making connections with others.

His dad had hugged Nathan and said he was proud. It meant a lot, coming from a man whose advice for any malady was to "walk it off." Nathan was glad his dad hadn't considered him a failure just because he'd fallen down.

He'd died of a heart attack six months later.

"Every kid is different," Abby said. "A few will succeed against all odds, like you said. Some respond well to criticism and others don't. What helped you might not help Leo."

"What are you, some kind of parenting guru?"

"No," she said, laughing. "Part of my job at the center is to counsel residents and their families. The transition into assisted living is harder on some than others. Most families have issues with no easy resolutions. Relationships between parents and adult children are full of conflict."

He heard a slight hitch in her voice every time she said "family." She was from a broken home, and she'd married young for the wrong reasons. Nathan couldn't judge, having rushed into matrimony as a teenager, himself. But Abby's story tugged at his heartstrings. He knew how it felt to lose everything. His anger toward Ray, which had faded over the years, flared up again. Nathan wanted to punch Ray in the gut for hurting her.

He also wanted to show Abby a good time. Not out of pity. She looked delicious, and he'd love to have her. His desire had selfish reasons as well as altruistic ones. She seemed interested in him as a man. If she let him, he'd touch every inch of her body and kiss her for hours. He imagined stroking her to the edge of orgasm and watching her quiver with need. The idea of getting her off without taking his own pleasure appealed to him. He could almost taste her, exploding on his tongue.

Of course, he hadn't been with a woman in so long, he'd probably come in his pants. Just thinking about it made his cock as stiff as a bat.

He turned to stare at the trees again, his pulse throbbing. He'd put on a pair of sweatpants over his shorts, so the layers of clothing disguised his arousal. Taking a deep breath, he struggled to pull himself together. This wasn't the time or place for inappropriate thoughts. Abby's teenage daughter was twenty feet away in a tent with his teenage son. Nathan couldn't spread Abby out on a sleeping bag and dive between her legs.

Nor would she allow him to, if he asked. Most women needed to relax to enjoy oral sex. She might take a bit more work than average to warm up, even in a private setting.

God, that was hot. He didn't know why, but it was. When he finally got his mind out of the gutter and his body under control, he noticed the water on the stove was boiling. He poured a cup of instant coffee and glanced in Abby's direction. She was curled up on her side, asleep.

With a wry smile, he stirred his coffee. There was no need to worry about keeping his hands off her. She wasn't panting over him or fantasizing about a naughty tryst by moonlight. He'd bored her right into dreamland. Either that or she was exhausted from the strain of the day and the difficult climb.

His chest tightened at the sight of her peaceful slumber.

Not wanting to disturb her, he retrieved the other sleeping pad from the tent and placed it a few feet away from her, on higher ground. Then he settled in for a long night. He had a clear view of the trail, the tents and Abby. He sipped his coffee while he kept watch, pondering her advice about Leo.

At nineteen, Nathan hadn't been ready for parenthood. He'd left the baby care to Lydia, sympathizing with her struggles but offering minimal help. The minor leagues were no picnic, physically and financially. His folks lived in Wisconsin, hers in Brazil. They'd had no support system. They were *kids*.

In hindsight, he'd been stupid. He'd thought being madly in love meant they could take on the world and win.

Somehow, they got through the hard times together. Or Lydia got through them by herself while Nathan traveled and trained nonstop. Moving to the majors improved their situation dramatically. Overnight, he had money and fame. New house, new cars, new outlook. For the next few years, everything he touched had turned to gold.

Back then, Leo had been happy to see Nathan. He'd called out "Daddy, Daddy!" and hugged him as soon as he walked through the door. Nathan could still feel his son's little arms clinging to his neck. Nathan wasn't home enough, but when he was, he'd been affectionate. He knew he'd kept Lydia satisfied in bed. They'd been good together.

He had regrets, of course. He could have helped her with Leo more, especially during those early years. He hadn't been able to comfort her after the miscarriage. And his drinking, more than anything, had ruined them.

Nathan could trace his problems with Leo back to the same source. Had he been too hard on Leo from the start? He remembered being annoyed by Leo's crying and whining, but only because Nathan didn't know how to calm him down. Lydia was a good mother, soft and gentle. Nathan considered it his job, as a father, to teach Leo guy stuff. He'd always felt a little guilty about Leo's disinterest in sports. Nathan had hoped that Leo would become more competitive with age and experience. He hadn't.

Maybe that was why Nathan had enjoyed watching Leo so much today. While Abby cringed with worry every time Brooke jumped, Nathan had marveled at his son's transformation. Leo had grown so much in the past few years. He seemed at ease with his body, and he was a fast swimmer. Surfing had done wonders for him.

Nathan had accepted the fact that Leo wouldn't follow in his footsteps and become a professional athlete. He'd given up on Leo playing a sport, period. Now the pressure was off, and Leo had found his own path.

Maybe Nathan could ask Leo to give him a surfing lesson. It was summer. Nathan liked swimming and lounging on the beach.

He finished his coffee and spent the next few hours planning a happier future. He knew it would be a challenge to win Leo over, but he was ready to meet it. Abby's distanced perspective was just what he'd needed. Nathan wished he'd had the opportunity to sit down with Lydia and talk things out the same way. Their exchanges were always brief. Ray had a jealous streak, which was ironic, considering his penchant for sleeping with other women, but also understandable. Before he went to rehab, Nathan had embarrassed himself by barging in on one of their dinner parties and trying to kiss Lydia.

He smiled again, shaking his head. What an idiot he'd been. That memory had always made him cringe. Now it struck him as funny, while the image of him stumbling around with a beer can at the tender age of twelve did not.

In the wee hours of the morning, his eyelids grew heavy and he started to nod off. Abby made a sound in her sleep, sort of a low moan. Nathan wondered if she was having a nightmare. He was tempted to stretch out next to her and put his arm around her.

Yawning, he rose to make himself a fresh cup of coffee instead.

Leo stirred inside the tent. He unzipped the front opening and came out, shivering in his shorts and T-shirt. After he pulled on a hoodie from his backpack, he walked away from the tent and disappeared behind a tree.

Nathan poured the hot water into a cup and added instant coffee, stirring it with a stick. Leo retrieved his sleeping bag, wearing it like a cape, and joined him.

"I'll have that," he mumbled, gesturing for the coffee.

Nathan had never seen Leo drink coffee before, just hyped-up soda and sugar-filled energy drinks. "It's black."

He took a sip and made a face.

"Add some cocoa to it," Nathan said.

While Leo fumbled for the cocoa packets, Abby straightened, rubbing her eyes. "Is it morning?"

Leo checked his watch. "It's 2:00."

"Why don't you go in the tent?" Nathan said.

"I'll stay out here with Leo if you want to get some rest," she said.

Leo exchanged a hopeful glance with Nathan. He'd rather hang out with Abby, a stranger, than his own father.

"No," Nathan said. "We're good."

She got up and walked to the tent, taking her sleeping bag with her. Leo stared at her retreating form until she ducked inside. Then he added cocoa powder to his coffee and stirred it. Nathan tried to remember the advice she'd given him.

Compliment him.

"You woke up," he said, as if this was a stellar achievement.

Leo took his coffee to the log and sat down, not responding.

Strike one.

Undeterred, Nathan sat next to him.

"You can go to sleep." Leo said. "I got this."

"I'll stay awake with you."

Leo muttered something under his breath. Nathan couldn't hear the comment, but that was probably for the best.

After he got sober, Nathan had apologized to Leo for all of the wrongs he'd done. Redemption was a big part of recovery. Addicts were asked to take responsibility for their hurtful actions and make amends. Nathan had acknowledged every mistake he could think of to Leo. The long absences and bitter fights, the drunken stupors and morning hangovers.

Leo hadn't forgiven him anything.

Instead of dwelling on past conflicts, Nathan reconsidered his strategy. He narrowed his focus to a recent, specific slight. "I'm sorry for telling you to pull it together in the woods."

Leo's eyes widened with surprise.

Base hit?

Nathan cleared his throat and continued. "The deer reminded me of my dad…your grandfather."

"I remember. He hunted."

Conrad Strom had displayed his trophies. He'd also invited Leo hunting, an offer Nathan had declined. It was the only sport Nathan hadn't encouraged his son to try. "He…hit me."

"Grandpa did?"

Nathan rubbed a hand over his mouth, his stomach churning with anxiety. He'd never told anyone this before. "Not hard, or with his fists. He hit me with a belt as punishment. When I was a teenager, he'd slap my face, just lightly, if I did something stupid."

"Like what?"

"Like, got a bad grade or made an off throw. I hated it. I hated the insult of being slapped in the face."

Leo pondered this, his brow furrowed.

"Sometimes I'm tempted to hit you the same way. I don't know if it's instinct or a learned reaction, but it bothers me. When we were searching the woods, I was scared and tense. That's why I lashed out at you, not because you did anything wrong. I'm sure it felt like a slap in the face, and I'm sorry."

"It's okay," Leo muttered, studying the ground. "I'm sorry I punched you."

"That was self-defense. Fair game."

"I didn't know Grandpa was such a shithead."

Neither did Nathan. The realization was a weight off his shoulders. His dad hadn't been perfect, and his parenting style left a lot to be desired. Nathan wasn't sure why he'd been trying to emulate him. "I love you, Leo."

Leo gripped the handle of his coffee cup until his

knuckles turned white. Although he didn't respond, his eyes glittered with unshed tears.

Nathan blinked his own tears away, clearing his throat. This was good. He'd gotten a few things off his chest. No need to ruin it by pushing his luck. "I'm sorry to hear about your mom and Ray."

"Really?"

"Sure."

"Ray is a dick."

Nathan couldn't disagree there.

"You're not going to try to get back with her, are you?"

"No," he said, frowning. Oddly enough, the thought hadn't even occurred to him. Nathan wished Lydia all the best, but he had no interest in reuniting with her. If she left Ray, he hoped she'd find someone who treated her right.

Nathan and Leo fell into a companionable silence. It was the first they'd shared in years. Nathan didn't mention Leo's drug use or failing grades. He was troubled by the idea of Leo traveling abroad, but he kept his mouth shut. He couldn't turn back the clock or change the past. He could only pray that Leo got his act together before he gained access to his trust fund. At twenty-one, he'd sink or swim.

"I can handle this watch," Leo said. "Go to sleep."

Nathan nodded, deciding to give Leo a chance to prove himself. Maybe Leo would return the favor. Instead of retreating into the tent, Nathan retrieved his sleeping bag and stretched out on the sleeping

CHAPTER TEN

ABBY WOKE JUST before dawn.

She'd dreamed about the earthquake again.

Heart racing, she sat up and searched for Brooke. Her daughter wasn't beside her. She wasn't inside the tent at all.

Abby scrambled out of the sleeping bag and shoved her feet into hiking shoes. She could hear voices outside the tent, a soft laugh and a low murmur. Her rapid pulse began to slow as she recognized the sound of Brooke chatting with Leo. The opening at the front of the tent wasn't zipped up all the way. After tying her shoelaces, she peeked out.

Pale light touched the edges of the horizon. Nathan was stretched out on the sleeping pad in front of the fallen log. Leo and Brooke were at least twenty feet away, cuddled up in a sleeping bag. While Abby watched, rubbing her eyes, Brooke climbed on top of Leo. She straddled his waist and tried to pin his arms above his head, without success.

Leo switched their positions in a flash. He flipped Brooke onto her back and trapped her wrists in his hands, holding her down. He wasn't smiling or being playful. The pose didn't remind Abby of puppies roll-

ing around in a meadow. More like a wolf biting a
too-aggressive mate to assert dominance.

Abby backed away from the front of the tent, conflicted. Should she interrupt? She felt guilty for spying on them. Brooke had instigated the contact. If she
didn't want Leo to touch her, she shouldn't touch him.

If she did want Leo to touch her…yikes.

Ray already thought Leo was stubborn and rebellious. A fling between Leo and Brooke could create
major problems.

Abby didn't want to make things worse by invad-
ing their privacy. Brooke wouldn't appreciate her
mother meddling in her love life. It was clear that
Brooke liked to tease Leo. The question was, did
Leo like being teased? In a reverse-gender situation,
Brooke's behavior might be considered sexual ha-
rassment.

Instead of bursting out of the tent and catching
them, Abby coughed several times to announce her
presence. Then she unzipped the flap opening and
crawled out. It was a foggy, chilly morning. Dew
clung to the grass and leaves. Her shoes were damp
before she reached the outhouse. It wasn't her worst
bathroom experience, but it wasn't pleasant. She'd
rather pee behind a bush.

By the time she returned, Leo and Brooke had broken apart. He appeared frustrated and embarrassed.
She'd busied herself with the camp stove.

"Why don't you get some more sleep, Leo?" Abby
said. "I'll keep watch with Brooke."

Nathan rolled over, his eyes bleary and his hair

sticking up. Now he looked his age, and more tired than rugged. But cute. Damned cute.

"You, too," she said, gesturing to the tent. "Go rest for another hour."

The sun wasn't up yet, but there was enough light to see anyone sneaking up on them. Nathan and Leo didn't argue about safety. They collected their sleeping bags and lumbered off, choosing separate tents.

"What time is it?" Abby asked. Without her phone, she was lost.

Brooke checked her watch. "Almost six."

"How long have you been up?"

"An hour."

Abby helped herself to a cup of coffee and sat down. "We need to talk."

Brooke straddled the log, petulant. She'd changed into jogging pants, a long-sleeved shirt and a colorful alpaca-wool hat with ear flaps, probably knitted by Peruvian Indians.

"I saw you and Leo," Abby said in a near whisper.

Brooke seemed more annoyed than surprised. "So?"

"Are you sleeping with him?"

"Oh my God, Mom," she said, rolling her eyes. "No."

"Would you like to be?"

Brooke couldn't answer this one as quickly. "I'm not a virgin," she announced.

Abby assumed this was a recent development. They'd had frank discussions about sex before, and Brooke had assured Abby that she wasn't "getting any." Brooke had started dating a fellow student at Berkeley earlier this year. She hadn't shared many details with Abby about their relationship. They must have done the deed before breaking up.

"I can have sex with whoever I want," Brooke said.

"That's true," Abby said. "As long as they're of age and say yes."

Her brows drew together, as if she couldn't imagine that a boy she picked would say no. To be fair, it was unlikely. Unless that boy was her stepbrother.

"I'm sure it's fun to wrestle around with Leo," Abby said. "But if he doesn't want you to touch him, you have to leave him alone."

Understanding crossed over Brooke's face, followed by more uncertainty. Maybe she didn't know how Leo felt about her, or how she felt about him.

Abby's heart went out to her daughter. Abby couldn't sort through these issues for Brooke or tell her what to do next. They'd already talked about her style of dress and her manner of presenting herself, both of which were provocative. But Abby had never scolded her about teasing boys or exploring her sexuality. If anything, she'd stressed the importance of safety.

"Did you use condoms?" Abby asked, hopeful.

"Yes, Mom."

"Every time."

"I know."

On impulse, Abby hugged her. "Is there anything else you want to talk about?"

"I didn't even want to talk about this."

"I'm always here for you."

Brooke sighed, as if Abby was there a little *too* much. It had been difficult for Abby to let Brooke go away to college. Not just because her only daughter was beautiful and naive and reckless. Brooke was the center of her universe. Abby knew she was over-involved and clingy. She'd been the same way with Ray, perhaps.

"Can we heat up some water for washing?" Abby asked.

Brooke smiled at Abby's compulsive cleanliness. She indulged Abby by bringing out a neat stack of toiletries and a collapsible plastic bowl. They spent the next twenty minutes soaping their faces, brushing their teeth and tidying their hair. Abby would have preferred a full shampoo but Brooke nixed the idea. Tomorrow, she promised.

After they freshened up, Brooke put more water on to boil and made two single-serving packets of oatmeal for breakfast.

"How did it go last night?" Brooke asked.

"Fine."

"I think Leo's dad likes you."

Abby blew on a spoonful of apple-cinnamon oatmeal to cool it. She should shut this conversation down and discourage Brooke from matchmaking. But feminine curiosity got the better of her and she asked, "Why?"

"He checks you out when you're not looking."

Abby took the first bite of oatmeal, her chest tight with pleasure.

"He even does it when you *are* looking," Brooke added. "Like yesterday morning, right after I said your favorite word was *fuck*."

"That wasn't true, Brooke."

She laughed, unconcerned with minor details. "It got his attention."

Abby let herself fantasize about that for a brief moment. He'd seemed amused and intrigued by the claim, as if he couldn't quite believe it. Abby assumed he'd heard women curse before. Did he have a thing for dirty talk? Her body tingled at the thought of telling him what she wanted him to do to her in graphic terms.

After breakfast, Abby treated herself to the rose-tinted lip moisturizer Brooke had allowed her to bring. Brooke laid out the map and studied it. The sun had broached the horizon, its rays filtered by the thick forest and muted by cloud cover. Overcast skies indicated the temperature would be comfortable today.

"So we survived the night," Brooke said. "No one attacked us."

"Are you saying that we should forget we were robbed?"

"Yes," Brooke said brightly. "Let's carry on and enjoy ourselves. If we push, we can get to the hot springs by early afternoon."

"Leo and Nathan are going to be tired from keeping watch," Abby said. "They might not want to hike deeper into the forest."

"These are our options," Brooke said, pointing out

their location. "We can head back the way we came, on the trail where we met the thieves. We can go to Lupine Meadow, where we told the thieves we were going. Or we can hike up this mountain and leave them in the dust. After the hot springs, there's an off-highway vehicle area and an old forest service road that leads into town. It's a good alternate route."

"Where we'll get run over by motorbikes."

"Bikers have cell phones."

Abby didn't want to go back the way they came. Nor did she want to spend another night in the woods without a cell phone. None of the options suited her. "Where is that four-star resort Leo was talking about?"

"Very funny," Brooke said.

Abby knew this trip was important to Brooke. Ray and Lydia had almost ruined it. Turning back after one night would disappoint her to no end. She might do something crazy like skydiving or rock climbing to cheer herself up.

Their last family excursion to the Channel Islands had been a disaster, but lightning didn't usually strike twice. Brooke and Abby had been through hell during the earthquake. What were the odds that they'd face another life-threatening circumstance out here in the middle of nowhere?

As much as Abby preferred to avoid crises, she had to admit that they didn't always end badly. Ella and Paul had fallen in love after getting stranded together. Now they were engaged. Abby frowned as she pictured her sister's one-of-a-kind engagement ring.

"What's wrong?" Brooke asked.

"Do you think Paul is right for Ella?"

"Of course."

"Why?"

"They're adorable together. He's smart and nice and superhot."

"So's your father."

Sorrow darkened her blue eyes. "Dad is a lot of things, but nice isn't one of them."

Before they got married, Abby had thought Ray was nice. A more apt descriptor would be *suave*. He had an engaging personality and knew how to put people at ease. His bedside manner was impeccable. Those qualities didn't translate into kindness or empathy, however. He was only nice when it benefited him.

"Paul is the faithful type," Brooke said.

"How can you tell?"

She touched a finger to her lips, considering. "He looks at other women openly."

"That's a good sign?"

"Well, he doesn't stand there with his tongue hanging out. Here's an example. The three of us went to the beach together a few weeks ago. There were girls in bikinis all over the place. Paul admired some of the sights. When Ella caught him, he just smiled and squeezed her hand. She smiled back at him."

"What does that prove?"

"That he's a guy who likes half-naked women, but she's not worried about it because he worships her. Now, if he was sneaky and creepy, or he put on his sunglasses to rubberneck every hot chick on the beach, that would be a red flag."

Ray was the sneaky type for sure. He was also a smooth liar. He denied looking at other women and often wore dark sunglasses. Abby wondered how many red flags she'd missed before Lydia came along.

Abby reminded herself that Paul wasn't Ray, and Ella wasn't Abby. Her sister had been born in a loving home. Ella's parents were still together. Children of solid marriages had a little less baggage to sort through when choosing a mate. They weren't as slow to trust. They had better role models for healthy relationships.

Abby studied Brooke's pretty face, aware that her daughter would have to overcome the same obstacles Abby struggled with. This was not the legacy Abby wanted to leave Brooke, and she was angry with Ray for perpetuating the cycle. With a father like him, how was Brooke supposed to believe love was anything but transient?

Abby didn't even believe it.

Brooke might not have internalized Ray's betrayal the same way, but she'd focused on sports and books for a reason. Her description of the boys at Berkeley suggested that she kept an emotional distance.

Though cautious, Brooke didn't seem pessimistic about relationships. She tried to pair Abby up with eligible bachelors, like Nathan, and she wasn't suspicious of Paul. Brooke took everything in stride. She was amazingly strong and resilient.

"It's too bad about Ray and Lydia," Abby said.

"You're not happy they're having trouble?"

"Of course not."

"Dad is an idiot."

"Yes."

"She knew she was marrying a cheater, so I don't feel sorry for her."

"I thought you liked her."

"I do like her," Brooke said, her eyes narrow. "I'm not going to make that mistake again."

"What mistake?"

"Getting attached."

Abby's heart twisted inside her chest. She didn't blame Brooke for being angry with her father and even Lydia. It was a messy situation, full of mixed feelings.

Nathan emerged from the tent thirty minutes later. He murmured a greeting, chugged some coffee and ate two packages of oatmeal. When he'd revived enough for conversation, he arched a brow at Abby. His hair was still disheveled and his eyes were bloodshot. She had a powerful urge to ease his fatigue with snuggling.

"Did you sleep at all?" she asked.

He scratched the stubble on his jaw. "Do I look like hell?"

"No," Abby said.

"Yes," Brooke said.

He laughed, taking no offense. "I got a few hours. What's the plan for today?"

Brooke gave Abby her pleading puppy-dog look.

Abby couldn't deny her. "It's up to Nathan and Leo."

"Yes!" She jumped to her feet and pumped her fist in the air. "I'll get Leo and we can gather for a family meeting."

Nathan groaned as she sprinted off toward the tent. "I can't remember having that much energy at eighteen."

"I can't remember *being* eighteen."

They exchanged a smile.

"Don't feel obligated to keep up with her," Abby said. "I told her that you and Leo stayed up most of the night and wouldn't want to hike all day."

"I can hike," he said, rotating his shoulder. "How are you, though?"

"I'm okay. Not too anxious."

"Good."

When she smiled again, his gaze lingered on her lips for a breath-stealing moment. Warmth bloomed in Abby's cheeks. She didn't feel like a teenager, but the butterflies in her stomach were oddly reminiscent of high school. The long glances and feverish thoughts brought her back to study hall. Nathan Strom's penetrating stare excited her more than half the sex she'd had in the past decade.

God. If they got together, it would be explosive.

Brooke dragged Leo out of the tent and made everyone gather around to study the map. She traced the route to the hot springs with her fingertip and discussed returning to Monarch via the old forest service road.

"The hot springs are totally awesome," she said, selling her cause. "There are three pools of various temperatures. They formed tubs with rocks and concrete in the 1920s. And it's right next to the river, so you can cool off."

"Will there be nudists?" Leo asked. "I can't vote until I know if there are nudists."

Brooke elbowed him in the ribs. "You wouldn't say that if you'd ever seen a nudist. Most of them are wrinkly and old."

"That's not true. I've been to a nude beach in Brazil, and the girls—"

Nathan gripped Leo's shoulder to shut him up. "Let's save that observation for a more appropriate time."

"Okay," Leo said. "I'm in."

"What do you say?" Brooke asked Nathan.

Nathan deferred to Abby. She knew he wanted this extra time with his son. He needed it. Leo was nineteen and under no obligation to foster their relationship. Nathan might not get another opportunity to connect with him.

What else could she say?

"Let's do it."

CHAPTER ELEVEN

BROOKE COULDN'T WAIT to get going.

She helped Nathan break down the tents and pack up the gear. They filled individual containers with filtered water from the collapsible jug. She was about to dump out the washbowl when Leo approached with his toothbrush.

Brooke walked away to give him the space her mother thought he wanted. The advice confused her, but so did Leo. He sent mixed signals, holding himself at a distance but following her with his eyes.

She studied him from across the camp, crossing her arms over her chest in annoyance. When a guy had a crush on a girl, he stayed close to her. He called and asked her out on dates. He kissed her and touched her as often as possible. At night, he didn't turn away and let her spoon him. He spooned *her*.

Based on these cues, Leo wasn't interested in her as a girlfriend. Yeah, he got hard when they were wrestling, but boys his age probably had nonstop erections. The fact that he tried to keep his penis away from her, instead of putting it in her, told her everything she needed to know. He might be attracted to her on a physical level, but he wouldn't act on it because their parents were married. It would be like having a one-night stand with a coworker and seeing them every day after. Her best friend had done that once. Awkward!

Leo wasn't going to sleep with her. Whatever. Brooke didn't see why she shouldn't play around with him. It was harmless. She wanted to be in his life no matter what they were to each other. Friends, step-siblings, or more.

Nathan joined Leo to brush his teeth and wash up. Brooke was glad they were concerned with basic hygiene. They didn't have to smell great, but at least they could have fresh breath. While she watched, they tugged off their shirts and splashed their arm-pits. Brooke turned to look for her mom and found her gazing at Nathan's chest.

Yes, her mom definitely approved of his…hygiene.

Leo caught them both staring and smirked. Brooke hadn't really meant what she'd said at the lake. His dad *was* pretty hot for an old guy, but she only had eyes for Leo. He had a beautiful body, smooth and strong. Although he resembled Nathan, he had his mother's skin tone and jet-black hair. He'd also in-herited her blend of ethnicities. Brooke knew he had a mix of Latin, European and Asian blood.

When they were finished at the washbowl, Brooke dumped out the water. Leo, who was still shirtless, hooked his arm around her neck. "I have some sexy body hair for you," he said, putting his wet armpit in her face.

"Eww, Leo!" She pushed him off, laughing. He

smelled nice, but it was disconcerting to have her nose shoved into a semiprivate place. She knew he meant to be funny and brotherly. Even so, the contact thrilled her. This was the problem between them. His humor wasn't quite appropriate. They both had boundaries issues.

"Quit messing around," Nathan said, throwing Leo his shirt.

He put it on while Brooke tucked the bowl into her backpack, glancing at her mother. Abby hadn't missed the exchange. Brooke lifted her brows to communicate her dilemma. *See? He's touching me first.*

The thought struck her as childish, bringing to mind some of the squabbles she'd had with Ella when they were younger. If she wanted Leo to treat her like a girl, instead of a friend or a sister, she had to change the way they interacted. Maybe Leo hadn't gotten the message. She wasn't being obvious enough.

Brooke started down the trail, taking the lead again. No one complained. The gory image of the dripping deer had faded, along with the fear that those dudes would sneak up on them. They were long gone.

She set a difficult pace, hoping to reach the hot springs early enough to enjoy an afternoon soak. It was a beautiful hike along the mountainside, climbing steadily in elevation. Although the day was overcast, rather than sunny, the temperature felt warm. The cool breeze and cloudy skies kept them from overheating.

When Abby started to lag behind, her cheeks

flushed, Brooke checked her watch. It was time for a lunch break.

She stopped in a nice shady area by the creek, shrugging out of her pack. They snacked on peanut butter crackers and banana chips. Her mom took off her shoes and put her toes in the water, making a sound as if her feet hurt. Brooke was itching to keep going, but she hopped across a few rocks and explored the opposite bank instead. Maybe Leo would follow her and give their parents some alone time. She glanced over her shoulder and found his eyes on her. Hiding a smile, she continued into the trees.

"What are you doing?" he asked when he caught up with her.

"Nothing." She flattened her palm against the bark of an oak, feeling its rough texture. "My mom saw us this morning."

"I figured."

"She asked if we were having sex."

His brows shot up. "What did you say?"

"I said yes, we're doing it every chance we can get. In the tent, behind the outhouse and on the back of your motorcycle."

Although she was clearly joking, he didn't laugh. "You shouldn't talk like that."

"To you, or my mother?"

He just stared at her, his lips pressed together in disapproval. For a pothead, he was sort of uptight. Maybe that was why she felt so compelled to brush up against him when he was near, to arch her back a little when he was watching.

"Did you talk to your dad?" she asked.

He looked away, scowling. "Yeah."

"How did it go?"

"Fine."

"You didn't argue?"

"No. He said he was sorry for telling me to pull it together."

"When you were puking?"

"Yeah."

"That was kind of jerky," she said, thinking back. "It's cool that he apologized. See, Leo? He's trying."

"I guess."

"We should totally get him together with my mom."

He grimaced. "Why are you so obsessed with that?"

At the cabin, she'd been pushing them together because Nathan seemed like a good guy. They'd make a cute couple. Now there was a different force driving her. The idea of her dad and Lydia splitting up bothered Brooke. She'd grown attached to Lydia. She didn't want to lose Leo. In her experience, the only way to hold on to someone was through family connections, and even those were tenuous.

"If they fell in love, my mom would be happy again...and we could still see each other," she said softly.

His eyes lit up with an emotion she couldn't identify. It was happy and sad at the same time, lost in a strange space between pleasure and pain. She suspected that he was uncomfortable with her affection, but also flattered by it. Maybe he didn't discourage her advances because he liked having his ego stroked.

She dismissed the notion as quickly as it popped into her mind. Leo cared about her; she was certain of this, if nothing else. He didn't want to hurt her feelings by rejecting her. So he played along and endured the push/pull between them, as if any move forward or back would send them both toppling over the edge they'd been balancing on.

He was afraid to let go of her, too.

"I won't stop seeing you, Brooke."

"You stopped seeing your dad."

His gaze narrowed. "That's different."

"Why?"

"He left me."

"Not by choice."

"He chose to drink."

"You choose to smoke."

"Goddamn it," he muttered, raking a hand through his hair. "It's not the same. I'm not hurting anyone!"

Brooke dropped the subject. She felt like a hypocrite because she'd asked him to share a joint with her at Mavericks. He'd never offered her pot or smoked it around her before. She'd caught him getting high in his room once when her dad and Lydia weren't home. He'd been drowsy and distracted, unable to concentrate on their conversation.

Her reaction to the drug wasn't what she'd expected. Instead of feeling mellow, she'd become jumpy and hyperaware. Sounds and sights were magnified. She was confused one moment and giggling the next. Leo had laughed with her when she was laughing, calmed her when she needed calming.

Hours later, she'd clung to him dreamily, lost in a trance. She'd pressed closer, touching her lips to his neck, and…

A flash of movement on the ground distracted her. She searched the leaves at her feet and located the source leaping onto a nearby boulder.

"Look," she said, grasping Leo's arm. "A frog."

He cupped his palm against the boulder, lightning-fast. Grinning, he turned his hand over, careful not to crush the tiny creature. It was about the size of a quarter, with a round body that was the color of speckled sand. When Brooke leaned in for a better look, it jumped again. She tried to find the frog among the scattered leaves, to no avail.

What she did find gave her pause.

Leo reached down and grabbed the arrow before she could pick it up. "This is from a crossbow." It was longer than his forearm, with yellow feathers at one end and a wicked-looking metal point at the other.

Covering the sharp tip with his thumb, he closed his fist around the point and brought it to the hollow of his throat. He lolled his head to the side, eyes dull. "Wouldn't it be funny if I stumbled out of the woods, pretending I'd been shot?"

"No," she said, appalled. "My mom would have a heart attack."

"So would my dad."

"Maybe this is the same kind of arrow they found in that dead boy."

"Nah," he said, taking the point away from his neck. "There's more than one hunter with a cross-bow around here."

Brooke glanced around the woods, chilled by the thought.

"Not right here, by the trail," Leo said. "In this forest."

"If they don't shoot near the trail, why is this arrow here?"

"Good question," he said. "I don't know if it's legal to shoot close to the trail or not. We could ask my dad."

She wrapped her hand around the shaft. "Let's just leave it here and not say anything."

"I want to keep it."

"Why?"

He shrugged. "To hunt with later. I can catch a fish for our dinner, Pocahontas."

Smiling, she released the arrow. "Okay, Captain John."

"I'm not Captain John." He held the arrow over his head like a spear. "I'm fucking Crazy Horse."

She laughed at his warrior pose. "Don't let my mom see it."

He tucked the arrow into the waistband of his shorts, sharp end up, before they returned to their parents. Her mom wasn't flirting with Nathan, to Brooke's disappointment. She was brushing the sand off her perfectly manicured toes while he stood nearby, his arms crossed over his chest. Leo wasn't the only one who seemed reluctant to make a move. Brooke was going to have to up her match-making game.

Time for a full-court press.

At the hot springs, Brooke and Leo could go exploring while her mom and Nathan soaked in the tubs. Leo's dad liked women in bikinis. He liked her mother in a bikini. He also seemed protective, so maybe Brooke could exploit that.

They resumed hiking at a moderate pace. Brooke didn't want her mom to get too tired for romance. She focused on the sights and sounds of the forest, enjoying the pleasant burn in her muscles. Physical exercise always put Brooke in a peaceful state of mind, sort of an altered consciousness. It was so much better than the type of high Leo preferred. Brooke didn't have anything against other people smoking pot, but she'd rather stay sharp. The woozy mixture of paranoia and hilarity had unsettled her.

About two hours later, Brooke could tell they were getting close. A hint of sulfur tickled her nostrils, and ribbons of steam threaded through the trees in the distance. She grinned at Leo over her shoulder, excited.

"Are we there yet?" he asked in a monotone.

"Almost," she said, walking faster. As she rounded the next corner, a naked woman sprinted toward her, dripping wet and screaming her head off. She was dark-haired and slim, her eyes wide with panic.

"Nay," the woman yelled, glancing behind her. In her hysterical state, she didn't see Brooke and Leo on the trail. Making a sound between a shriek and a sob, she continued running and almost collided with them.

The scene went from frightening to bizarre in two seconds flat. A tall blond man crashed through the bushes, holding a snake. He was naked and wet, like the woman, but neither small nor slim. Thor had a wide chest, thick arms and a very impressive piece of male equipment between his legs.

Brooke didn't have the faintest clue how to react. While she stood there, dumbstruck, Leo sprang into action. Moving in front of Thor, he brandished the arrow he'd tucked in his shorts. The terrified woman collapsed on the path, whimpering. Leo held the impromptu weapon in a challenging manner, as if ready to charge.

Nathan caught up with them a second later. When he saw the cowering woman and buck-naked giant, he did a double take. Thor had six inches and at least fifty pounds on Leo. "What the fuck is this?" he asked, gaping.

Thor tossed the snake aside and cupped his junk, flushing. It was a harmless little water snake, nothing compared to his manhood. One hand didn't even cover him. Brooke didn't mean to stare, but she couldn't help it.

Her mother crouched down next to the nude woman. "Are you all right?"

The woman answered with a rush of foreign words, her teeth chattering. She didn't look scared anymore, just angry and cold.

"I play," Thor said. "She is friend. Girlfriend."

Leo relaxed his stance. "Do you speak English?" he asked the woman.

She continued to scold the man in her native tongue. Brooke couldn't guess what it was. Leo tried Spanish, which she seemed to understand. Finally she said, "I am okay," in heavily accented English. "Sorry."

Thor apologized also, seeming chagrined. Leo exchanged a few more words with the woman in Spanish. Brooke guessed that she was afraid of snakes, not her boyfriend. Thor had been chasing after her as a joke.

Leo turned around to give them some privacy, gesturing for his dad to do the same. Brooke and her mom followed suit. As the woman scampered away with Thor, Brooke peeked at his retreating backside. Not bad.

When the couple was out of sight, the four of them exchanged incredulous glances.

"I think we found the nudists," Nathan said.

They all burst out laughing. Brooke felt dizzy from a mixture of tension and relief. She'd assumed the woman was being attacked, but she'd just stood there. Leo was the one who'd stepped forward to protect her. He was still holding the arrow.

"Where did you get that?" her mother asked.

"In the woods," he said, tucking it away again.

The couple returned, covered with beach towels, a moment later. They must have left their belongings by the hot springs. The man said they were visiting the U.S. from Croatia. Their names were Jakov and Petra.

"Do you have a cell phone?" her mother asked, cupping a hand to her ear.

Jakov nodded. *"Ya."*

"Can I use it? *Por favor?"*

They followed Jakov and Petra to a nearby campsite. Jakov found his cell phone and handed it her mother. Although she couldn't get a voice call through, she was able to send a text message to Ray detailing their whereabouts and asking him to report the theft to the local authorities. Leo communicated with the couple in a combination of languages, explaining that they'd been robbed at Echo Lake.

Her mom returned the cell phone with a profuse thank-you. Instead of staying in the campsite, the couple got ready to leave. They waved goodbye and set off down the trail.

"Do you think they understood you?" Nathan asked.

"I don't know. Their Spanish wasn't much better than their English, and they didn't speak Portuguese."

"What were you going to do with that arrow?"

"I have no idea," he replied, smiling.

"He could have swatted it away from you like a fly."

Leo arched a brow. "I think he could have beaten me up with his dick."

They all laughed like crazy at this exaggeration, unable to pretend they hadn't noticed Jakov's male endowments. Brooke almost died. Nathan doubled over and staggered sideways. Even her mother joined in, giggling until she cried.

"I don't blame her for running away," Brooke said, sending them off again.

"Remind me not to go to Croatia," Leo added. "I can't compete."

Brooke hadn't laughed so hard in months. The humor was adult and juvenile at the same time. It felt weird to share this moment as a family, but good. If they could make fun of penises, they were getting comfortable with each other.

"Seriously though," Nathan said, sobering. "That was brave of you."

Leo stopped laughing. He looked bewildered, as if he couldn't believe his father was actually giving him a compliment.

"He's right, Leo," Brooke said. "That girl was screaming bloody murder and I just froze. I didn't know what to do."

"That's a common response to a dangerous situation," her mom said. "Most people move slow instead of hurrying to help. Some can't move or think at all."

"Where did you hear that?" Nathan asked.

"I've read a lot of books about survival psychology," her mom said.

"She's obsessed with worst-case scenarios and disaster prep," Brooke said. "If you need to know how to escape a submerged vehicle, she's your girl."

Nathan smiled in approval. "I'll remember that."

"You can't predict how anyone will react during an emergency," her mom said to Leo. "It takes a special sort of person to push aside their fear and be a hero."

Leo's eyes watered as he listened to her. They all fell silent, watching him with interest.

He must have been embarrassed by the display of emotion, because he walked away, pinching the bridge of his nose.

CHAPTER TWELVE

LEO STAYED AT the edge of the campsite for a few minutes.

Pulling himself together.

He wasn't a hero, and he hadn't done anything special. He didn't enjoy being put on the spot or patted on the back. It was better than getting criticized for puking, he supposed, but the situations felt similar. Both of his reactions had been instinctive, rather than deliberate. If he'd stopped to consider the size differential, he wouldn't have jumped in to help.

His dad was trying to win him over with nice words, and Leo wasn't going to fall for it. He didn't like this pressure in his chest. With some difficulty, he blinked the tears away. He didn't like crying, either.

When he was dry-eyed and guarded, he returned to the group. This campsite was even more primitive than the last one, with a single fire pit and a small clearing for tents. There was no outhouse; they were going to have to dig holes. Gross.

His dad was setting up a tent in the shade. Brooke went to gather water with Abby. Saying nothing, Leo approached his dad and started helping. When Brooke returned to camp, she passed out a handful of pistachios and dried apricots. Leo would have killed for a burrito. Even a bowl of cereal or some fresh fruit sounded good.

Anything but more nuts.

"What else is there?" he asked Brooke. "I'm still hungry."

She gave him two sausage sticks, which he devoured. Abby opened a bag of pretzels and shared those, also.

"We'll have a heartier meal tonight," Brooke promised.

They finished the snack and drank tepid water. The sun had burned through the late-day clouds, bringing a muggy, hazy heat. Leo felt like stretching out in the shade and napping until dinnertime. His dad sat down with his back to a tree trunk while Brooke and Abby ducked inside the tents to change. Leo found a low-lying boulder to use as a recliner.

A few minutes later, Brooke emerged from the tent in her bikini and flip-flops. She had a towel draped over one arm. Abby's towel was wrapped around her waist in a more demure, ladylike fashion.

"Are you guys coming?" Brooke asked.

"We'll catch up in a minute," his dad said.

Leo was too lazy to protest. He tucked his hands behind his head, following the sway of Brooke's hips as she left camp.

"Has Ray talked to you about her?" his dad asked.

Leo knew what he was getting at. "Yes."

"What did he say?"

"That he'd cut off my balls if I touched her."

"Is that why you haven't?"

Leo didn't answer. It was a trick question, and he wasn't stupid. "I guess you don't think I'm gay anymore."

His dad looked puzzled. "I never thought you were gay."

"You asked me if I was once."

"When?"

"After soccer practice. I was eleven."

His dad squinted into the distance, as if trying to place this conversation. "The coach's son called you a name on the soccer field."

"Faggot," Leo supplied.

"I told you it didn't matter if you were gay."

"If it didn't matter, why bring it up?"

"I couldn't just let an insult like that slide."

"Because you were afraid it was true."

"No," he said, frowning. "I wasn't."

"Come on," Leo said. "I sucked at soccer, and at baseball, and at football. You know you were looking for a reason."

"You didn't try hard enough. That was the reason."

Leo's temper flared. He straightened, pushing away from the boulder. "I did try, but you were never satisfied. You wanted me to be the best on the team because you were the best. Average wasn't good enough."

His dad stared at him with a confused sort of guilt, as if he knew what he'd done, but not why it was wrong. He was a superstar athlete; of course average wasn't good enough for him. The problem was that Leo had never been better than average.

"I did try," he repeated. "I just didn't have the passion for it that you did. I felt out of place on the field."

"What do you mean, out of place?"

He wasn't sure how to explain it. "I didn't belong."

"You feel like you belong when you're surfing?"

Leo shrugged. "I can surf on my own, at my own pace. There's no pressure to score. It just fits me better. So does playing music."

"Then why did you change majors?"

"I decided music was more of a hobby for me than a career."

"Wow," Nathan said, shaking his head.

"What?"

"That sounds very mature."

"You think I'm incapable of acting like an adult."

"No. I just can't believe how grown-up you are. I missed so much."

Leo fell silent, wary of another emotional upheaval. He could handle his dad's criticism, not these…warm fuzzies.

"Do you remember my friend John Christie?"

"No."

"His son committed suicide when he was fourteen. Six months before I had that conversation with you."

Leo hadn't known that. He looked at his dad, curious. "Why did he do it?"

"He was getting bullied at school. Other boys called him gay."

"Was he?"

"I don't know. John didn't think he was, but they'd never talked about it. He told me he wished they had."

"Oh."

"I wasn't worried about you being gay, Leo. You seemed aware of pretty girls at a young age. That doesn't necessarily mean anything, I guess. It never occurred to me that you might like both boys and girls."

"I don't."

His dad smiled wryly. "The important thing was that you knew it was okay with me. John had no idea that his son was depressed. He'd assumed Jordan was straight, maybe for some of the same reasons I assumed you were. But I didn't care either way. I didn't want you to hate yourself or decide you'd rather end your life than be who you are."

Leo wondered how he could have misinterpreted the discussion so badly. He rose from the ground, full of resentment and ambivalence. He didn't like feeling sad about their shitty relationship.

"I can see that I should have communicated this to you back then," Nathan said.

"Too late," Leo replied. "For everything."

His dad stood up to face him, his eyes full of pain. It felt good to hurt him, good and bad and mean at the same time. Leo told himself to walk away before he started crying again. His dad looked sort of choked up, too.

Fuck *this*.

"I was thinking," his dad said, clearing his throat.

"I've never been surfing. Maybe you could give me a lesson."

Leo wanted to say no way, but his mouth wouldn't form the words. "You're too old," was the best he could manage.

His dad laughed, wiping his eyes. "Let me know if you change your mind."

"I won't," Leo said, but his voice wavered. Shit.

He stormed into the tent and changed into his board shorts. Leo was determined to sit in the hot springs until his inner turmoil soaked away. Not bothering to wait for his dad, he took off down the trail.

Brooke met him halfway there. She was wet and flushed, carrying a long walking stick. "Look what I found."

"A stick?"

"I thought we could tie the arrow point to the end and make a real fishing spear."

His dad passed by in his swim trunks, glancing at Leo over his shoulder. Leo knew that Brooke was trying to arrange for their parents to be alone together. She clasped his hand in hers, pleading silently for him to go along with it.

Damn her pretty blue eyes.

Smothering a sigh, Leo followed Brooke back to camp. He had a leather cord in his pack that they could use to affix the arrow to the end of the stick. While he was searching for it, his fingertips brushed the plastic container where his pot was stashed and a wave of longing hit him. He hadn't smoked weed for two full days. If only he could sneak away. He needed the escape, the instant mood lift.

After stashing a bud in the pocket of his board shorts, he pulled out the leather cord and attached the arrow to the stick. It made a wicked-sharp spear.

Brooke grinned at the sight. "Will it work?"

He doubted it. "Maybe. Do you have any aluminum foil?"

"Yes."

"Give me some."

"What for?"

"To use as a lure."

She rifled through the supplies and located a square of foil, which he placed in his pocket. Good thing she was clueless about drugs. She didn't have any idea that he could mold the foil into a disposable pipe.

They hiked down the trail until they found a convenient fishing hole. A huge pine log had fallen across the river and become lodged horizontally, blocking the flow. The deep, calm area on the other side was perfect.

"This is so awesome!" Brooke gripped his biceps. "Maybe we can stay here tomorrow. Take a break from hiking."

Leo wouldn't mind staying an extra day, but not if it meant more heartfelt discussions with his dad. He'd rather return to his regularly scheduled summer. Surf, sun and smoke. He couldn't wait to sleep in his own bed and listen to music. He had to figure out a way to get his car back, too. Doing yard work or chores usually sufficed. As long as he promised to drive sober, he didn't see the problem.

He followed Brooke across the log with caution. It felt steady, but the surface was slippery. She stopped short, fighting for balance. When he put his hand on her waist, she bent forward, as if aligning her ass to his crotch might help. He felt like shoving her into the water. Or urging her down on her knees.

Instead, he let go and she leaped to the other side of the log with nimble grace. Her blond hair was loose and wavy today, her swimsuit striped with earth tones. She reminded him of a wood nymph. *La belle dame sans merci,* from the poem he'd read in high school.

"What did you and your dad talk about?" she asked.

"Nothing important."

They spent the next twenty minutes trying to spear a fish, with no luck. Brooke kept distracting him by pressing her breasts to his arm. He told her she was crowding him and she wandered off. When she didn't come back, he straightened, searching the shore for her.

"Brooke?"

No answer.

Pulse racing, he ducked into the copse of trees beside the river. There was no sign of her. "Brooke?"

Maybe she'd gone to the hot springs. He hadn't seen her leave, but there could be an alternate route. Frowning, he headed toward the fallen log. Just before he reached it, she jumped out from behind a boulder and scared the hell out of him. He stumbled backward in the mud, tossing the spear away. When she tried to help him stay upright, their legs got tangled up. Forward momentum propelled them both to the wet ground.

She fell on top of him, laughing.

Leo pushed her onto her back. "You did that on purpose."

Unrepentant, she scooped up a handful of mud and dropped it on the center of his chest with a splat.

It wasn't funny. He'd been carrying a sharp object. This stunt could have resulted in one or both of them getting hurt. She'd also hidden from him and made him worry about her. He'd had it with her playful manipulations.

Did she think she could jerk him around with no consequences? Tease and taunt him just for kicks? He wasn't much taller than her, but he was stronger and heavier. He had greater upper body strength. He could hold her down and teach her a lesson.

Sweeping mud into his hand, he deposited it on top of her head, smearing it all over her lovely blond hair.

There. Take that.

Her eyes went wide with shock. Then she gritted her teeth like a feral animal and began to wrestle him in earnest.

This meant war.

She locked an arm around his neck and tried to shove him into the mud. He laughed at the feeble attempt, evading her easily. But Brooke was a force to be reckoned with. She scrambled to her feet and tackled him from behind, determined to take him down. He hooked his arm around her thigh and tried to shake her loose. They broke apart, rolling around in the mud and throwing it in each other's faces. No dirty trick or body part was off-limits. If she could have kneed him in the groin, she would have.

In the end, he came out on top. She was pinned underneath him, panting from exertion. His belly was flat against hers, his fists buried in her gritty hair. Every inch of her skin was splattered. Her bikini strings had come loose in the melee. He could feel her breasts against his chest, slippery and bare.

He groaned, fighting the urge to grind against her. He wanted to grip her hair tighter and slide up and down, back and forth, creating delicious friction.

Instead, he released her and crawled away.

She didn't bother to cover her breasts. They rose and fell with every breath, mud-speckled and perfect.

He became painfully aroused. Gripping his dick to keep it from sticking out at a 90-degree angle, he hobbled to the edge of the water and submerged his filthy, overheated body. The cold shock withered his hard-on. He winced at the unpleasant sensation.

Brooke fumbled with her bikini top and followed him into the river. "You cheated."

"I won fair and square."

"You untied my top."

He might have gotten his hand tangled in it, but not on purpose. "You put mud in my shorts."

Smiling, she ducked under the surface.

Leo scrubbed at his face, his neck, down his shorts and behind his ears. He had mud everywhere.

Brooke was in worse shape, with thick clumps in her hair. She swished her hair around in the water and threaded her fingers through the strands to remove the dirt. When she was finished, she straightened and turned toward him. Her bikini top was still untied. Her breasts were exposed, nipples like cherries. While he watched, mesmerized, she gathered the loose strings and secured a knot at the nape of her neck. He backed away, wading toward the shore. She joined him on a flat rock in the late-afternoon sun.

He reached into his pocket for the pot he'd stashed there. It had crumbled into mush.

Brooke put her head on his shoulder, shivering. She probably wanted him to put his arm around her. He'd tried to teach her a lesson about teasing him, but she'd enjoyed it. He didn't know what else to do. He couldn't even smoke pot to fade away. When she snuggled closer, seeking warmth, he leaped to his feet.

"Can't you find someone else to fuck you?"

She stared at him in shock. "What?"

"Maybe try getting yourself off every once in a while. Or can't you figure out how to come that way, either?"

To his dismay, tears filled her eyes.

"Shit," he said, raking a hand through his wet hair.

She drew her knees to her chest and wrapped her arms around her legs, making herself as small as possible.

He sat down next to her again, his gut clenched in regret. It wasn't her fault that he was sexually frustrated. And there was nothing wrong with *her* that a generous boyfriend couldn't cure. "I'm sorry."

"I can come on my own," she said, wiping a tear from her cheek. "But doesn't it feel better with a partner?"

Leo didn't answer right away. Being with a girl was more pleasurable, and infinitely more exciting, than using his hand. It also had the potential for failure and disappointment. Jerking off was like going to McDonald's. He always got exactly what he ordered. There were no surprises, no fireworks. "It feels good either way. When you're with another person, the closeness is what makes it special."

"Can't we have that? The closeness, if not the... other?"

He wanted both, the closeness and the coming. She was asking for sexual intimacy without sex, which was impossible, like touching her without getting aroused. But he had such a hard time saying no to Brooke.

Smothering a sigh, he put his arm around her.

CHAPTER THIRTEEN

NATHAN CONTINUED DOWN the trail, his palms sweaty and his throat dry.

He was nervous about being alone with Abby. In warm water, mostly naked. It was a recipe for temptation.

The path from the campsite to the hot springs was short. There were three small pools at the river's edge. Abby was in the closest one, which was round and encircled by a rock wall. In the middle there was a rectangular tub, clearly manmade. On the other side lay a second oval-shaped pool. All three looked inviting, with crystal-clear water.

"The middle tub is the hottest," Abby said.

Nathan could use a good soak. His leg muscles ached, especially his quadriceps. He placed his towel on a nearby rock and joined her in the closest pool. It was warm, but not too warm. Perfect.

Abby moved over a few inches to make room for him. Then she settled back against a flat rock, one arm draped over the side of the pool. He could see the shape of her body beneath the rippled water. Her hair was piled into a knot atop her head, and her skin was dewy with moisture. He could have studied her face for hours.

She stared back at him, her gaze trailing down his chest.

"I don't measure up to Jakov, if that's what you're wondering."

She choked out a laugh. "I wasn't."

"No? I thought women were obsessed with size."

"Who told you that?"

"Late-night infomercials."

"You're funny," she said, smiling. "Leo gets it from you."

He sobered at this observation, which had never occurred to him. "We haven't laughed together in years."

"That was a nice compliment you gave him."

"Yeah?"

She nodded, biting her lower lip.

Nathan had to admit that she'd been right. Praise was exactly what Leo needed, and his response to it had been heart-wrenching. Nathan supposed that boys didn't believe they were good or brave or manly unless their fathers told them they were.

Nathan hadn't given Leo enough credit, and he wasn't proud of that. The picture Leo painted of Nathan's competitive spirit had been pretty ugly—and accurate. Nathan had always had a monster inside him, a cold mixture of drive and aggression. His inability to accept average or second-best in himself had transferred to Leo, with unfortunate results.

Leo had said he didn't belong on the team. Nathan

related this to Abby's comment about not belonging in her own family. Nathan couldn't fault either of them for feeling this way. Maybe he'd mistaken Leo's lack of passion for poor sportsmanship. This disconnect had colored so many interactions between them. Nathan hadn't realized that Leo had misunderstood their conversation about sexuality.

Jesus. Was there anything Nathan hadn't fucked up?

Although it wasn't easy to face his mistakes, discovering how and where he'd gone wrong felt like a revelation. Being able to communicate with his son was priceless. Leo didn't want to forgive Nathan, but they were making progress, and he owed it all to Abby.

"Thank you," Nathan said simply. "Your advice was excellent."

She flushed with pleasure. "I'm glad to help."

He responded to her on many levels. He appreciated the kindness she'd shown Leo. He liked her smile, her elegance, her sense of humor. Yesterday at the lake, he'd admired her daring while also recognizing her vulnerability. She inspired his protective instincts. Plus, she looked hot in a bikini. "Are you seeing anyone?"

Her lips parted in surprise. "No."

"Why not?"

She glanced across the river, as if searching for an answer.

"I'm making you uncomfortable."

"No, it's fine."

"You're a beautiful woman," he said, digging himself in deeper.

She seemed embarrassed by the attention. Instead of answering, she fingered the damp tendrils of hair at her nape. Damn. He'd struck out already. Maybe she didn't like superficial compliments. Maybe she thought he was a moron.

"I'm sorry," she said, meeting his gaze. "It's been a long time since I...did this."

"Fended off a come-on?"

"Accepted a compliment."

That was a shame. She was either avoiding men, or talking to the wrong ones. "None of your strip poker friends get fresh?"

"They have bad eyesight."

"I don't."

"I'm not dating anyone," she said finally.

"I assumed you weren't, based on Brooke's attempts to throw you at me."

She laughed, covering her forehead. "You noticed?"

"She's not subtle."

"I was involved with someone at work until recently."

"A resident?" he joked.

"No," she said in a chiding tone. "A physical therapist."

"What happened?"

"I decided to break it off. It wasn't going anywhere."

"Why not?"

"It was just that kind of arrangement. Neither of us wanted a committed relationship. He was newly divorced and spent weekends with his kids. We weren't exclusive."

"What do you mean?"

"He saw other women."

"You're kidding."

"No."

"You didn't mind?"

"I preferred it. His honesty was refreshing."

"You don't think men are capable of being faithful," he said.

"Some are. I just don't trust myself to pick one who is."

His chest tightened at those words, spoken sincerely. He'd been betrayed, like her. The difference was that he felt responsible for his failed marriage. Abby's only mistake was in giving her heart to the wrong man. "Did you care about this guy?"

"I liked him as a friend. That's one of the reasons I ended it. I thought he'd meet someone else if I wasn't in the picture."

"What about you?"

"What about me?"

"Don't you want to meet a man you can fall in love with?" When she didn't answer, he pressed on. "How old are you…thirty-five? There are plenty of women your age who are just now getting married and starting families."

"I'm thirty-six. And thank you for letting me know

I still have value due to my youth and childbearing capabilities."

"Anytime," he said, aware that he'd annoyed her. "You're hot, too. Don't forget the most important part."

She gripped his arm to steady it and punched him in the shoulder. It was his bad shoulder, but he didn't mind. He liked the contact, the hard slap of flesh against his and the way her breasts jiggled enticingly. "Why aren't you dating anyone?" she asked, turning the tables on him. "You're young and hot and capable of fathering children, I imagine. Plenty of men your age are starting their *second* families."

Ouch.

"I dated a lot of different women after the divorce," he said.

"You mean you slept with them."

He inclined his head. "In rehab, I took a vow of abstinence."

"For how long?"

"A year."

"Did you make it?"

"No. Six months after I got out, my father died. I drove to a bar. I wanted to drink. Instead, I nursed a club soda and went home with a woman." She'd been tipsy and distant, participating with the feigned enthusiasm of a prostitute. Nathan had rushed to the finish and left. "It wasn't good."

She smiled at the understatement. "But you stayed clean."

"Yes."

"Was the next time better?"

"There hasn't been a next time."

"What do you mean?"

"I can't sleep with strangers anymore. The bar scene is a trigger for me. I don't want to hang out at clubs or meet women for cocktails."

"You could date a nondrinker."

"I could."

"Why haven't you?"

He shrugged, unsure of the reason. He'd been focused on managing the Toros and repairing the rift with Leo. Casual sex was out. Real relationships required work. He hadn't met anyone who tempted him to take on another challenge. Until now.

But just because he wanted to, didn't mean he should. Their kids were stepsiblings. He might screw up and hurt her. She should find a nice guy to have babies with. She deserved that. The perfect little family she'd always dreamed of.

As much as he'd like to have her, Nathan couldn't give her what she needed. Starting over and having more kids wasn't in the cards for him.

Movement in the woods caught his attention. He put his hand on Abby's arm, his heart racing. Then he saw a flash of blond hair and realized it was Brooke, ducking behind a tree. "I think your daughter is spying on us."

Abby groaned, glancing in that direction. "She's relentless."

"We should just make out. Then she can tell Ray and Lydia we hooked up."

She chuckled at the suggestion. "Okay."

Okay? He'd been kidding.

"But we have to really go for it, with lots of groping and tongues."

Nathan couldn't bring himself to say no. If she wanted to get groped, he'd grope her. "You're on."

She turned toward him, resting her hand on his shoulder. They were only pretending, so he didn't have to worry about making it special or impressing her with his seduction technique. Even so, he didn't feel right about moving too fast. Despite his promise to "really go for it," he eased in, brushing his lips over hers.

She laughed at his chaste kiss. Making a scolding sound, she threaded her fingers through his hair and opened her mouth for him.

Nathan had no choice but to pick up the gauntlet. He braced one hand on the edge of the pool and slid the other around her waist, bringing her body closer to his. Her breasts settled against his chest, plump and warm. Already aroused, he dipped his tongue into her mouth and got down to business.

She was sweet, hot, acquiescent. Her lips were soft. Water lapped between them, urging him to delve deeper. He switched angles and explored the recesses of her mouth. She moaned in encouragement, tangling her tongue with his.

Twenty seconds ago, he'd worried about being too aggressive. Now he was ready to peel off her swimsuit and bury his face in her breasts. Her response to him didn't seem feigned. He hoped Brooke would go away and give them some privacy.

Abby made a breathy little sound that went straight to his cock, swelling him to full mast. He couldn't get on top of her in the shallow pool. With a low groan, he pulled her over his lap. She gasped at the contact, digging her fingernails into his shoulders. When he raised a hand to her breast, squeezing her soft flesh, she squeaked a protest.

Tearing his mouth from hers, he glanced into the woods. He didn't see Brooke or Leo lurking in the trees, to his relief. He returned his attention to Abby. Her cheeks were flushed with arousal, her eyes smoky and half-lidded. Did she want him to stop or keep going? She wasn't shying away, so he didn't move an inch. His hand was still glued to her breast, his erection nudging the cleft of her thighs.

She covered his hand with hers. "They're not real."

He stared at her stupidly for a moment, his brain sluggish. Her breasts weren't real? Huh. "I can't tell."

"You can't?"

He shook his head, testing their pliancy again. She felt natural to him, not that he cared either way. She wasn't lumpy or oversize. Heart racing, he brushed his thumb over her hardened nipple.

A pulse fluttered at the base of her throat. She removed his hand and eased off his lap, returning to the other side of the pool. "Ray didn't do them. I went to a female plastic surgeon after the divorce."

He smiled at this confession, shared with an impish grin. It didn't matter to him, but it clearly mattered to her. He was glad she didn't have to carry around a physical reminder of Ray. He liked her style. The chemistry between them was off the charts. She might not be the one-night-stand type, but damn.

He wanted her.

Before he could decide what to do next, Leo and Brooke appeared at the edge of the trail. Nathan didn't know if they'd seen anything, but Abby looked embarrassed. The encounter hadn't gone as planned. They hadn't been pretending.

"Sorry for cock-blocking," Brooke said with a wink.

Nathan smothered a laugh at her graphic language. There was something funny about an angel-faced girl with a mouth like a sailor. Leo climbed into the middle tub and leaned back, resting his arms on the rim. He didn't appear sorry in the least. Brooke perched on the side of the pool with Abby, swishing her long legs in the water.

"You have mud in your hair," Abby said to Brooke.

She inspected the damp tangles. "Still?"

"We had a mud fight," Leo said.

"Who won?" Nathan asked.

Brooke and Leo exchanged a weighted glance.

"Nobody did," Leo said flatly.

After an awkward silence, Abby launched into a conversation with Leo about foreign languages. She seemed genuinely impressed with his knowledge. Nathan admired her communication skills. She had a way of making Leo feel comfortable and smoothing things over. It would have been easy for her to snub him or make catty remarks about Lydia. Instead, she'd placed blame where it was due, on Ray. She'd pointed out Nathan's mistakes, but she hadn't judged him for making them. He would never forget that.

They stayed in the hot springs for about thirty more minutes, until the sun went down. Then they returned to camp. No longer concerned about the thieves, he collected wood for a roaring fire. They shared a hearty meal of chicken and rice with vegetables. Brooke made instant pudding for dessert. When Nathan complimented her on the dish, she thanked him and sat down. She was quiet for a long time. He didn't realize she'd been crying until she got up, wiping the tears from her cheeks.

Abby followed her away from the fire.

"What did I say?" Nathan asked Leo.

"Nothing," Leo replied. "You were nice. Her dad isn't."

"He's mean to her?"

"No, he just never has time for her. He checks his messages during dinner and skips dessert."

It dawned on Nathan that Leo was Brooke's only male family member, besides Ray. Leo had the power to give her the love and attention she craved. Going beyond that would probably reinforce any negative feelings she had about men. Leo's responsibility toward her was more serious than Nathan realized.

Brooke and Abby returned a few minutes later. Leo teased Brooke into serenading him by the campfire, as promised. She agreed to sing "Take Me Out to the Ball Game." Her voice was terrible, scratchy and off-key.

"You sing like an angel," Leo said when she was finished.

"Shut up," she said, rolling her eyes.

"I mean it. You should try out for *American Idol*. Wasn't she great, Dad?"

Nathan couldn't come up with a polite answer. Brooke elbowed Leo in the ribs, but she was smiling. His joke had lightened the mood.

Before they went to bed, Brooke exacted her revenge. She pointed at Leo's shoulder, claiming she saw a huge, hairy spider crawling on him. When he jumped up and took off his shirt, throwing it on the ground, she laughed so hard she fell over the log.

Nathan laughed along with her, enjoying the moment. It was the best day he'd had in a long time. He was making progress with Leo and getting to know Abby. They were all healthy and happy. Coming on this trip had changed his life.

He crawled into the tent, exhausted but hopeful, wondering what tomorrow held.

CHAPTER FOURTEEN

ABBY WOKE WITH a start, her pulse racing.

She'd been dreaming about Nathan, not earthquakes. Well, maybe little earthquakes. Sexual earthquakes. They'd been naked in the hot springs at night, mouths melded together, skin slick with moisture.

Whew.

Suppressing a moan, she stretched her arms over her head. Need throbbed between her legs and every muscle in her body ached. The light outside the tent indicated that the sun was already up, but the sky was overcast and it smelled like rain. Once again, Brooke wasn't in the sleeping bag beside her.

Abby slid her hand down her stomach. She remembered the feel of Nathan's hard body against hers, his strong arms and seeking tongue. His erection, straining the fabric of his swim trunks. God.

She cupped one breast, mimicking his firm grip. Her implants were on the small side, but she could feel them. She'd only been with a few men since the surgery. It wasn't a secret. She assumed they'd noticed, though no one had complained.

She wasn't sure why she'd blurted it out to Nathan.

He'd probably seen more fake breasts than real ones. She felt silly for bringing it up.

Brooke had grilled her mercilessly about Nathan after they'd gone to bed. Abby had been tempted to confess to the ruse. Had it been a ruse, or runaway hormones? She didn't know what had possessed her to make out with him, but she couldn't do it again. He had heartbreaker written all over him. Which was a shame, because he also had an irresistible personality and great hands. He kissed like a champ. Although he'd joked about not measuring up to Jakov, she didn't think size was an issue for him. He'd felt big and deliciously stiff against her.

Groaning, she crawled out of the sleeping bag. She put on her fleece pullover and hiking shoes at the front of the tent. Nathan and Leo were standing by the fire pit. There was no outhouse at this site, so she ducked into the woods and found a bush to squat behind. Before she joined the others for breakfast, she rinsed her hands, brushed her teeth and washed her face. Abby didn't want to share her morning breath with Nathan. She considered taking a quick glance in a mirror, but she was afraid the sight would kill her confidence. Brooke had promised they could wash their hair today, so she left it down.

Tugging on her hat, she approached the guys. Nathan was wearing dark trousers with a gray T-shirt and checkered flannel. His stubble was thick, his hair disheveled. Leo was teenage-dream scruffy in a hooded sweatshirt and skinny jeans.

"Morning," Nathan said, giving her a crooked smile. "How did you sleep?"

She flushed at the memory of their kiss. "Fine. You?"

"Good. Better than the night before."

He looked relaxed, well-rested and ready to satisfy her womanly desires. Tension sizzled between them. Abby had to remind herself that last night hadn't meant anything. She couldn't seriously consider dating him. He was too dangerous to her peace of mind. The only place they'd be having sex was in her dreams.

Leo had fired up the propane stove. He was reading the directions on a packet of oatmeal, as if unsure how to prepare it.

Abby glanced around. "Where's Brooke?"

Nathan's brows rose at the question. "She's not in the tent?"

"No."

"We haven't seen her," Leo said.

"How long have you been up?"

"Thirty minutes."

She wondered if Brooke had ducked into the woods to use the bathroom. Abby strolled around the perimeter of the campsite, but she didn't see Brooke. She wasn't at the hot springs. She wasn't within yelling distance.

Abby took deep breaths, trying not to panic. Where was her daughter? She hadn't heard Brooke leave the tent this morning.

When Abby came back from the search empty-handed, Nathan and Leo abandoned the attempt to make breakfast to help her look. "She did this yesterday," Leo said. "She was playing around and hiding in the woods. I called out and she didn't answer."

That sounded like Brooke. "Where was this?"

"Upriver a few hundred feet. I'll take you there."

A horrible idea occurred to Abby, chilling her blood. "What if she fell in?"

"I'm sure she's fine," Nathan said, but he started walking faster.

They were all worried.

Leo guided them to a fishing hole not far from camp. It was quiet and serene, with water rushing under a fallen log.

"Brooke," Nathan yelled, cupping his hands around his face. "Brooke!"

Only the chirping birds and rustling leaves answered.

The articles Abby had read about drowning victims and missing girls swam in her mind. She was about to jump in the water and start dredging its depths when Leo walked across the fallen log. There was a muddy bank on the other side of the river. As he inspected the ground, his forehead crumpled. Abby hurried toward him, with Nathan's help.

"Brooke and I were barefoot yesterday," Leo said, crouching down by the mud.

The surface area showed signs of a wrestling match, as well as something far more disturbing: fresh footprints. It appeared that two sets of boots had trampled through here as recently as early this morning.

"Oh my God," Abby said. Her empty stomach pitched with nausea.

Nathan measured his foot against the prints. "These are about my size. One is bigger, maybe a thirteen."

Her eyes filled with tears. Brooke wore a ten in women's. The only other people they'd seen in the area were Petra and Jakov—and the thieves. "It was those hunters," Abby choked. "They've been following us, waiting for an opportunity to grab her."

Leo straightened and glanced toward the woods. "We don't know that. Someone came through here, maybe them. That doesn't mean they…they *took* her."

"Then where is she?"

"Brooke is a fighter," Nathan said. "We would have heard her scream."

Abby strode into the forest, searching for her daughter. She couldn't hear above the thundering of her heartbeat, couldn't see through the blur of tears. Nathan and Leo accompanied her, hollering for Brooke.

They hadn't gone far when Abby stumbled over one of Brooke's hiking boots. She picked it up with shaking hands. Her heart twisted as she imagined Brooke trying to kick free from her captors. Less than ten feet away, Nathan found a dingy white cloth on the ground. It resembled a folded dish towel.

He brought the fabric to his nose and grimaced. "Smells like starter fluid."

Abby touched the damp cloth and sniffed her fingertips. She recognized the substance immediately. "It's ether," she said, feeling faint.

"What's that?" Leo asked.

"An anesthetic. Rarely used, but easier to get than chloroform."

This was why no one heard Brooke scream. She'd probably gone outside to pee during the night and not bothered to lace up her hiking boots. The men had attacked, smothering her with the ether rag and dragging her away from camp. Once they reached this area, she was unconscious. The boot had slipped from her slack foot.

Abby inspected every inch of the sturdy leather hiking boot as if it might offer a hint of Brooke's whereabouts. No blood dotted the tawny brown surface. The inside of the boot was worn smooth from Brooke's slender foot. One of the red laces was knotted at the end, its tip frayed from overuse.

Abby clutched the boot to the center of her chest, smothering a sob. She'd felt this way during the earthquake. It had been total chaos. She remembered the spectacular crash on the freeway, the lifted sections of concrete and pileup of cars. Fire. Exploding gas tanks and shattered glass. Her door had been smashed shut, her left arm pinned at her side. Even before the ground stopped shaking, all of her thoughts had centered on Brooke.

Brooke, alone at the house.

She'd considered calling in to work that morning. Brooke didn't have school, and Ray had brought her

home a day early. Abby didn't usually leave Brooke
unattended, but she was a little too old for a babysit-
ter. Brooke had made plans to spend the afternoon
with a friend. Abby had assumed she'd be fine for a
few hours.

A man with a pickup truck, also demolished, had
saved Abby's life. He'd used a crowbar to rip the door
open. She'd climbed out on unsteady legs, her teeth
clacking from anxiety. The view of the collapsed freeway just behind them had floored her. Brooke had
been on the other side of that rubble, in a neighborhood ten miles away.

The man had nudged her toward a group of survivors, who were already walking the opposite direction.

"My daughter," she'd cried, pointing south. "I have
to go home."

"Someone else will help her," the man had said.
"You can't go that way."

Even with a broken arm at her side and an insur-
mountable obstacle in front of her, Abby had wanted
to go after Brooke. Then a powerful aftershock had
struck, causing huge slabs of concrete to fall. When
it was over, Abby had joined the other survivors and
fled. Abandoning her daughter to the care of strangers was the hardest thing she'd ever done. For the next
three days, she'd agonized over the decision.

Never again.

"We have to look for her," Abby said, blinking
away those awful memories. "We have to find her!"

Nathan shook his head. He had another idea. "I'll

run down the trail until I reach Jakov and Petra. I can get to them today, maybe this afternoon. I'll use their phone. They are our best chance to rescue Brooke."

Abby knew he meant well, like the man with the crowbar. But she couldn't be dissuaded. "Go ahead."

He seemed relieved. "You'll stay here with Leo?"

"No. I'm tracking those men down right now." She headed back toward camp, planning to get water and some kind of weapon. There was nothing she wouldn't do for Brooke. No mountain she wouldn't climb, no fire she wouldn't walk through. No one could take her daughter away from her.

"You can't," Nathan said, chasing after her.

"Why not?"

"They have a huge head start. Even if you caught up with them, which I doubt, what could you do? How would you fight them, a woman against two men? You'll only get hurt and put Brooke in more danger."

"They might kill her. Those other girls disappeared—"

"Do you want to end up like them?" he asked in a gravelly voice, gripping her upper arm. "Maybe that college kid tried to save his girlfriend instead of going to the authorities. He got an arrow in his chest!"

Abby jerked her arm from his grasp. "We're days from civilization. I can't wait that long for help to arrive."

"I'll get the authorities back here tonight," he promised. "I'll run all the way to Monarch if I have to."

"I can't wait until tonight. They might only keep

her alive long enough to—" She broke off with a strangled sound, too upset to finish that sentence. But she didn't have to. He knew very well what happened to female victims.

"If you go looking for her, Leo will follow you," he said.

Leo didn't argue this point.

"I won't let you put my son at risk," Nathan said. "You're not thinking clearly, Abby."

"Fuck you," she said, pushing by him. She scrambled across the fallen log and sprinted back to camp. When she arrived, she removed every unnecessary item from her backpack. She tossed in some snacks, water and a jacket.

"Goddamn it," Nathan shouted. He yanked the backpack away from her and threw it. "I'll tie you to a tree if I have to."

Leo moved in front of him. "Don't touch her."

"Or what?" he said, getting in Leo's face.

Abby stepped between them. She braced her palm on Nathan's chest to hold him back. His heartbeat hammered against her hand, furious and fast. "Where's that spear you made?" she asked Leo, swallowing hard.

"Hold on a second," Leo said. "Let's vote on this as a family."

More tears stung Abby's eyes at this request. Brooke would have wanted them to work together, but Abby wasn't backing down. She didn't care what they decided. "I'm going after my daughter no matter what." Walking away from both of them, she picked up her backpack. "You two do whatever you feel is right."

Nathan pointed at Leo. "You're staying with me."

"Hear me out," Leo said.

"No!"

"We can all go."

"And all die?"

"We might be able to catch up with them," Leo said. "It's not easy to carry someone, and she's heavier than she looks."

"She only weighs a hundred pounds," Nathan said.

"A hundred and twenty-five," Abby corrected.

"They'll share the weight," Nathan said. "Any fit man can handle sixty pounds."

"We're only a few miles from the old forest service road and off-highway vehicle area," Leo said. "It's in the same direction they took Brooke. If we don't find her, we can continue on that route. We could run into someone with a phone or transportation faster that way, and we don't have to split up."

Swearing, Nathan raked a hand through his hair.

"That sounds reasonable," Abby said.

Nathan must have known he didn't really have a choice, unless he wanted to fight Leo. He couldn't stop Abby. Leo wouldn't let him. "Fine," he said. "Fuck!"

They gathered enough food and water for one day. Leo kept his spear and Nathan had a utility knife. The only weapon Abby could find on short notice was a fist-sized rock. On impulse, she put it in an athletic sock.

Leo nodded his approval. He bumped his knuckles against hers, like they were bros, before they set off.

The trail wasn't difficult to pick up, once they found it, but staying on track required close attention to detail. The ground wasn't damp enough to show muddy footprints, and they weren't experienced trackers. Abby didn't know how to read broken leaves or bent twigs for clues. They were in luck, however, because Brooke's alpaca wool hat seemed to be shedding. Every quarter mile or so, they found a bundle of colorful threads.

Nathan got suspicious after the third bundle. "I don't like it."

"What do you mean?"

"I think we're walking into a trap."

"Why?"

"They left footprints and an ether rag at the river crossing. Now these threads. It's like a trail of bread crumbs. No one is this sloppy."

"So they're luring us out here?"

"Maybe."

"Why not kill us in the camp?"

"I don't know."

"They might not want to kill all three of us," Leo said, glancing at Abby.

His meaning was clear. These men could be planning to capture Abby, along with Brooke. It was a risk Abby was willing to take. She'd rather die alongside her daughter than live without her.

Another possibility occurred to her. "What if

Brooke left the threads? They wouldn't have noticed her dropping them in the dark."

This must have seemed plausible to Nathan, because he shut up and kept going.

BROOKE DIDN'T KNOW what hit her.

She'd woken with a full bladder in the wee hours of the morning. After stumbling away from the tent to take care of business, she'd pulled up her pants and *bam*. Someone grabbed her from behind.

Before she could open her mouth to scream, a man clamped a wet cloth over the lower half of her face. Powerful fumes burned her throat and triggered her gag reflex. She'd struggled to break free, to no avail. She couldn't breathe or move. Her nose and mouth felt crushed, her arms trapped in a cruel grip.

As her vision blurred, strange thoughts assailed her. Dizzy and weak-kneed, she pictured herself with a snout for a nose. When the man took his hand away from her mouth, she'd be transformed into a cartoon animal, like the naughty boys in *Pinocchio*. The imagery terrified her. She tried to bite down on the rag, but everything went dark.

For the next few hours, she drifted in and out of consciousness. She couldn't piece together the fragments of reality to create meaning. There were only disembodied sensations. The sting of a needle in her arm. A foul-smelling sack over her head. Her back resting against something, like a hospital stretcher. *Bump, bump, bump*. Had there been another earthquake? Floating up and coming down. Wrists and ankles tied.

She could see a crisscross of night between the threads of coarse fabric covering her face. It was... burlap.

Brooke moaned, closing her eyes. "Mom, I'm thirsty."

So thirsty.

No one answered.

"Let me up, Leo. You win."

The journey continued, rhythmic and bizarre. She conjured more disturbing animated creatures, a man-horse carrying her into a thorn-snarled forest. Her inability to control her imagination frightened her, but she couldn't keep her mind alert or focus on anything. She felt like she had a head injury. She was afraid to sleep, afraid to stay awake.

Something bad was happening. She couldn't grasp what.

Don't speak, a voice whispered. *Play dead.*

She wasn't dead. She wasn't dead. She wasn't dead.

At semiregular intervals, she was placed on the ground. Footsteps circled her like musical chairs and she was lifted again. After the third or fourth—or tenth?—time, it occurred to her that the footsteps belonged to more than one person. She could ask one of these man-horses where she was.

Don't speak.

Why not?

Her head lolled to the side and her thoughts scattered. Just go with the flow. Float away on the carousel to Pleasure Island. Braying donkeys smoking cigars. Leo, passing her a joint in the backseat of his car.

Take me out to the ball game...

Her back hit the ground with a jolt. *Hey. Watch the merchandise, boys.* She opened her bleary eyes and sputtered, trying to get the disgusting gunny sack away from her mouth. She was so thirsty. Poison apple.

Someone tugged on her hoof. Boot.

"Shh."

The sound was real. It came from a real person. She was sure of it. She tried to lift her hand to grab the voice, as if touching this real thing might ground her. But her arm was immobile, her wrists bound together. Her ankles were tied, also. Another pull and her boot slipped off. She was only wearing one, she realized. Now both feet were bare.

Don't speak. Shh.

She tried to wiggle her toes and—success!—she did it. Tears flooded her eyes at this tiny victory.

Up again and into a closed space. Dark, dry, dirt. Down again, up again, bump-jostle-bump. After a series of odd twists and turns, vertical and horizontal angles, linear equations, she landed like an airplane.

The horsemen, possible satyrs, trotted off. Without the constant motion, Brooke drifted into her subconscious. She slept in fits and starts, her dream sequences plagued by landslides and wild animals and diving board vibrations.

On your mark, get set...go!

She couldn't run at the whistle, too sluggish. Instead of finishing the race, she stumbled to the sidelines to rest.

CHAPTER FIFTEEN

NAUSEA FORCED HER AWAKE.

Unable to roll over, Brooke turned her head to the side and retched, emptying her stomach of its meager contents. She hadn't felt this sick or disoriented since the San Diego earthquake. Her wrists and ankles were tied, her face covered. Hot tears leaked from her eyes and saliva trailed down her cheek. Ugh.

Where was she? Not at home. Not in a tent.

Blunt fingertips fumbled with the burlap sack, removing it with care. Colors melted together and came apart. A nubby washcloth on her skin. It smelled like mildew.

"Drink," a voice said, helping her raise her head.

It was the "shh" voice. She swallowed several mouthfuls of water. Creek water, probably filtered, but with the same gritty aftertaste.

When her vision cleared, she saw a boy sitting beside her. Dark hair, tangled and dirty. Thick, heavy brows. She recognized him as one of the hunters they'd met on the trail. He had a camouflage bandanna around his neck and a wispy mustache. Although young, he looked feral. His irregular features and big ears gave him an awkward, Picasso-esque appearance. If she passed him on the street, she'd avoid eye contact.

She struggled to match his intimidating visage with the careful touch and kind voice. He'd drugged her and kidnapped her.

Brooke tore her gaze from his and tried to focus on the room they were in. It appeared to be a bunker or underground cavern. It was a cramped space with a dank, earthy odor. The walls were brown and bare. There were scratch marks...

The boy. She studied the boy again, swallowing her fear. He was sitting on a plastic crate. There was no other furniture, other than the bed she rested on. It was hard and narrow, with pine boughs as bedposts.

"Who are you?" she asked.

He flushed, as if the question embarrassed him. Despite the circumstances, he seemed more skittish than threatening.

"What's your name?" she said, softer this time.

"Wyatt."

"I'm Brooke."

He stared at her for a long moment. Then he glanced at the open doorway. She couldn't see what lay beyond. Whatever it was scared him more than he scared her. There was a monster lurking in the shadows.

"Is this where you live?"

Wyatt nodded.

"How old are you?"

"Sixteen."

"I'm eighteen," she said. "Do you go to school?"

"No."

Brooke felt sorry for him. He had to live in this dirt-packed hovel like an animal, miles from civilization. If she got the chance, she'd bash this hillbilly over the head with a rock, but she could sympathize. "I go to Berkeley."

"What's that?"

"It's a college in Northern California."

He gave her a blank look. Maybe he'd never been out of these woods.

Her wrists ached from the bindings. She tried to rotate them, flexing her fingers. "Will you untie me?"

He glanced away, denying her. *Shh.*

"Where are you from?"

"I can't remember."

"Were you born here?"

"No."

"How long have you been here?"

"Five years."

"Is that man your father?"

He didn't answer.

"Where's your mother?"

"Dead."

Tears filled Brooke's eyes. She wanted her mother. So much. She wanted to read one of her mom's annoying text messages and accept her cushiony hugs. She wanted to be coddled, and smothered, and spoiled. She wanted to feel her mother's cool palm on her forehead, checking her temperature. "Do you miss her?"

Wyatt nodded.

Brooke moistened her lips. "Will you...will you hold my hand?"

After a short hesitation, he reached out, entwining his fingers with hers. They were numb from lack of circulation. Pinpricks of sensation tingled in the swollen digits. The contact stung as much as it comforted her.

"Why didn't you tell me she was awake?"

Wyatt jerked his hand away from hers. It was the monster. She recognized him as the other hunter they'd met on the trail near Echo Lake. He was larger than Wyatt. More powerful, with a full beard and craggy features. His gaze gleamed with cold relish, something the boy lacked. This man-horse was in his element, doing exactly what he wanted. He inhabited this space with confidence.

"She threw up," the boy said.

"Take off her clothes."

Terror coursed through Brooke, cold and bright. Of course this was the reason she'd been brought here. It was the same reason any girl got taken and tied up against her will. She would be raped and murdered, like the other victims. The ones who'd tried to claw their way out of this grave with their fingernails.

She turned to Wyatt in a silent plea. He wasn't a monster. Or maybe he was a skinnier, less-experienced monster.

Would he help her?

The older man spoke again. "I said, take off her clothes."

Wyatt moved his gaze from Brooke. "No."

"No?"

"I want this one."

The monster clenched his hand into a dirty fist. "You what?"

"I want her for myself."

The monster looked back and forth between them, incredulous. Clearly they worked as a team, but Wyatt must not have asserted himself this way before. "I wouldn't have gone to all this trouble to bring you a little friend."

"You can get another woman. The older one."

Wyatt meant her mother. Brooke's heart twisted at the thought.

"This one's mine," he insisted. "I like her."

"You don't know what to do with her."

"Yes, I do."

"Show me."

"No," Brooke said, squeezing her eyes shut. She didn't want to belong to either of them. Intuition told her Wyatt would be kinder and easier to escape from. But she couldn't just lie here while he violated her. "Please, don't."

"See? You're not ready to break her."

"I can do it," Wyatt said, glowering at him. "She's young. I can let her get used to me. Then maybe she won't run away, like the others."

The monster grasped her bare foot. His fingernails were ragged, with dark crescents of dirt beneath them. "The last one ran away because you got lazy with her shackles. Do you remember what happened to her?"

Wyatt paled. "Yes."

"You won't make that mistake again, will you?"

"No, sir," he said, bowing his head.

"If you want her, you can have her after I'm done. Now move aside."

Brooke's stomach lurched at his words. She panicked, trying to kick her legs and jerk her wrists free of the bindings. When the man tightened his grip on her foot and gave it a hard yank, she screamed out loud.

"Where's her boot?" the monster asked.

"It fell off at the campsite."

He backhanded the boy across the face. Wyatt went sprawling. Brooke gasped in dismay. She'd seen fights after school, and the not-so-playful scuffle between Nathan and Leo. But she'd never witnessed this kind of abuse.

"She was wearing one the whole way here," the man said.

Blood dribbled from Wyatt's lip. He cowered in the corner. "I didn't notice."

That was a lie. Brooke remembered someone removing her boot and telling her to hush. Wyatt must have done it. She didn't know why this was important, but she kept her mouth shut, trusting her instincts. *Shh.*

"I'll go look for it," Wyatt said.

Brooke shuddered at the thought of being left alone with the older man.

"No," the monster said, after a pause. "I'll go. You stay here and guard the hatch."

"Yes, sir."

"And don't you dare untie her—or you'll both end up in the pit."

BY MIDDAY, THE TRAIL had gone cold.

Abby scoured the forest for wool threads. Leo studied the map as if "villain's lair" might be marked with an X. They backtracked and changed routes. Nathan wanted to continue to the off-highway vehicle area in hopes of finding some bikers with cell phones. Leo said they were at least five miles from that location. Nathan glanced at the map and disagreed. The two of them argued in urgent whispers that set her nerves on edge.

Abby was hanging on to sanity by a thread. She'd been this way for several days after the San Diego earthquake. Hope that Brooke was still alive kept her going, then and now. She couldn't rest until she knew where her daughter was. She wouldn't stop looking.

She would not quit. Ever.

"We need to get to higher ground and study the land formations to orient ourselves," Nathan said.

Abby seconded this idea. They climbed the nearest hill and looked around. Leo didn't believe that Nathan knew where the hell they were, but they reached a truce nevertheless. The tree-lined ravine in the distance indicated Silver Creek, which flowed east. According to the map, the creek skirted the edge of the old forest service road, which led south, to the off-highway vehicle area. If they traveled east along the creek, they should find something resembling a dirt road within miles.

As plans went, it was sketchy, but she wanted to keep moving. She couldn't stop to think. She'd fall apart.

Abby trudged down the other side of the hill towards a copse of trees. She'd only taken a few steps when a hint of red caught her attention. She gripped Nathan's wrist, unable to speak. Brooke's brown hiking boot was lying at the base of a short cliff, less than a hundred feet away. The red laces were untied, dangling loose.

He followed her gaze to the boot. A muscle in his jaw flexed. He signaled Leo with a curt gesture and they ducked into the trees. Abby crouched down in the leaves beside Nathan. Her heart was pounding in her ears, her mouth dry. She wondered if Nathan's suspicions were right. Perhaps they *had* been lured into a trap.

The boot appeared perfectly placed, like a flag on a putting green. There was also something odd about the area. It resembled the rest of the Monarch wilderness, with boulders and foliage and pine trees. The cliff was more of an escarpment, a rift between two levels of earth that rose about twenty feet high.

"If anyone was going to ambush us, they'd be waiting right here," Nathan murmured.

"Then we're safe to proceed," Leo said.

"I don't know how her boot ended up at the base of that cliff. The dirt is rocky and the ground is uneven. It's not a natural footpath."

"Maybe it fell from the top."

"Maybe."

"Let's check it out," Leo said.

"I'll check it out," Nathan said. "You two stay here."

When Leo opened his mouth to protest, Abby elbowed him to shut up. As long as they kept moving and making choices, she could hold her emotions at bay. Too much discussion and strife would wear down her defenses. "Good idea."

Leo and Abby kept watch while Nathan crept forward. Abby studied the woods for movement, though she wanted to see what Nathan was doing. When he disappeared from her peripheral vision, she felt lost.

He returned a moment later, his face tense. "We have to go."

"Why?"

"There's a door in the escarpment," he said. "A fucking door, hidden inside a crevice. It's covered in clay or some kind of material that matches the dirt."

"Let's break in," Abby said.

"They're waiting on the other side, armed and ready to kill us," he hissed. "That's the only reason they aren't out here."

"So you want to just leave, after coming this far?"

"I thought we'd find them in a camp or someplace open. This is a fortress. Our chances of getting in and out alive are minimal." He paused to let that sink in. "We need help, Abby. We can lead the authorities straight to her."

Abby stared at her daughter's boot, remembering the long hours after the quake. The aftershocks. The agonizing walk to the football stadium, which had acted as an evacuation center. The hours spent sitting on the floor of an overcrowded east-county hospital. Sleepless nights and endless days. Piles of dead bodies.

"I'm not leaving," she said.

"If we don't go now, we won't *get* to go. We'll all die. Brooke, too."

"I'm not leaving," she repeated.

"Me, neither," Leo said.

Veins formed in Nathan's flushed neck. "Mother-fucker," he said through clenched teeth. "I knew you two would do this."

"She's getting raped in there, Dad," Leo said quietly.

"You think I don't know that?" Nathan whispered, rage in his eyes. "You think I don't *care?*"

Abby understood why he was angry. Her insistence on staying put Leo's safety at risk. She'd be dismayed if their situations were reversed, and Brooke wanted to rescue Leo. But the only thing that mattered to Abby right now was saving Brooke. Leo was an adult who could make his own decisions.

"I'm going in after her," Abby said.

Leo bumped his knuckles against hers again, showing solidarity.

Nathan looked as if he wanted to throttle them both. She thought his head was going to explode. Finally, he took the knife out of his pocket and stood.

"Bring your fucking spear, hero. We have to case the perimeter first."

Abby rose with them, her heart racing.

Nathan stopped her with a blistering glare. "You can keep watch. We'll be right back."

"What should I do if I see someone?"

"Run."

After issuing that curt dismissal, he walked away with Leo. She studied the swaying grass on the hillside, her heart in her throat. Anxiety coiled inside her like a spring. Although she wasn't a religious woman, she prayed for her daughter with fervent desperation.

When Nathan and Leo reappeared, Abby almost wilted with relief. Nathan gestured for her to follow him through the copse of trees. "I think there's another door at the top of the cliff," he said, pointing in that direction. "You stay here and guard the exits. If Brooke comes out, don't wait for us. Just run as fast as you can."

"Where?"

"To the creek. It will lead you to the forest service road."

Abby didn't like it. "I'd rather go in with you."

"No."

"Why not?"

"What do you think we're going to do in there, ask nicely for Brooke to be released? Have tea and discuss our options?"

Abby's palm itched to slap his face. She crossed her arms over her chest, smothering the urge to respond with a violent outburst. "She's my daughter. I should take the greater risk."

"We have to overpower them, and Leo is stronger than you are."

"I don't want him to get hurt."

"Neither do I," he said coldly. "But here we are."

"Leo can keep watch."

He narrowed his eyes. "Do what I fucking said or we're leaving."

Abby looked to Leo for help and found none. He stood by his father for once. She had no choice but to nod her assent.

Taking a deep breath, she ducked behind a tree. From there, she could see the side of the escarpment and its grassy plateau. As Nathan and Leo approached the door, her fear skyrocketed. He'd never forgive her if this plan went terribly wrong. The tenuous connection they'd made over the past few days had just snapped, unable to bear the strain of the horrific circumstances.

She waited, knees trembling, for all hell to break loose.

AFTER HIS FATHER LEFT, Wyatt got up and wiped his chin with the same washcloth he'd used on Brooke.

He didn't seem shaken by the abuse. This was the way he expected to be treated. There was a slamming sound and movement overhead, as if the monster had ventured aboveground. Dirt rained from the ceiling of the bunker, which had been reinforced with log beams. It settled in her hair and tickled her nose.

Blinking the grit from her eyes, she examined Wyatt's homely face. He was in that awkward stage between man and boy. One day he might grow into his big ears and shaggy brow. Would he also develop into a psychopath? She couldn't count on him to free her. He hadn't lobbied for her release or fought back when challenged. If he had his way, she'd be *his* captive. But still, a captive.

"Are you all right?" she asked.

"I'm fine."

"That looked like it hurt."

He returned to the crate beside her. His gaze met hers for a moment before he flushed and glanced away.

"I don't like my dad," she said, trying to appeal to him.

"Does he hit you?"

"No. He ignores me."

"I wouldn't ignore you."

"Untie me," she whispered. "Please."

He studied the bloodstained rag, making no move to help her.

She tried again. "You don't have to stay here with him. We can leave together. I'll help you run away."

Wyatt didn't look at her. "He hunts down runaways."

"And brings them back?"

"No."

Brooke grimaced at the thought, fighting another wave of nausea. She didn't see a way out of this predicament. She felt weak and sick. Even if she could loosen her bindings, she couldn't run or fight until the drugs wore off.

She might die in this room after a prolonged torture session, perhaps years of captivity. The possibility loomed before her, nightmarish.

Wyatt watched her in silence. She got the impression that he was waiting for something. As if he was counting on her to be his salvation, instead of the other way around. They were both helpless, trapped here together, and she couldn't think of a solution. Her brain was sluggish. Whatever drug they'd given her was strong and long-lasting. She could only stay alert for a few moments at a time.

"You took off the boot," she murmured, drowsy.

He squeezed her hand in warning. "Shh."

When the footsteps returned, Wyatt broke the contact. Their captor burst into the room, carrying two guns. She guessed that one was a shotgun because it had twin barrels. The other might be a rifle. "They're outside."

"Who?" Wyatt asked.

"Her family. I can't believe they found us."

Brooke let out a whimper of distress. *No. Please God, no. Not a shoot-out.* She could live through another earthquake. She'd dodge cartoon creatures and floating heads. This was too real, too violent. If her mom tried to get in, they'd kill her or capture her. "Don't hurt my mom," she begged Wyatt.

"They're in the tunnel," the man said, handing Wyatt the shotgun. "Take this and get down there."

He accepted the shotgun with reluctance. "I can't."

"You can't what?"

"Shoot people."

"You can and you will," the older man said. "Just fire a warning round to send them running the other direction. Your birdshot won't kill them."

"What if they're armed?"

The older man turned to Brooke. "Does your dad have a gun?"

"He's not my dad."

"Answer the question."

She hesitated, uncertain. Nathan didn't have a gun, and lying about it might put them in more danger. "I—I don't know."

"Is he a tracker?"

"A what?"

"Does he hunt?"

Brooke wasn't sure how to respond. She had no idea.

"They're tree huggers," the man said to his son. "No balls and no weapons. They'll run as soon as you fire at them."

Wyatt glanced at Brooke. His hands trembled as he held the barrel of the shotgun in a white-knuckled grip.

The monster pointed the rifle at her, but spoke to Wyatt. "Don't forget what happens when you disappoint me, boy. Maybe you need three more days in the pit with your new girlfriend, after I put a bullet in her pretty little head."

"No," Wyatt said. "Please."

"Get down there!"

The man opened a hatch in the floor that she hadn't

seen before. While Wyatt descended into a dark space, his father stood in the doorway, rifle trained on Brooke. She stared back at him, terrorized into silence. He had crease lines in his forehead and stains on his shirt. His fatigue pants were torn. Threads of silver snaked through his unruly beard and mustache.

Although she wanted to spit in his face, she looked away, trembling. She couldn't even scream to warn her mother. He was large and filthy and probably insane. She supposed he had a mental illness, but she felt no sympathy, only fear. Wyatt had a sense of decency she could appeal to. There was a caring person behind those stark eyes and odd features. In the older man, there was nothing. No humanity.

Following his orders, Wyatt opened fire.

CHAPTER SIXTEEN

THEY CREPT TOWARD the hidden door, side by side.

Leo's heart hammered against his ribs with every step. He'd never been so afraid—or so pumped up with adrenaline—in his entire life. The thought of Brooke being terrorized by two psychos made him crazy. He wanted to tear those guys apart with his bare hands, to pop out eyeballs and rip off arms. He'd chew through their fucking necks.

Even through the haze of bravado and bloodlust, he understood why his dad had lobbied to play it safe. This was a scary situation, and it could end badly. Leo was worried about their chances for survival. The odds were stacked against them. Their opponents might be armed with a crossbow and an arsenal of other weapons. Leo had only a hastily made fishing spear, his dad a hunting knife.

They were taking a big risk. Maybe a stupid one. But they had no other choice. Leo couldn't walk away while Brooke was in danger. Abby *wouldn't* walk away. Leaving both women behind would be disastrous.

In a dark corner of his mind, Leo wondered if this was partly his fault. He hadn't been the best stepbrother to Brooke. His gut tightened at the memory of their wrestling match yesterday. He regretted being rough with her and using harsh words. The idea that he might never see her again rocked him to the core.

His feelings for her went deeper than he'd realized. All of the emotions he'd kept buried had rushed to the surface. His attraction to her wasn't just about hormones and rebellion. It was stronger than their wavering family connection.

Leo wished he'd done things differently. He'd failed to protect Brooke. He also shouldn't have lied to his dad about the bag of weed. The deception had made the thieves seem like stoner opportunists, mercenary but harmless.

When they arrived outside the door, he studied its composition. It appeared flat, and was covered with clumps of dirt. Someone had spackled the door with mud to make it blend in to the hillside. There was no doorknob or handle. Leo tried to pry it open with his spear, to no avail.

His dad grew impatient and motioned for Leo to step aside. He started kicking the middle of the door. It only took a few tries before the clay-caked wood splintered. This fortress wasn't designed to keep out intruders; invisibility was its main defense. Behind the door lay a tunnel. Leo had figured that this entrance led to some kind of larger dwelling. It was almost pitch-black inside.

Leo took a cigarette lighter out of his pocket and pantomimed the sparking motion. His dad nodded and entered the tunnel. They had to duck their heads to accommodate the low ceiling. The squat, narrow space invited feelings of intense claustrophobia. Leo continued into the dark with caution, sticking close to his dad. After about ten feet, he sparked the lighter and held his arm out. The flame flickered and wavered, illuminating the passage. It reminded Leo of an animal burrow. The acrid smell of piss assaulted his nostrils. Perhaps this tunnel was an emergency exit that doubled as a latrine.

Sick.

Wrinkling his nose, Leo shuffled forward. Around the next corner, he paused, lifting the flame higher. The passage widened into a dugout with a reinforced ceiling. The wooden planks appeared to be ax-chopped, with rough edges and no uniform size.

Leo lowered his arm too quickly. The flame went out, casting them into darkness. He smothered a curse as the hot metal singed his thumb.

His dad gripped his shoulder, holding him still. There were muffled voices overhead. Leo heard an ominous scraping sound. He waited, his pulse thundering in his ears. Then he caught a flash of motion about ten feet in front of them. Light filtered in from the ceiling near the end of the tunnel. It was some kind of hatch, he realized. A figure climbed down the short ladder and raised the barrel of a shotgun.

Oh, shit.

"Run," his dad said, pushing Leo in the opposite direction.

Before they could get around the corner, the gun blasted. Bullet fragments peppered the tunnel walls.

Fire struck his right leg, ripping through his jeans and flaying his skin. Leo stumbled sideways and dropped the spear. He gripped his thigh with a strangled yell, shocked by the searing pain.

He'd been shot.

ABBY ALMOST COULDN'T bear to watch.

She suppressed the urge to clap one hand over her eyes as Nathan and Leo broke down the door. It appeared to be locked from the inside, and solidly built. After five or six blows, the door split open. So much for stealth.

No one came out. Was Brooke even in there?

Nathan moved the ruined door aside and stared into the dark space. He entered the passageway with Leo following close behind. Abby bit the edge of her fist, terrified. Her heart was beating as fast as a jackrabbit's, threatening to burst from her chest. She took deep breaths and tried not to faint.

Waiting was such a sharp misery. She couldn't stop thinking about Brooke and picturing worst-case scenarios. This path led to madness; Abby knew that from experience. It led to soul-deep anguish and mental collapse. The third day after the earthquake had been the most challenging. There was no long walk to focus on, no helpful distractions. Her injured elbow had been set and cast. She'd reunited with Ella and spoken to her parents. There were so many survivors with horrific tales of the utter devastation downtown.

But…no Brooke.

Boom!

The sound of a gunshot brought her back to the present and turned her blood to ice. Nathan had been right—the men were armed. Had he been shot? She smothered a scream, plagued by visions of torn flesh and bloody mayhem. The ground seemed to shift beneath her feet, like a phantom earthquake.

Movement on the hillside divided her attention. Oh, no. She'd forgotten to keep watch! Racked with anxiety, she peered around the tree she was hiding behind. A camouflage-clad figure emerged from a cluster of boulders. Gunmetal glinted in the sunlight.

No. Oh, God. This couldn't be happening! What should she do?

Nathan had told her to run, but she was frozen. She couldn't leave them. She couldn't leave Brooke.

Gripping the tree bark, she looked again. The man was crouched on top of the cliff with his rifle trained on the broken door. With a sinking stomach, she realized he was going to shoot whoever came out. Maybe there was no alternate exit, or he'd blocked it. He was waiting for his targets to appear so he could pick them off.

There was only one way to stop him.

She slipped off her backpack and reached for the sock weapon inside. When she had it in her trembling fist, she scurried through the trees, putting distance between her and the gunman. As soon as she'd gone far enough to escape detection, she circled around and climbed along the backside of the cliff.

He thought he could ambush *them?* She'd ambush *his* sorry ass.

There wasn't much cover on top of the cliff, just low-lying rocks and bushes. She crouched down and moved forward quickly. The weighted sock felt heavy, the cotton hot in her sweaty grip. A breeze ruffled the damp hair at her temples. That was a good thing, she supposed. The wind was blowing away from the gunman, so he probably couldn't hear the sound of her approaching footsteps.

Abby didn't give herself time to hesitate.

Don't overthink it.

When she reached the man in camouflage, she knew she had to act fast, before he sensed her presence. She rushed at him, swinging her sock weapon like a wild banshee. She aimed for the side of his head and missed by a wide margin, connecting with his right shoulder.

Oops.

He roared in surprise and scrambled to his feet. Although he'd left his weapon on the ground, Abby was paralyzed with fear, unable to strike again. She recognized him from the trail. His countenance was menacing, his eyes devoid of light.

Making a pathetic noise, she stumbled backward and almost fell down. Another plan was born out of desperation: run away and hope he gave chase.

Somehow, it worked. When she turned to flee, he abandoned his post and followed her. The sneak attack must have rattled him as much as it had her. Maybe she'd sparked his predator instincts. He couldn't resist hunting her.

She bolted away from him as fast as possible, fighting to stay upright on the rocky slope. She wasn't a track star like Brooke or a pro athlete like Nathan, but she was able to put distance between them. Adrenaline increased her speed and kept her going. She reached flat ground and tore through the trees, her legs pumping. If she could lure him far into the woods, Nathan and Leo might have a chance to rescue Brooke.

She didn't see the exposed root until it was too late. Her shoe glanced off the edge. Although she tried to recover her balance, it was no use. She tripped and went flying, arms outstretched. After a short tumble, she landed on her back in a pile of dirt and damp leaves. The oxygen squeezed from her lungs.

He was on top of her in a flash. Before she could gasp for breath. Before she could swing the sock-mace again.

Grabbing her by the hair, he rolled her over and shoved her face into the leaves. Her arm was wrenched backward with shocking pressure, almost to the point of breaking. She struggled for air, tears stinging her eyes.

While she sucked in a lungful of oxygen, he trapped her wrists together and cinched them with a plastic tie.

Abby couldn't believe it was already over. He'd captured her in less than two minutes. She was winded, her shoulder throbbing. Her hands and knees felt raw from the fall. Her scalp ached from the hair-pulling. She didn't know where her sock-weapon went. It wasn't clutched in her fist anymore.

"Get up," he said, jerking her to a standing position. He squinted at her and smiled, as if she pleased him. "Move."

She wanted to make things more difficult for him by refusing to walk. But when he nudged her, she stumbled forward, too shaken to resist. Her knees felt like jelly and her body trembled with tension. She'd used up all her bravery in the attack. There had been a lifetime's worth in that one swing.

Up close, the hunter was scary enough to star in a horror movie. He wasn't hideous or disfigured, as far as she could tell. It was hard to imagine what he looked like underneath the dirty clothes and overgrown facial hair. What disturbed her wasn't his unkempt appearance, but the perverse enjoyment he seemed to take in her fear. He reminded her of a cult leader or a religious fanatic. There was a Manson-like glee about him.

And he smelled bad. Like chewing tobacco and dead animals.

Remember Brooke, she whispered to herself as she trudged forward. *Focus on Brooke. Pray for Brooke. Never give up.*

Abby was a survivor. She could get through this. As long as Brooke was still alive, she could endure anything. She would keep a firm grip on hope, grasping it with both hands until she could hold her daughter again.

NATHAN HAD KNOWN that breaking in was a stupid idea.

He couldn't believe he'd let Abby talk him into it.

He was so scared and pissed off that he didn't even want to fuck her anymore. Unlike Leo, he had no interest in playing hero. He was too old for this shit.

He hadn't agreed to do it for Abby, though. Not for Leo, either. If he'd wanted to, he could have kicked his son's skinny-jeans-wearing ass and dragged him out of here. He was still stronger than Leo. He wasn't *that* old.

He hadn't walked away for one reason: Brooke.

Damn it all to hell. He liked her. She needed help. Her quiet tears over that throwaway compliment last night had undone him. Ray was a deadbeat dad, despite his buckets of money. He was an even worse parent than Nathan, and that was saying something.

If Brooke was his daughter…he couldn't imagine making any other choice. That didn't mean he thought barging into the fortress was a good strategy. But, emotionally, he understood Abby's point of view. The longer Brooke stayed in captivity, the more harm would come to her. She might suffer multiple attacks. There was a strong possibility that she would be killed before help arrived. She could be dead already.

Nathan hoped he hadn't sealed his own doom with this decision. Or worse, Leo's.

As soon as the shots rang out, Nathan grabbed Leo and hauled him around the corner. But it was too late; they'd both been hit. A searing pain tore through his forearm, white-hot. The dark seemed to close in around them.

Grimacing in pain, Nathan reached out with his free hand to touch the tunnel wall. "Come on," he said, dragging Leo toward the exit. Leo loped along beside him, making a hissing sound between his teeth. Blood trickled down Nathan's forearm. It felt like a flesh wound, but he was too pumped up to judge.

"I got shot," Leo said, his breathing labored. "That motherfucker shot me."

"Can you run?"

"No!"

Nathan couldn't hear anyone coming after them. He hoped the other hunter wasn't waiting outside the door. That would be a game-changer, even more than these inconvenient gunshot wounds. But staying in the tunnel wasn't an option, so he moved forward, his gut clenched with dread.

He didn't say "I told you so." Nor could he bring himself to choke out, "I love you." There were no fitting words for this situation. Trying not to panic, he kept going. He refused to believe it would end this way.

They broke out of the tunnel into daylight. Nathan didn't slow down. He helped Leo through the copse of trees and beyond, heading toward the creek. They stumbled across the forest as quickly as three good legs could carry them.

When they reached Silver Creek, Abby wasn't there. He'd assumed she would start running at the sound of gunfire. In his rush to get Leo to safety and evade the hunters, he hadn't thought to look for her.

Leo took a seat on a flat rock, groaning. His jeans were dotted with red patches, but not soaked completely through. The spread-out pattern indicated small ammunition, which didn't cause as much damage. He wasn't going to die or lose his leg. Nathan tried to smother a sob of relief, and couldn't quite manage.

"What's wrong with you?" Leo asked.

He swallowed hard, shaking his head.

"Are you hit?"

"No, I'm not hit."

"Your arm is bleeding."

He glanced at the minor laceration. "It's fine. I was just…worried."

"You should be worried. I'm all shot up!"

Wiping his eyes, he bent down beside Leo to inspect his leg. The wounds were seeping and probably hurt like hell. He needed emergency medical treatment, but it would have to wait. "It's just birdshot."

"What's that?"

"Tiny bullets." They were lucky. Buckshot might have broken bones or severed arteries. "You'll be okay."

Leo flexed his knee experimentally, wincing.

"We have to keep moving."

"We have to go back."

Nathan couldn't believe how quickly Leo had overcome the trauma of getting shot. He was already willing to risk his life again.

"Abby got captured," Leo said.

Nathan's heart sank. "How do you know?"

"She's not here."

He raked a hand through his hair, stricken by Leo's

logic. The hunters could have caught up with them, but they hadn't. They'd gone after Abby instead. Or they'd gone after her *first*. That didn't mean they wouldn't come for Leo and Nathan.

Within minutes, perhaps.

Those men knew every inch of these woods, and they weren't wounded. Nathan was quite certain they would kill to protect their lair. If Nathan and Leo continued to flee at a sluggish pace, they'd probably be shot before the sun went down. Returning to the fortress didn't seem wise, either. Leo was in no shape to attempt another rescue, and they might meet up with the hunters on the way there.

"We're vulnerable out in the open," Nathan said, glancing around. "We have to hide and hope they pass by."

Leo studied their surroundings. The rock he was sitting on had blood smears on it. Anyone with half a brain would know they'd been here. "They'll expect us to go downriver. It's the path of least resistance, and it heads to the road. Let's leave some footprints along the shore and double back. Maybe we can climb that tree."

Nathan followed his gaze to a sturdy live oak, nodding in approval. Finally they were seeing eye-to-eye. "Good plan."

"While they're on a wild-goose chase, we can save Brooke and Abby."

Nathan didn't agree or disagree. They'd cross that

CHAPTER SEVENTEEN

THE HUNTER SHOVED ABBY into the dark, keeping one hand on her bound wrists.

"Wyatt?" the man called out.

Nathan and Leo weren't inside the tunnel, so maybe they'd escaped. Another figure met them in the narrow confines. He held an old-fashioned kerosene lantern, which illuminated his face from below, transforming it into a ghoulish parody. She was afraid to stare at either man closely or study her surroundings, even though she knew those details were important. She'd also studied and practiced dozens of self-defense maneuvers, but she hadn't used them. She'd cooperated out of desperation.

Her brain rejected any attempt to focus. She wanted to see nothing, hear nothing, experience nothing. Her natural instinct was to withdraw from this horror, not to fight back or plan her escape.

"What happened?" the man behind her asked Wyatt.

"I think I hit one of them."

Abby's emotions shut down. She couldn't process any more bad news. She pictured herself curled up

on the ground with her hands clapped over her ears.
Oblivion was another method of survival.

Remember Brooke, she said to herself. *Stay alert
for Brooke.*

"You *think* you hit one?"

"I'm not sure," Wyatt said. His voice wavered, as
if he was scared.

"They got away," the other man said, urging her
forward. "This mama bear attacked me with a rock
before I could shoot at them."

Wyatt's tense brow relaxed at this statement, but
he didn't offer any comment. Turning around, he led
the way to a trapdoor in the ceiling of the tunnel. He
climbed up a ladder and set the lamp inside to help
Abby. She ascended on cue, her knees quaking and
her mind numb. The room they entered looked like
an underground bunker. Her daughter was lying on a
rough-hewn cot with her wrists and ankles tied. She
was fully clothed and appeared unharmed. Her large
pupils indicated she was still under the influence.

"Mom," she cried, struggling to sit up.

A resurgence of hope flowed into Abby, bringing
back her strength and willpower. Brooke was alive.

Brooke was *alive.*

Nothing could keep them apart.

Abby stumbled forward, intent on reaching her
daughter. But the hunter shoved her sideways before
she could get there. She would have gone sprawling
if Wyatt hadn't been there to catch her fall. Brooke
made a whimpering noise, but Abby didn't look at
her again. Intuition told her that her captor would

enjoy female distress. Every scream would be music to him, every tear a triumph. So she found her balance and stayed still.

Wyatt didn't smell as bad as his friend. The odor of smoke and fish clung to his clothes, unpleasant but bearable. When he released her, she realized he was just a teenager. Judging by his strong physical resemblance to the older man, they were father and son.

"Maybe you were right about taking them both," the father said, coming up beside her. He touched her cheek, making her flinch. "This one suits me. She's all woman."

Brooke let out a strangled sob. Wyatt stared at the ground and said nothing.

Abby didn't know if the father liked her maturity or her softer curves, but she'd take it. Anything that kept him away from her daughter. She'd sacrifice herself for Brooke without a second's hesitation.

"If you want the other one, you have to earn her," the father said.

"How?" Wyatt asked.

"Come on. It's time to make your first kill."

Abby didn't hear the boy's response to this chilling statement. His father gripped her arm and guided her through the open door while Brooke continued to weep. They traveled down a short tunnel to another small dugout. There was a sleeping pallet at one end and a trapdoor in the ceiling with a wooden ladder beneath it. A strange-looking box, about the size of a large dog crate, sat in the corner. Her stomach lurched with terror as he dragged her toward it. He was going to cage her like an animal.

She dug her heels in the dirt floor. "No, please."

The man smiled in response, his teeth tobacco-stained but straight. The more she fought, the more excited he'd get. Although Abby sensed that, she couldn't control her panic or summon any degree of calm. Her detached docility had snapped. She started thrashing back and forth, kicking to get free.

He grabbed her by the hair again and swept his foot in front of hers. She went down hard on her knees, gasping in pain as he opened the cage door and shoved her in. Her cheek slammed into the perforated metal floor. She collapsed on her belly, too stunned to move.

Her legs were sticking out of the cage door. He made a chopping motion at the back of her heel that caused excruciating pain. Biting back a scream, she rolled onto her side and drew her knees to her chest to avoid another blow. He slammed the door shut and locked it, tucking a key into his pocket.

The crate was made of stainless steel with quarter-sized ventilation holes along the sides and a barred door at the front. She couldn't stand up or stretch out. She could probably sit up and turn around, but it was a very tight fit.

The hunter crouched beside the door, squinting at her. "Give me trouble and I'll make your daughter pay."

Abby was ready to tear him apart with her teeth and fingernails. He wanted an animal? She'd be one.

"Do you understand me?"

"Yes."

"Good."

She watched, her scraped face burning and her ankle on fire, while the hunter drank water from a gallon container. Thirst overwhelmed her, but she knew better than to ask for a drink. He might give it to her in a dog bowl.

"Bring the shotgun and the crossbow," the man said to his son.

An icy hand trailed down Abby's spine. They were going to hunt for Nathan and Leo, who were both unarmed, maybe injured, stumbling around in unfamiliar territory. The odds were stacked against them, and there was nothing she could do about it.

This was all her fault. She'd been wrong to insist on a half-cocked rescue attempt. They'd taken a gamble and lost. She should have listened to Nathan and gone to the authorities. Now they'd die here, just as he'd predicted.

The trauma she'd experienced during the San Diego earthquake had caused this predicament. She couldn't have endured another agonizing separation from Brooke, uncertain if she was alive or dead. Those days had been the worst of her life.

Until this.

How sickeningly clear hindsight was. How cruel and precise. And how unfair to survive one horrific tragedy, only to be struck down by another.

The hunters left the dwelling through the trapdoor, wearing camouflage from head to toe and armed to the nines. She was trapped and helpless, unable to move. Her arms ached from the uncomfortable position, and the sharp zip-tie cut into her skin. To her utter frustration, tears wouldn't come. The emotional breakdown she'd been expecting remained elusive.

She yelled for Brooke until her voice grew hoarse. There was no response. Her daughter was tied up and drugged, probably locked behind a door. Even if Brooke could get up, which seemed doubtful, she wouldn't be about to get out.

Abby was in a similar, impossible position. She couldn't escape the cage with her hands bound behind her back. She couldn't escape the cage, period. It was a heavy-duty piece of torture equipment. When she tried kicking the door, her left ankle screamed in protest. Grimacing, she braced her left foot against the corner and kicked with her right. The cramped space didn't allow much range of movement, which made her blows ineffective.

You'll die here.

Brooke *will die here.*

A choked sob escaped her lips, as weak and unsatisfying as the escape attempt. Her ankle throbbed and her wrists hurt.

The miserable confinement reminded her of the third day after the earthquake. There was still no word from Brooke. The entire city had been evacuated, and civilians were barred from reentering their own neighborhoods. In addition to massive structure damage, there had been secondary disasters in the form of fires, floods and landslides.

She'd felt so helpless.

Abby hadn't broken down until later, however. She'd been reunited with Brooke, finally. The joy of seeing her daughter alive had lifted Abby's spirits into the stratosphere. While the downtown area was being rebuilt, they'd stayed in a hotel. Brooke had to attend a satellite school. On her first day back, Abby had dropped Brooke off at the site, which was a big parking lot with trailer classrooms.

After she drove away, Abby had experienced a debilitating panic attack. She'd pulled over to the side of the road and called Ella. She couldn't remember much after that. Apparently Ella had picked her up and taken care of her for the next several hours. Abby didn't know what she would have done without her sister.

Unfortunately, Ella wasn't here with her now. No man with a crowbar would free her. She couldn't count on Nathan and Leo to return. Abby had only herself to rely on. And she couldn't quit. Not after everything they'd been through.

Brooke's life was in her hands.

It occurred to Abby that she knew how to break a plastic zip-tie. She'd seen a video demonstration on the internet. A friend of hers had shared a link to the clip on Twitter. Abby couldn't resist clicking information about survival techniques.

The self-defense expert had used leverage and body positioning to snap the plastic. He'd bent forward, pushing his arms down his lower back as far as they could go and pulling apart at the same time.

Abby couldn't stand up, like the man in the video. Her muscle mass was decidedly lower. But her motivation to succeed was unparalleled. She had to free herself and save Brooke. Failure was not an option.

She didn't get it on the first try. Or the second. After about ten minutes, she lost count of the attempts made. She flopped on her back, on her belly and on her side. Sweat dripped from her hairline and the plastic sliced into her wrists, which became slippery. Panting from exertion, she switched tactics, squirming to slide her wrist out. That didn't work, either. In a desperate burst of energy, she strained against the zip-tie until black spots danced before her eyes.

It snapped.

She lay against the grated floor of the cage, breathing hard. When she'd recovered enough to glance at her wrists, she groaned. They were red and swollen, cuffed in blood. She stretched her arms over her head and rolled her shoulders, grateful for the range of movement. Her hands were free. Now she needed to get out of the cage.

The inside of the door offered no solution, and the bars were too narrow for anything but her fingertips to fit through. She couldn't reach the lock or feel the keyhole. Without a tool of some kind, she'd be out of luck.

She grabbed the broken zip-tie, struck by another wave of inspiration. It was skinny, sturdy and stiff enough to use to pick the lock.

Score.

Although Abby tried multiple angles and hand formations, the zip-tie didn't work. It was too straight, and not quite long enough. She needed another tool. Or a miracle.

"Brooke," she shouted. "Brooke!"

No answer.

Abby didn't think her daughter could hear her, let alone come to her rescue. She sat on the floor of the cage with her legs crossed, taking inventory of the situation. There was nothing near the cage she could try to lasso with a shoelace. There was nothing inside but her. She had hiking shoes. Jogging pants with no zippers, buttons or pockets. A tank top, because she'd taken off her jacket earlier today. Underwear.

Under*wire*.

Her bra had a thin, semiflexible piece of wire sewn into the cup. It was curved to follow the shape of a breast. She could use the underwire to pick the lock! A flexible piece of metal would be perfect for reaching the keyhole.

Moving quickly, she removed her bra and tore into the fabric with her teeth. She preferred well-made lingerie, so biting through the material wasn't easy. Thirst and fatigue assailed her. She tasted blood and gagged.

"Don't stop," she whispered. "You've got this."

She'd given Brooke that pep talk a hundred times. The difference was that Brooke had magic legs and a winning spirit. The girl never quit, never slowed, never let up. Abby smothered another sob at the thought of her, drugged and disoriented in this hovel. Growling like an animal, Abby ripped through threads and reinforced lace.

When the underwire popped out, she removed one shoelace and tied the metal to her wrist. She was worried about dropping the tool and being unable to retrieve it. One false move with shaking fingers might put the object on the other side of the bars.

Taking a deep breath, she extended the wire through the bars and found the keyhole. It was a contortionist exercise, destined to induce madness. She couldn't see what she was doing. Her arms and shoulders were already tired, her muscles aching.

Within minutes, her wrist cramped.

She alternated between using her left hand and right hand. Neither felt strong. Sweat dotted her hairline and beaded on her upper lip. The tool kept slipping from her fingers. She stifled the urge to bang her fists against the cage.

Instead of losing her cool, she experimented with different techniques. She chewed off the tiny plastic nub from the tip of the underwire and tried again. She used the strap of her bra to hold the wire in place with her left hand while she cranked it with her right. When she heard the tiny click of gears—finally—she almost wept with joy. After a bit more finessing, a spring released inside the lock and the door opened.

Victory.

She had no idea how long she'd been in the cage. It felt like hours, but her accelerated heart rate and spiked anxiety might have warped her sense of time. She stared at the square-shaped doorway, her pulse pounding with fear. Although freedom beckoned, she didn't move. She was shocked and ashamed by her urge to stay put. This awful crate was a known entity, both a trap and a protective shield. Outside, she'd have to evade the hunters, maybe attack them again. She wasn't sure she could do it.

The same insecurities that had plagued her for years welled up, holding her captive. She had anxiety issues. She'd been abandoned by her father and her husband. She was broken, unworthy of love, incapable of keeping a man.

Leaving this cage meant taking a risk. Fighting for her life, rather than accepting her fate. It was difficult to trust herself enough to move forward. Her rescue plan had backfired. Maybe cooperating would be safer. If she got caught trying to run away, she'd be killed. Like the other women who'd been terrorized here.

Abby didn't know anything about the previous victims. She didn't know about their families or their romantic relationships. But it didn't really matter. None of them deserved this. No one deserved to be locked up and abused.

She scrambled out of the crate, tears stinging her eyes. She had to escape and survive, for those victims. For her daughter.

For herself.

NATHAN HELPED LEO onto a higher branch, wincing at the familiar tug in his shoulder.

Damned rotator cuff.

When they'd climbed as far as they could go, they found secure hiding places. Leo chose a perch between two sturdy branches on the west side of the tree trunk. Sitting on the lower limb, he gripped the upper one with his right hand. Nathan settled onto a more exposed branch, facing the creek bed so he could keep watch. They were both wearing dark clothing, so they'd be hard to spot from a distance. The foliage wasn't thick enough to cover them at close range. If the hunters happened to look for them up here, instead of following the footsteps downriver, they'd be in trouble.

They had to be very quiet and very still.

Getting to this point had been tricky. Nathan had stomped through the mud, with Leo hobbling alongside him. Then they'd entered the creek and doubled back. They'd traveled against the current until they reached the lower tree branches and climbed up. Now they had nothing to do but wait.

Nathan glanced over his shoulder, evaluating Leo's condition. His black hair was damp with sweat. He didn't appear pale, but he rarely did. He had Lydia's olive skin tone. The patchy stubble on this jaw reminded Nathan of his younger self.

"I'm thirsty," Leo said.

"Me, too."

"I guess you were right about going to the police."

Nathan wished he'd been wrong. He'd have given his life savings for a better outcome. And he was quite rich, so that was a lot of money.

"Now that we know where the hideout is, the girls don't have a chance."

He'd already figured that. These men didn't want anyone contacting the authorities. If Nathan and Leo got away, the kidnappers might kill the women and flee. Brooke and Abby could be dead before help arrived.

There was a long silence. Nathan did another sweep of the area, keeping a close eye on the bloody rock.

"They didn't steal my pot," Leo said.

Nathan gripped the trunk for balance. "What?"

"I lied about that."

"You lied about bringing it?"

"No, I brought it. I lied about it being stolen."

"Why?"

"I thought you'd take it away."

"I would have tossed it in the fucking lake."

"Right."

Nathan studied the water's edge, his ire rising. He should have been too focused on survival to get angry. Somehow, he wasn't.

"I just wanted you to know. In case we die."

"If we don't die, you're in trouble."

"I'm too old to be in trouble, Dad," Leo said in a calm voice. "I don't live with you, and I don't want your money."

Nathan could stop contributing to Leo's trust fund, but it wouldn't make much difference. Lydia was wealthy enough to care for him in style, with or without Ray. Leo didn't need anything from him. "So you don't care what I think?" Nathan asked, glancing over at his son. "I don't matter to you?"

"That's not what I said."

"You know why I'm worried, don't you?"

"You think I'll turn out like you."

The words were painful to hear, so plainly stated. Nathan hadn't realized that Leo understood his greatest fear.

"I won't," Leo promised. "I don't even drink."

"Since when?"

"I've never been drunk."

"You think being stoned is better? All natural and good for you?"

"It's not addictive."

"Bullshit."

"Would you care if I was drinking a few beers here and there?"

Nathan scowled, rubbing a hand over his mouth. "Yes."

"Bullshit," Leo said, tossing the curse back at him. "I'm not driving under the influence—"

"Then why are there joints in the ashtray?"

"There was one roach, not multiple joints. I don't get all blasted and drive. I'm more responsible than you think."

Nathan didn't mention Leo's academic problems. Hopefully switching majors would help motivate him. "If you expect me to give you the green light on pot smoking, I won't."

"That's fine. I'm an adult. I don't need your approval."

Nathan examined the hills in the distance, tamping down his anger. His natural instinct was to guide and protect Leo. To control him a little…for his own good. But maybe it *was* too late. Leo had grown up before Nathan had the chance to be a proper father. The missed opportunity weighed heavily on him.

Then again, at least they had a relationship now. Leo had admitted to lying, which indicated a certain amount of maturity. This type of open, honest communication felt like progress. They were developing mutual trust and respect. They'd made headway. Nathan also had to consider his own tendency to be overcritical. Was he upset about Leo's drug use because it was harmful, or because it didn't align with his vision of an ideal son? Nathan couldn't expect Leo to be perfect. Nathan sure as hell wasn't.

He had to accept Leo for who he was.

It was possible that the near-death experience had mellowed him. Nathan didn't want their last conversation to be contentious. There were more important things to worry about—like surviving the next few hours.

Leo nudged his shoulder and pointed behind Nathan, upriver. The hunters were making their way along the creek about a hundred yards west of the bloody rock. His heart dropped at the unexpected approach.

Nathan had been counting on the men to follow their tracks in a straight line from the fortress to the creek. Instead, they'd taken a sneaky detour. They'd be passing right by the tree Nathan and Leo were hiding in. If either man happened to glance this way, Nathan and Leo would be spotted. The branches weren't leafy enough to disguise them. They had to get out of sight immediately.

Nathan gestured for Leo to move from his perch to the other side of the trunk. They found a sturdy limb for Leo to stand on. Nathan took the space below him, bracing his left foot on a weaker branch. It felt questionable, but he didn't have a choice. With both hands he grabbed the limb above his head that Leo was standing on.

It was an uncomfortable position. Leo's wet shoes dripped on his temple at infrequent intervals. Nathan shifted in discomfort, unable to escape the water torture. When a mosquito landed on his neck, he released the branch with one hand to slap it away. The limb below him cracked. Before he could readjust his grip, it gave out, leaving him dangling by one arm, twenty feet above the ground.

Shit.

He didn't know how long he could hang on. He let go with his right hand, which was attached to his injured shoulder. Reaching straight up had been difficult for him since the surgery. If he couldn't get a more secure hold, he'd be fucked. The fall wouldn't kill him, but the hunters would come to investigate.

Leo solved the problem by crouching on the tree limb and extending his left hand. Nathan met him halfway. Leo pulled him up, and Nathan was able to grab the limb with both hands, without a second to spare.

The kidnappers must have heard the branch snap. One of them splashed across the creek and approached the tree. He stood almost directly underneath Nathan, who tried not to sway or make a sound. It was the teenager. Nathan could see the top of his scraggly head. He had a crossbow and quiver strapped to his back.

Another drop of water from Leo's shoe splashed the tip of Nathan's ear, startling him. That tiny, insignificant sensation was almost enough to break his concentration. He clung to the tree limb, gritting his teeth. He willed the boy to go away. If he didn't, Nathan would have to jump on him before he raised his weapon.

Suddenly, the kid glanced up. Their eyes locked.

Nathan had to attack him or risk being shot by the crossbow. Even so, he hesitated. It was a long way down. He might break his leg. Also, the boy was young and skinny and dirty. His ears were too big for his face. He looked scared.

Nathan couldn't do it. He couldn't imagine stabbing this kid or strangling him to death. The idea of killing anyone, especially a scrawny teenager, turned his stomach.

The boy didn't load his weapon. He didn't call out to the older man. His eyes moved past Nathan, to Leo, and beyond. He did a visual sweep of the area and retreated in silence, as if he hadn't seen anything.

Nathan gripped the tree limb for several minutes after the boy left. His biceps quivered from the strain. He held on for five seconds longer, counting them like weight reps. Then he found another branch on the other side of the tree and shifted his weight to it.

He caught a glimpse of the hunters heading downriver. Overwhelmed with relief, he helped Leo maneuver to a lower limb.

"That was close," Leo said.

"He looked right at me."

"I know. I thought he was going to shoot us."

Nathan placed a hand over his galloping heart. He couldn't believe what just happened. "He must have been afraid to do it."

"We're lucky it was him, and not the old guy."

He nodded. The incident gave him hope for rescuing Abby and Brooke. The kid wasn't as much of a threat as they'd figured. He might be a reluctant participant in the kidnapping, even another captive.

Nathan waited for his breathing to calm and reevaluated their situation. The past few hours had been a maelstrom of stress. He'd gone from furious to fearful and back again. Now that the hunters had passed, he could focus on their next step. Although they were still in danger, they were alive. They were capable of fighting. Nathan was a practical man and a protective father, but he wasn't a coward. Abby and Brooke needed their help. He couldn't leave two defenseless women to die.

When this was over, Nathan wanted Abby to be his. Maybe fear had amplified all of his emotions. Maybe he was getting old and sentimental. Either way, their connection was undeniable. He'd like to keep seeing her—assuming they survived.

As soon as it felt safe to abandon their hiding spot, Nathan climbed back down to terra firma and crossed the creek again. Leo was still favoring his right leg, but he didn't complain about the pain. He *had* become a man in the time they'd been apart. He was strong-willed, with a quick mind and fast reflexes. Nathan had come on this trip to save Leo from himself. Instead, Leo had saved them both.

"Thanks," he said to Leo, still rattled by the close call.

"For what?"

"Helping me get a grip."

Leo frowned at his gratitude. "You think I'd let you fall?"

"No. I'm just glad you were there."

CHAPTER EIGHTEEN

ABBY HAD NO IDEA when the kidnappers would return.

Casting a nervous glance at the trapdoor, she picked up the kerosene lamp and crept down the tunnel hallway. She assumed the men were still hunting Nathan and Leo, but the fortress was an underground maze with multiple exits. Their captors could be lurking around any corner. With each step, a dull ache radiated from her ankle to her hip. She reached the first door, which was locked from the outside. It had a hasp and a padlock attached to the wood frame. She'd have to find a key, pick the lock or break it down with a heavy object.

"Brooke?" she murmured, rattling the door. She rapped her knuckles against the wood. "Brooke!"

"Mom?" She sounded groggy, as if she'd been asleep.

"I'm going to look for a key," Abby said. "I'll be right back."

"Okay," Brooke said. "Hurry."

Abby hadn't seen any personal belongings in the main room, so she continued down the tunnel, her throat dry. There was another door on the left, unlocked. She stuck the lamp inside and peered into the dark recesses. It took several seconds for her to make sense of the shapes and shadows. What appeared to be a large, empty birdcage hung from a hook on the wall. Another sleeping pallet sat in one corner, next to a wooden chest.

Abby entered the room with caution. She didn't have time to let fear overwhelm her. Clearly these troglodytes enjoyed torture. The chest was open, revealing a coil of rope and some metal chains. Sick bastards. Nothing in the chest could be used to break down the door, so she lifted the lamp again. There was a short, circular rock wall at the opposite end of the room. Feeling nauseous, she approached the edge and glanced over. It was a pit or well, dug so deep she couldn't see the bottom.

What if someone was down there?

Heart racing, she knelt and braced her hand on the rock wall. "Hello?" she ventured, trying to illuminate the abyss. When she leaned out a little more, a rock shifted under her weight, startling her. She narrowly avoided toppling over the edge.

Good job, Abby. Fall into a pit and break your neck.

She took a deep breath and repositioned her hand before looking again. She didn't see anyone, but her stomach churned with dread. This place gave her the creeps. They had to get out of there *now*. Before she left the room, it dawned on her that the loose rock would make a good bludgeoning tool. She removed it from the wall and hurried back to the locked door.

Setting aside the lamp, she held the skull-sized

rock with both hands and slammed it against the padlock. Nothing happened. She hit it again and again, trying to keep her fingers out of the impact zone. Soon the wood frame splintered. Although the padlock stayed intact, the metal hasp gave way.

Abby wrenched the door open. She rushed inside and found Brooke on the cot, trying to chew through the rope at her wrists.

"Let me," she said, untying the knots. It seemed to take forever. Every second that ticked by felt like an eternity. The hunters were coming for them.

When Brooke's wrists were free, Abby knelt to take care of her ankles. Her fingers were clumsy, her entire body shaking. Her mouth was so dry she couldn't speak. Finally she worked the knots loose. Brooke threw her arms around Abby's neck and hugged her close, sobbing. Abby's chest swelled with hope. They were both okay.

They were going to make it.

"Are you hurt?" she asked, studying her daughter's pretty face. Her eyes were glassy and unfocused, her pupils huge.

"I'm fine," Brooke said.

Abby wasn't sure Brooke would be able to remember any abuse she'd suffered, but they could worry about that later. There was a cup of water sitting on a crate by the cot. Brooke drank half and gave Abby the other half.

"Can you walk?" Abby asked, trying not to panic.

Brooke stood, wobbly in her bare feet. "I think so."

Taking her by the hand, Abby picked up the lamp

and guided them through the tunnel. Brooke stumbled along, sluggish.

Beyond the main room was a kitchen with a wood table and a cooking area. It was disorganized. Dirty dishes and bags of trash were piled in a corner. Large sacks of rice and beans were stacked in a haphazard fashion. Abby found a set of ignition keys on the table and a paring knife on the floor. Abby pocketed both items on their way out of the kitchen.

In the main room, Abby climbed the ladder and pushed open the trapdoor. Daylight assailed her, burning her eyes. She made a shield with her hand and squinted at her surroundings. This exit appeared to be disguised among a cluster of boulders. She crawled out and did a quick sweep of the area before gesturing for Brooke to follow. Brooke ascended the ladder with clumsy motions, her usual coordination gone. When she reached the top, Abby pulled her through the opening.

They scrambled down the grassy slope with Abby supporting Brooke on one side. Her ankle throbbed from the additional weight, but she ignored the pain. She had to encourage Brooke to keep moving.

It was now or never.

Nathan had told her to follow the creek east. Although she was terrified of running into the kidnappers, she didn't know what else to do. She guided Brooke toward the copse of trees where she'd been hiding before chaos erupted. Her backpack was still there. When she stopped to retrieve it, Brooke slid to the ground, half-conscious.

Abby retrieved Brooke's boots and shoved them on her feet, tying the laces tight. Then she put on the backpack. "We have to go," she said, urging her upright.

"I'm too tired."

They'd drugged her with something besides ether. A strong depressant, judging by Brooke's level of intoxication. She'd be groggy for hours. Abby slid one arm around her waist and shuffled forward. Their progress was agonizingly slow. She tried coaching Brooke, pinching her, even slapping her cheek lightly.

Nothing helped.

It wasn't Brooke's fault. She was just too dazed to respond to the danger, and Abby didn't have the physical strength to drag her along. Her ankle hurt like hell. After several hundred feet, they both collapsed.

Abby smothered a cry of frustration. She'd come too far to give up, but her options were limited. She couldn't carry Brooke. She wouldn't leave her. There weren't any convenient hiding places nearby, just pine trees and clusters of green shrubbery. Abby did the only thing she could think of: she dragged Brooke behind a shrub and started digging with her bare hands. If she could carve out enough room for them to lie down, she could cover them with dirt and pine needles. The sun would go down in a few hours and the drugs would wear off. Until then, they had to blend into the scenery.

It was a disturbing process. Of course she thought of shallow graves and wild animals. She was burrowing to survive, tears streaming down her face.

Her manicure was ruined.

Twigs snapped in the distance, startling her. The kidnappers were coming! She shoved Brooke into the dent she'd created and piled debris on top of her. "Stay silent," she hissed. The space wasn't large enough for two, so she scurried under a nearby bush. Tiny thorns tore at her bare arms, piercing her skin. She crouched there, wild-eyed and feral. Anyone who reached in to grab her would get a nasty bite.

Remembering the knife, she drew it from her pocket and held it ready. Brooke didn't move or speak. Abby hadn't spared much thought to Nathan and Leo. She'd been too focused on escape. Now her throat closed up as she imagined father and son, their faces slack with death. Reunited in tragedy.

The kidnappers' return didn't necessarily mean that Nathan and Leo had been killed, but it didn't look good. Her breath hitched as if an arrow had gone through *her* chest. Over the past few days, she'd grown attached to Nathan and Leo. They were like family to her. Nathan was something more, something special. They'd both risked their lives for Brooke—at Abby's insistence. She was responsible for this tragic turn of events.

Tears pricked her eyes, but she blinked them away. Her palms grew damp with perspiration and her heartbeat thundered in her ears. She could barely hear the sound of approaching footsteps. The quiet, intermittent crunch of leaves indicated stealth or uncertainty. She stayed still and prayed that the men would pass on by.

They didn't.

A pair of boots paused beside the bush she was hiding behind. She gripped the knife handle in her sweaty fist, poised to attack. When a second figure limped toward Brooke's burrow, Abby emerged with a strangled cry. She was so ready to face their foes that she almost didn't recognize Leo and Nathan for the friends they were. The knife slipped from her hand and a relieved sob escaped her lips.

Brooke sat up in the leaves, her hair a tangled mess. Leo crashed through the bushes to help her to her feet.

Nathan strode forward and cupped his hand around Abby's face. He kissed her trembling mouth and brought her head to his chest, embracing her in a fierce, protective way. Tears flooded her eyes at the feel of his strong arms around her. They weren't safe, not by a long shot, but they were back together.

Like a family.

When they broke apart, Nathan studied her appearance. His dark eyes took in her scraped cheek, bloody wrists and general disarray. "Those motherfuckers," he said, his jaw clenched. He glanced over his shoulder, as if expecting to see them coming.

"Where are they?" Abby asked.

"By the creek."

"Brooke can't walk," she said in a rush. "She's drugged and I didn't know what to do."

"I'll carry her," Leo said.

"You're hurt," Nathan said. "I'll carry her."

"I want Leo," Brooke murmured.

Nathan ignored this and lifted her into his arms. She rested her head on his shoulder and closed her eyes. Leo led them back toward the underground hideout. Once they passed it, they could start heading east, towards civilization. Abby tried not to grimace as she followed him. Leo had a rash of shrapnel wounds on his left leg that had to hurt more than her ankle. Nathan was carrying 125 extra pounds.

She was terrified that the hunters would catch up with them.

"We need to build a travois," Nathan said. He sounded short of breath already. "I can't carry her the whole way."

Abby remembered the ignition key. She removed it from her pocket, wondering if the men kept a vehicle hidden. "I found this inside."

Leo took the key from her. "It's for an off-road vehicle. Maybe a dirt bike."

Nathan glanced around for a stash location. Now that they knew there were underground structures nearby, everything looked like a possible garage. "There," he said, jerking his chin toward a short, rounded hill.

Abby and Leo ran to investigate it. A square door was hidden in the side of the hill, cleverly disguised with mud and dry moss. Nathan set Brooke on her feet and helped Leo break down the door. There was a four-wheeled vehicle inside.

"It's an ATV," Leo said.

"Will it take two riders?" Nathan asked.

"Hell, yeah."

Nathan and Abby exchanged a glance. They didn't even need to discuss who would go. "Have you driven one before?"

"No, but it's easier than a bike."

"Do you think you can get Brooke to Monarch?"

Leo nodded. "You'd better tie her to me, so she doesn't fall off."

They took the four-wheeler out of the parking spot and made sure it was fueled up. After Leo hopped on, Brooke climbed aboard, hugging his waist. Nathan used his knife to cut the sleeves off Leo's hooded sweatshirt and adjust the neck opening. Abby put it on Brooke and Leo, securing them together.

"Go to a hospital," Nathan said. "Or flag down anyone you see and call the police."

Leo gave him an impatient look, as if he already knew what to do. "You should hide. They'll hear the engine."

"I know."

"What about tonight? You need shelter."

"We'll have to go back to camp," Nathan said.

Abby was too choked up to say anything. She kissed Brooke's forehead and touched Leo's dark hair, trusting him to take care of her baby.

"I'll keep her safe," Leo said to Abby.

"Keep yourself safe, too," she said, blinking back tears.

Leo looked at Nathan. It seemed like a thousand words hung in the air between them, unspoken. He cranked the key and started the ignition. Then Brooke and Leo were off, traveling toward freedom.

The sound wasn't as loud as Abby had figured, and the ATV went faster than any person could keep up with on foot. As long as the four-wheeler didn't break down, Brooke and Leo had an excellent chance of getting out alive.

Nathan led Abby to a nearby hill several hundred yards away. It was the same one they'd climbed earlier to get a better view of the area. "Let's wait here to make sure they aren't followed. Once they reach the forest service road, which is probably close by, they'll be able to go thirty or forty miles per hour."

Abby agreed to the plan, getting down on her belly beside him. They could see the trees lining the creek and both entrances to the underground structure. The thrum of the ATV engine had already faded into the distance. She shared the water from her backpack with Nathan and put on her fleece jacket. The late-afternoon sun had gone behind a group of dark clouds, and the air had a damp smell. Rain was coming.

"Did they rape you?" he asked, keeping his eyes on the area by the creek.

"No."

"Brooke?"

"I don't think so."

He glanced at her face once again. "How did you get out?"

She told him about the zip-tie and picking the lock. After he studied her raw wrists, he moved his gaze back to the forest. Her voice shook as she detailed the disturbing sights in the torture room. She broke off, unable to continue. "I'm sorry."

"It's not your fault."

"I should have listened to you."

"You escaped. You saved Brooke. That's what matters."

Abby withheld comment. They weren't safe yet. The tension inside her wouldn't ease until they were all together again. "What happened with you and Leo?"

"We went to the creek and hid up a tree."

"Did you see them?"

"Yes. The boy saw us, too. But he didn't say anything."

"Why?"

He shook his head. "I think the older one is the psychopath."

"It's his father."

"How do you know?"

"Just a hunch," she said, shivering.

Time ticked by, and the sky darkened with the threat of precipitation. Abby wasn't sure if it was getting late, or just stormy. With each passing moment, Brooke and Leo got farther away from danger. But what about Abby and Nathan? They'd have to return to camp and hope the men didn't come after them.

It was going to be a long night.

A crack rang out through the trees, like an ax splitting wood or a thunderclap. "That's rifle fire," Nathan said, gesturing for Abby to stay low.

"From where?"

"Close. The creek."

They watched and waited. Ants crawled along her

arms and under her clothes. The wind picked up. Her anxiety rose and rose and rose. She wanted to curl up in a little ball and wish everything away. To go to sleep and end this nightmare. After the terrifying, traumatic events of the day, her strength was sapped.

When it started to drizzle, they rose from the hill and fled into the trees. Abby couldn't stop shaking. As soon as they reached the woods, Nathan gripped her arm and jerked her behind a tree. He pressed a finger to his lips, his eyes darting sideways. She followed his gaze to a hooded figure in a camouflage rain jacket.

It was one of the hunters—and he was coming right toward them.

CHAPTER NINETEEN

LEO DIDN'T HAVE any trouble handling the ATV.

At first.

It was slow going, with a lot of boulders to skirt around and no discernible path for several miles. He jumped when he heard the faraway crack of a rifle shot, but he didn't stop. Even though Brooke was only half-lucid, the sound scared her. She clung to him tighter and kept looking over her shoulder.

Once they reached the old forest service road and headed south, it started to rain. Then it got dark. The headlamp on the Rincon was too dim to illuminate more than a few feet. Brooke pulled the hood of his sweatshirt over her head and slumped against his back. She dozed off, lulled by narcotics and the sluggish pace.

Leo drove as fast as the conditions would allow. He knew time was of the essence. His dad and Abby were out in the middle of nowhere on a stormy night, being hunted by a mountain man and a circus freak.

The road got increasingly bumpy and muddy. It was full of potholes, which turned into rain puddles of various depths. He lost count of the number of times his wounded leg got splashed. He'd probably develop a nasty infection. The off-highway vehicle area might be easier to navigate, but he didn't want to get lost on an interconnected network of recreation trails. If he stayed on this simple route, they'd make it to town.

He was punching it a little too fast on a straight-away and hit a pothole. When the vehicle listed to one side, Brooke couldn't help him countercorrect. Her slack weight tipped the already-precarious balance of the ATV. They both tumbled off the seat and hit the mud with a splat, while the heavy vehicle crashed down an embankment.

Leo landed on his shoulder with a hard slam. He rolled over into a mud puddle. Sputtering, he tried to free them both from the hooded sweatshirt that had kept Brooke from falling but also helped cause the accident. Escaping the fabric was beyond his capa-bilities. He finally tore the neckline down the front and scrambled upright.

Brooke was sprawled beside the puddle. Her hair was wet and bedraggled, her face pale. Although her eyes were open, he feared the worst: Internal injuries. Broken bones. Slipped disc. Fractured skull.

"Are you okay?" he choked out.

She sat up and lifted both arms, as if checking to see what still worked. "I think so. Nothing hurts."

He collapsed with relief, his breaths ragged. His *entire body* hurt. He'd read somewhere that drunk people were less likely to be injured in a car accident because they didn't tense up before the impact. That statistic had always bothered him. When he'd recov-ered well enough to stand, he slid down the embankment to turn off the vehicle's engine. The Rincon was wedged on its side in the ditch. Leo attempted to push it out, with no luck. He found a tree branch to use as a lever, but that didn't help.

After a few minutes, Brooke joined him. Although she seemed more alert, she was too uncoordinated to contribute. The rain continued to fall, complicating the process. Leo started to think *he* was going to get stuck in the mud and die there.

"Fuck," he yelled, shaking the stick at the sky.

"Let's just go," she said. "I can walk now."

They didn't have much choice. He threw the branch down and helped her up the embankment.

"Do you think we're close to the main road?" she asked.

It was hard to judge. They might be two miles away or ten. Either way, it would be a grueling journey. His leg throbbed in misery. He felt bruised and sore from head to toe. Brooke had none of her usual pep. They were in for a long haul.

He didn't ask what the men had done to her. He was afraid to find out. The idea of anyone hurting her filled him with impotent fury. If she told him they'd raped her, he might lose his mind. In some ways, she *was* like a little sister to him. She was his family. He'd seen her in braces, gangly and flat-chested. She'd never been an ugly duckling, but she'd definitely become a swan. Although he found her sunny personality annoying at times, he couldn't stand the thought of her light going dim.

They trudged forward in the mud. It was dark and

dreary. The rain transformed into a steady drizzle, then a fine mist cloaking the trees. Leo became increasingly weak, wincing every time he set his foot down. Brooke supported him on one side and murmured words of encouragement.

"I can give you a piggyback ride," she said.

He didn't doubt her. She was a tall girl with strong legs and the endurance of a horse. But he outweighed her by forty pounds, and the ground was slippery. If she fell and broke her ankle, they'd both be screwed.

"I need to rest," Leo said.

"Let me carry you."

"No, Brooke—"

"There's a light up ahead," she exclaimed, pointing through the trees. "Do you see it?"

Leo squinted at the faint glow in the distance. "Hurry," he said, picking up the pace. They lumbered away from the main road and across a hill that had to lead to the off-highway vehicle area. There was a big white RV parked next to a cliff, along with several ATV trailers and a black Jeep. Light filtered through the flowered curtains in the RV's side window, welcoming them like a beacon. He almost wept at the encouraging sight.

Brooke started calling out to the inhabitants when they were about twenty feet away. "Is anyone there? We need help!"

Before they reached the door, a man opened it. He was wearing an American flag T-shirt and a frayed baseball cap. There was a can of beer in his hand. He looked from Brooke to Leo, dumbfounded. "What the hell…"

"Please," she said. "My stepbrother's been shot. We need a phone."

Another man came up beside him to gawk. They must have resembled a pair of wet rats. But Brooke was beautiful, even while covered in mud, and a face like hers opened every door. "Let 'em in, Bud."

Bud let them in.

Brooke went up the short row of steps first, accepting the second man's helping hand. Leo followed her inside. There was a third man at a built-in table and booth. He stood to offer them a place to sit. Leo lowered himself into the space with a grimace. Brooke took the seat beside him.

The three men stared at them with bleary eyes. They were drunk, Leo realized. Drunk rednecks. Bud's T-shirt said Love It or Leave It. Lynyrd Skynyrd was playing on the radio. In addition to a mountain of crushed beer cans, there was a half-smoked joint in the ashtray. For once in his life, Leo had no urge to spark up.

"Do you have a phone?" Brooke asked.

The guys fumbled for their devices, none of which had reliable service in this location during a storm. Leo hoped one of them was sober enough to drive. Maybe he was paranoid from the day's harrowing events, but he felt vulnerable. He didn't like rednecks, for various reasons. He couldn't protect Brooke against three men. They were in their forties or fifties, and they were all large, if not physically fit.

"What happened to you two?" Bud asked Leo.

He tried to deliver a condensed, easily digestible version. "We ran into some weird guys. They kidnapped Brooke at our camp. My dad and I fought them and I got shot." He swallowed hard, adding, "Our parents are still out there."

"This is your sister?"

"Stepsister," Leo said.

"You don't look alike."

"We're not related by blood."

Bud inspected Leo's muddy, torn-up leg before narrowing his eyes at Brooke. "Did somebody hurt you, girl?"

"No," she said. "They would have, if Leo hadn't helped me get away."

The three men exchanged glances.

"Where are your parents, exactly?" Bud asked.

Leo explained that they'd been camping at the hot springs and pointed out the general location of the hidden fortress on a map. The men knew the area well. After a short argument, it was decided that Bud would drive Leo and Brooke to town while the other two took ATVs to the hot springs.

Bud's friends introduced themselves as Alan and Jeff. Leo shook their hands gratefully, fighting back tears.

"What's your dad's name?" Jeff asked.

"Nathan Strom."

"Like the baseball player?"

"That's him."

"No shit?"

"No shit."

Alan and Jeff didn't waste any more time talking. They put on rain jackets and grabbed a pair of shotguns. Maybe running into rednecks was lucky. Men like this were serious about exercising their right to bear arms.

"Thank you," Leo said.

"I have a daughter your age," Jeff said to Brooke, and left it at that.

After the rescue crew ventured out into the rain, Bud exchanged his beer can for a soda from the fridge. "Are you two thirsty?"

Leo and Brooke both said yes. Bud passed out sodas and the three of them exited the RV. Brooke climbed into the backseat of the Jeep while Leo sat passenger. They drove out of the off-highway vehicle area, toward the main road. Bud was careful not to go too fast or get stuck. Although inebriated, he wasn't reckless.

"I can't believe your father is Nathan Strom," Bud said.

Leo could anticipate the next question with 100 percent accuracy.

"Do you play baseball?"

"No."

"He speaks three languages," Brooke said.

"Is that right?"

Leo just shrugged. He knew his accomplishments weren't as impressive as being a superstar athlete in America's favorite sport, but so what. He'd helped rescue Brooke. He hadn't given up. If his dad could accept him the way he was, he could accept himself.

"Are you okay?" he asked Brooke, glancing back at her.

She looked out the window. "I will be."

THE ROUGH TREE BARK bit into Abby's spine as Nathan crushed his body against hers.

She trembled with fear. The soft rain had turned into a torrent, flooding the branches overhead and soaking through her clothes. Puddles gathered among the leaves at their feet. While she stood motionless, watching a pulse throb in Nathan's rain-streaked neck, the hunter in the raincoat passed by them.

He stopped at the edge of the trees, less than five feet away. She couldn't see his face, but she assumed it was the older man. There was a rifle slung over his shoulder, and he had a lump under his jacket, like a backpack. It was smart of him to take an indirect approach to the dugout instead of walking straight to the entrance.

Where was his son?

Nathan and Abby were in plain sight. It was too late to find a better hiding place. She was sure they'd be spotted. The boy might cut through the woods and discover them at any moment. Her heart thumped against Nathan's as she imagined the hunter turning around, raising his rifle, and taking their lives.

Nathan drew his knife. The wet blade glinted in the muted light. She knew he was thinking about going on the offensive. Striking first, cutting the hunter's throat. But instead of pouncing, he waited.

She held her breath until black spots danced across her vision. Again, she was reminded of the earthquake. Chaos. Pressure. Entrapment. When her car had stopped shaking, she'd wondered if she was dead. The magnitude of the event had been unfathomable, the destruction massive. It was end-of-the-world brutal.

"Abby," Nathan said, snapping her back to the present.

The hunter was gone. His retreating form was barely visible in the downpour. He disappeared amidst the cluster of boulders at the top entrance to the dugout. She couldn't believe he hadn't seen them.

They were still alive.

"We have to go," he said, studying her carefully. She could guess how she looked to him. Pale, freckled skin. Panicked eyes. Blue-tinged lips.

She took a few deep breaths, dazed. When she was ready to move, Nathan tugged her deeper into the woods. The rain was relentless, inescapable. He urged her to keep walking. She hobbled along as fast as she could.

"Are you hurt?" Nathan asked.

"I'm okay," she said, her teeth chattering. She was chilled to the bone and her ankle ached with every step, but she forced herself to continue. Carrying a full-grown woman was no easy task, even for someone as strong as him. He'd had enough trouble with Brooke. If Abby collapsed, they'd both suffer.

After what seemed like hours, they stopped to rest and take shelter under a large oak tree. Night was falling. She slid to a sitting position, hoping they weren't lost.

"I couldn't tell if that was the father or the son," Nathan said.

"Why would they separate?"

"I don't know. Maybe the shot we heard was…" He paused, as if reluctant to voice his thoughts out loud.

"What?"

"The father had the rifle."

"You think he killed his son?"

He stared into the rain, wiping the moisture from his face. It was a disturbing suspicion. Abby was already cold and scared, fighting off a mental breakdown. The short break eased the pressure off her ankle, but it didn't help her core body temperature. She began shivering uncontrollably.

They started hiking again. She endured the journey for as long as she could, retreating to a meditative state where fear and pain couldn't touch her. There were no guns, no kidnappers. No threats to Leo and Brooke. No worries.

Suddenly Nathan was standing over her, his eyes dark with concern. She could see his lips moving but she couldn't hear what he was saying.

His image faded as the door to reality closed, immersing her in oblivion.

CHAPTER TWENTY

NATHAN CARRIED ABBY all the way back to camp.

After about fifteen minutes, his right shoulder burned like fire. Then the strain spread to his biceps and calves. Near the end, he couldn't tell what was hurting anymore. His entire body was a quivering mass of jelly.

She was limp and incoherent in his arms. She asked for Brooke, for Ella, even for Ray. Sometimes she seemed to know who he was and where they were. Once she mistook him for a kidnapper and struggled against him in a short, ferocious burst of energy.

"It's me, Nathan," he'd said. "You're okay."

Then she clung to him again, trembling.

Nathan didn't know if she was hypothermic or having an anxiety attack. The rain had let up a little, but they were both soaked. He wasn't cold because his muscles were working hard and his blood was pumping. He had no idea what to do, other than try to get her warm. If her condition didn't improve after they took shelter, he couldn't help her. Rescue services wouldn't send a helicopter during a storm at night. He doubted the hunters—or hunter, singular—would come after them, either.

"Mr. Papadakis, keep your hands to yourself," she mumbled.

Nathan focused on putting one foot in front of the other. When he finally reached camp, he didn't take Abby to the tents. He went straight to the hot springs. It seemed easier to dump her in a warm pool than to fumble around for dry clothing.

His shoulder screamed for relief as he set her down at the edge of the tub. He tugged his shirt over his head and removed his boots. Then he unbuttoned his pants and stripped to his boxer shorts. He took off Abby's shoes but left the rest of her garments intact before easing her into the water.

The heat permeated his sore muscles, making him groan. Abby started shivering again. He held her to his chest, praying she'd be okay. Praying Leo and Brooke would make it to the hospital. Praying help would arrive, come morning.

After a short soak, she seemed to rouse. She pulled the soggy fleece over her head and flung it to the side of the tub with a splat. Then she turned to look at him. It was still drizzling and quite dark, with a mix of clouds in the moonlit sky.

"What happened?" she asked.

She looked and sounded lucid. He wasn't sure where to start.

"How did we get here?"

"I carried you."

"You did not."

"I did."

"Was I conscious?"

He shifted his sore shoulder, considering. "Sort of. You called me strange names, punched me in the ear and asked for Ray."

Her face crumpled at this news. She scooted away from him and burst into tears.

Nathan regretted being flip about her condition. He wanted to put her at ease, but he didn't know if he should reach out to her. Lydia had once told him not to touch her when she was crying. Abby stayed on the other side of the tub, weeping into her hands. Keeping his distance didn't seem right, so he got closer. He slid his arm around her waist and pressed his lips to the top of her head. "I'm sorry."

"You must think I'm crazy," she said, drawing a ragged breath.

"No."

"I can't believe you had to carry me."

"It made me feel very manly, if that helps."

She wiped her eyes.

"I don't think you're crazy, Abby."

"I don't like falling apart...being weak."

"You're not weak."

"I had a breakdown."

"So what? You were beaten and shoved into a fucking cage. There's no wrong way to react to something like that."

Frowning, she touched the mark on her cheek. "I wasn't beaten. My face hit the bottom of the crate."

Nathan didn't see the difference. It was no accident, and the details of her ordeal made him furious.

"The important part is that you and Brooke survived. You held it together when you had to."

She rested her head on his shoulder and fell silent.

He stroked her back for a few minutes, considering his own preconceptions about strength. He did equate physical power with masculinity, to some extent. His father had raised him on that belief, and Nathan had passed it on to Leo. He'd told Leo to "man up" on a number of occasions and encouraged him to be more aggressive in sports.

After John Christie's son committed suicide, Nathan had worried about Leo. Like many adolescents, he'd seemed sullen and withdrawn. Nathan had wanted to make sure he was okay. The conversation he'd instigated about sexuality had been sincere and well-intended, but maybe it was also an attempt to undo any damage he'd done. Nathan had known his be-tough attitude was the kind of thing that might make a boy question his self-worth. It was no wonder that Leo had felt inadequate. Nathan had meant it when he said he'd love Leo no matter what, but he'd also criticized every weakness.

"I used to throw up before every game," he said, remembering.

She raised her head to look at him. "Really?"

"It started in high school. I got sick one day when I thought a talent scout was watching in the stands. During the minors, I spent half of every pregame warm-up with my head in the toilet. The majors were even worse. I couldn't sleep or eat before my first start in the show. And I still threw up, twice."

She smiled at this admission. His teammates had ribbed him about it often, but they'd respected him enough not to share his secret with the press.

"It was just nerves," he said.

"Did it get better?"

"My nausea got better, but the way I dealt with pressure didn't." He'd gone from throwing up before games to drinking himself into a stupor after.

"When Leo got sick, did it remind you of those days?"

"Maybe subconsciously. I didn't think of it until now."

She slipped out of his embrace and rested her back on the opposite side of the tub, studying him. "Why did you tell me about it?"

"Because having anxiety doesn't make you weak. Neither does showing emotion. It's a hell of a lot healthier than drowning your feelings in alcohol, or burying them so deep you can't recognize them."

"You're too hard on yourself."

"I thought I was too hard on Leo."

"It comes from the same place."

She was right. Even though he'd already thought of this, it was an uncomfortable insight to hear out loud. He felt like a fool for failing to see things that were so obvious to her. Then again, she was more observant than the average person. He interpreted body language; she interpreted emotional histories.

Nathan reached for her backpack, which held a bottle of water and a bag of trail mix. They shared both, watching the rain-splashed river rush by.

"What else did I say when I was out of it?" she asked.

"Suggestive things," he said, wagging his brows.

"Like what?"

"You wanted to tear off my clothes and have your way with me." He pretended to reconsider. "Either me, or Mr. Papadakis."

"Mr. Papadakis is ninety years old."

"Probably me, then."

Her lips twitched with humor, even though the circumstances were inappropriate for it. "What are we going to do?"

"I can't keep hiking."

"Neither can I."

"The trail is too muddy, and I'm beat."

"We can't sit here all night."

Staying in the campsite wasn't a good idea, either. "When I'm capable of moving again, I'll grab some sleeping bags and dry clothes. I'm sure we can find a spot nearby to hide and wait out the rain."

Murmuring an agreement, she reached under the water and removed her jogging pants, placing them by her sweater. Then she peeled off her wet socks and lifted her foot to the rim of the tub to massage her sore ankle.

"Is it sprained?"

"Maybe."

"Let me see."

"I'm a nurse."

"I know all about sports injuries."

Instead of disputing this exaggeration, she extended her leg to him. It looked smooth and pale in the hazy moonlight. Her skin was warm. Although her ankle didn't appear badly swollen, she winced at his touch.

"Did you twist it running away?"

"No. He hit my heel with the edge of his hand."

His gut contracted with unease. "How did he get you?"

She pulled her foot from his grasp.

"You don't have to tell me."

"No, it's okay," she said, swallowing. "I saw him at the top of the cliff, pointing the rifle at the broken door. He was going to shoot you and Leo as soon as you came out. So I circled around and approached him from behind."

"You sneaked up on him?"

"He was going to kill you. I had to."

Suddenly the tub felt too hot, too smothering. The idea of her taking such a shocking risk rattled him more than he cared to admit. He boosted himself to the edge and sat there, wiping the mist from his face.

"I tried to hit him over the head with the rock, but I missed. It bounced off his shoulder. Then I freaked out and ran."

"He chased you?"

"Yes. I didn't get far."

"You got far enough to save my life. You saved Leo."

"I was the one who sent you in there," she said. "I couldn't just watch you die."

Nathan stared at her for a long moment. It took a

lot of guts to attack a gun-toting psycho. He didn't know if he would have done the same thing in her position. A lesser man—his former self—might have been intimidated by her audacity. He might have rejected her personal advice. But the man he was now felt only concern and admiration toward her, along with a huge amount of gratitude. She'd helped him repair his relationship with his son. She'd rescued them. "You're an amazing woman, Abby."

"You carried me several miles," she added. "That's more amazing."

He disagreed. His feat required brute strength, rather than heroics. What she'd done was extraordinary.

She moved to sit on the edge of the tub, directly across from him. Her thin cotton tank top clung to her breasts, revealing the circles of her nipples. She was braless. Her lacy panties were soaked to transparency. It would be rude to ogle her after the horrifying abuse she'd endured, so he forced his gaze away.

Heat suffused his neck as he remembered cursing at her during their argument. He didn't feel good about losing his temper, but he wasn't flushed from embarrassment. His anger had faded. Thinking about their exchange sparked a different reaction in him now. Her strength of will excited him. She was a passionate woman. She might be hard to handle in bed. He assumed she wasn't the type to fake an orgasm or stroke his ego.

He was up for the challenge. Way up.

Although his desire for her had intensified, so had

his reasons for keeping his distance. She'd been assaulted and thrown into a crate. Her daughter had been kidnapped. There was a madman on the loose. She'd just recovered from a serious panic attack. They were exhausted and still in danger.

This was *not* the time to put the moves on her. At all.

Unfortunately, logic didn't work on his libido. He hadn't been with a woman in years. Most of the sex he'd had since his divorce had been emotionless and impersonal. After the traumatic events of the day, his need to connect with another person, to reaffirm life and share pleasure, was overwhelming.

He clenched his hands into fists, aching to touch her.

Part of the attraction between them was physical. But there was something deeper, too. He had a connection with her that transcended chemistry and evaded definition. They just *fit*. He liked the way she matched him. They'd be explosive together, like flint and steel. She'd give as good as she got and then some.

He also wanted more from her than anonymous sex. Any guy could make her come, if she let him. Her coworker could clean her clock. Nathan wasn't interested in a no-frills servicing. He wanted her begging and sobbing. He wanted to fuck the memory of Ray out of her. He wanted her complete surrender.

He imagined her legs wrapped around him, her face contorted in pleasure. The fantasy was so erotic, he almost groaned. He blanked his mind, concentrating on the cool mist and willing his dick not to get hard.

Her eyes trailed down his chest, where droplets of moisture had collected on his skin. Although the night air was cold, steam rose up from the hot springs to counter the chill, and his legs were submersed in warmth below the knee. When she nibbled on her lip, his cock swelled with arousal, straining against the wet fabric of his boxer shorts.

Instead of flushing and glancing away, she moved from the edge of the tub and came toward him.

ABBY HADN'T CHANGED her mind about getting involved with Nathan.

The circumstances were far from ideal. They needed to leave the area as soon as possible. She'd just had a disturbing blackout, and he was exhausted from carrying her. Initiating a sexual encounter wasn't a good idea.

On the other hand…they could stay here a few more minutes. The air was still heavy with moisture. If the kidnappers were smart, they'd be hiking deep into the mountains to escape the authorities. Brooke and Leo had probably reached town by now.

Even if Abby had felt completely safe, giving herself to Nathan would be risky. He wasn't the type of man she could manage. She couldn't keep him on a friend shelf or hold him at a distance. If she opened this door, she'd be ceding control. Letting him in. She hadn't done that with Jeremy. She hadn't allowed any of the men since Ray to touch anything but her body.

Nathan would take more.

That was part of his appeal, if she was being honest with herself. She needed human contact *and* an emotional response. Just this once. The hurt that might come later didn't matter. Right now, she had to feel pleasure.

She didn't care how foolish her decision was. They were alive. Their children were alive. He wanted her, judging by the erection straining his boxer shorts. He'd become aroused just by looking at her. That was a powerful draw.

She studied him from beneath lowered lashes as she came forward. The moonlight was muted by mist, giving the night a grainy, grayish cast. Steam from the tub rose up in foggy wisps and a fine sheen coated his skin, like sweat. His jaw was taut, his eyes half-lidded. He wiped his face again, his biceps flexing.

Her gaze trailed down his lightly furred chest and hard stomach. His upper thighs were heavy with muscle, a shade paler than his hair-dusted calves. The contrast struck her as absurdly sexy. She imagined pressing her lips to him, dragging down the waistband of his boxer shorts to take him in her mouth.

As she stood before him, her pulse racing, his eyes skimmed her breasts and the wet fabric between her legs. Her flesh tingled at his perusal, her nipples tightening. Although her invitation had to be obvious, his fists stayed clenched at his sides. He seemed reluctant to stare at her body, let alone touch it. Maybe he was worried about taking advantage of her precarious mental state.

She turned around, presenting him with her disheveled hair. "Can you help me?" she asked over her shoulder. She'd tried to comb her fingers through the tangled strands, but they were full of leaves.

He didn't respond right away. She could feel heat coming off him in waves. Her white panties were so transparent she might as well have been naked. She indulged in a vivid fantasy of him tearing the lace and bending her over the tub.

Instead of doing what they both wanted, he removed the debris from her hair. When he tugged on a stubborn knot, she swayed toward him. Her bottom brushed his crotch. Making a strangled sound, he locked his arm around her waist and urged her down on his lap. He was rock-hard, throbbing against her.

Abby's pulse raced with excitement as he swept her hair aside and placed his mouth on the tender skin at the nape of her neck. Kissing her there, he moved his hands to the front of her body. One cupped her breast. The other slid between her legs.

God. Three seconds in and he was already on third base.

"I want you," he panted against her neck. His fingertips rubbed the soaked fabric at the apex of her thighs, wrenching a groan from her lips. She was swollen and sensitive, already aching for him.

"I can tell," she said, her voice hoarse. Once again, she thought of him stripping off her panties and taking her from behind. That was another intimacy she hadn't shared since Ray. Catching him with Lydia that way had soured her to the position.

"We shouldn't…"

Abby knew all of the reasons they *shouldn't,* and she didn't want to hear them. Turning in his arms, she removed her wet tank top, exposing her breasts. He was a man, and therefore susceptible. When he saw her naked flesh, his eyes darkened and his mouth went slack. Resistance was futile.

She twined her arms around his neck. Her breasts plumped against the hard wall of his chest, making her shiver. She flattened her palm on his cheek and brought her lips close to his. They were both shaking with need. His erection nudged her belly. Her fingertips pressed into his shadowed jaw. Their ragged breaths mingled. When their mouths met, it was like a flash of lightning. She'd never felt anything so raw and sexually charged. Once he decided to go for it, he really went for it. His kiss wasn't gentle. He was hungry and demanding, taking full possession of her mouth. His tongue plunged in and out, delving deep.

With a low groan, he groped her bottom with big hands. She squirmed against him, kissing him back with enthusiasm. Desperate to get him inside her. His fingertips slipped beneath the waistband of her panties and between her cheeks, touching a base no other man had ever been on with her. She went still, bracing her palms on his chest.

He stopped kissing her. His hand froze.

Her lips tingled with sensation and a heavy beat pulsed between her legs. She wasn't pushing him away or saying no. She was so turned on, she wouldn't deny him anything. Her body was his for the taking.

Instead of continuing into uncharted territories, he removed his hand from her panties. Throat working in agitation, he peeled the wet fabric down her hips. When she was completely nude, he stared at her for several seconds. Then he molded his hand to the back of her neck and brought her forward, kissing her mouth again and again.

Abby lost track of everything after that. Drunk with desire, she focused on him. His mouth, his hands, his hair-roughened skin. Nothing existed except this pool and this moment. She was pliant in his arms. He cupped her breasts, squeezing her stiff nipples. They were still sensitive, but she preferred more pressure, even pinching when she was near climax. He had no trouble finding the perfect balance. His hand slid between her legs again, strumming her cleft with his fingertips. By the time he set her on the side of the tub and pushed her thighs apart, she was melting for him.

He kissed his way down her quivering belly. Normally she was shy about oral sex, more comfortable giving than receiving with a new partner. With Nathan, she seemed to have no inhibitions. She vibrated at his touch, taut as a bowstring.

When his mouth closed over her clitoris, sucking gently, she groaned. It was so good, she wanted it to last and last. She lay back against the cool rock and gripped the side of the tub, watching him work. Rain drizzled down on her like a caress, collecting in beads on her skin. He flicked his tongue over her clit and circled it lazily, in no particular rush. The orgasm built to a spectacular crescendo. She clutched his hair and cried out, bucking against his mouth as waves of pleasure washed over her.

Afterward, he lifted his head and studied her sex. She felt like a wanton on display, flushed and spread-eagled. He moistened his lips, as if tasting her on them.

"Do you have a condom?" she asked.

"If I did, I'd be buried inside you right now."

She straightened and reached for the waistband of his boxer shorts. When she lowered it, she had to smother a moan. He was wonderfully thick and hard. Her insides shivered with longing as she wrapped her hand around his shaft, stroking him up and down slowly. Torturing him, she placed the tip of his cock against her soft inner thigh. Dangerously close to the place he wanted to be buried.

"You're killing me," he said, lifting his hand to her cheek. He traced her parted lips with his thumb. When she drew his thumb into her mouth, applying sweet suction, he groaned. "I'm dying to fuck you."

She was tempted to let him.

He removed his thumb from her mouth, dragging it down her chin. She continued to caress him with her legs spread wide and his cock poised at her opening. His restraint was impressive. Covering her hand with his, he urged her to use a firmer grip. She pumped him with her slippery fist. Then she heard a strange noise, like shouting voices.

Someone was coming. And it wasn't Nathan.

CHAPTER TWENTY-ONE

BROOKE WAS SOBER by the time they arrived at the hospital.

Monarch had a small urgent care facility, which was closed. They had to continue to the larger town of Bishop. Leo used Bud's phone to call the police. He stayed on the line for almost thirty minutes, sharing every detail of their experience. When he hung up, he said that officers would meet them in the emergency room. They were organizing a search-and-rescue crew for Abby and Nathan. The rain had abated.

"Don't worry," Leo said, looking over his shoulder at Brooke. "Everyone jumps when they hear my dad's name."

That was true. Nathan Strom was a baseball legend.

Bud parked his Jeep and stayed in the waiting room with them. He was a nice man. He offered to buy her a coffee after they sat down.

"She doesn't drink coffee," Leo said.

He looked terrible under the harsh fluorescent lights. His clothes were splattered with mud and his jeans were torn, showing bits of ragged flesh underneath. His complexion appeared more gray than

olive. She realized that he'd been running on adrenaline for the past few hours. Now that they were safe,
he'd crashed.

A pretty nurse took them both to the treatment
area. Leo's bed was separated from hers by a cur-
tained partition. Brooke didn't think she needed medical care, but the nurse drew blood and took her vital
signs. Leo was wheeled to another room for an X-ray.

The nurse wouldn't let Brooke shower until after
she'd been examined. Two uniformed police officers
came to interview her. They asked if she wanted to
speak with a rape counselor or a female detective.
She said no.

The interrogation process was long and unpleasant. She answered the same questions over and over.
Her memory of the events was fractured from whatever drugs she'd been given. Fear and stress might
have warped her reality. By the end of an hour, she
was half-convinced that the kidnapping had been a
figment of her imagination. She couldn't tell if the
officers believed her or not. One was much older than
the other, with a weathered poker face. The younger
officer seemed surprised that she hadn't been sexually assaulted. She shuddered to think of how much
worse she'd feel if she *had* been.

Both officers thanked her and left, saying they
were checking up on some information. The nurse
brought her a package of graham crackers and juice.
Brooke was ravenous. She wanted a full-course meal,
not a snack.

Leo had to go into surgery. They were going to remove bits of shrapnel from his thigh and calf. Brooke wasn't allowed to accompany him to the operating room. She held his hand and kissed his forehead, distressed.

The officers returned with a laptop. They showed her photos of a clean-cut soldier named Gary Nash. He was a decorated veteran, trained in combat. He'd done a tour of duty in Iraq. He'd also been a prisoner of war in Afghanistan. Brooke studied his picture and saw little resemblance to the wild mountain man who'd taken her captive.

"I don't recognize him," she said, exhausted. She wanted her mother.

The younger, more tech-savvy officer brought up a second photo on the screen. "This is Wyatt Nash, his son."

Brooke examined the boy's face. It appeared to be a school picture. He had dark brown hair that stood up on top. Dark brown eyes. Goofy, gap-toothed smile. Big ears. "That's him. That's the boy I met."

"How sure are you?"

She looked again. "Ninety percent."

"This was taken six years ago, when he was ten."

"He told me he was sixteen. He said his mother was dead."

The officers exchanged a glance. "Elizabeth Nash was killed in a household accident in Petaluma, Florida. There wasn't enough evidence to press charges. Nash brought his son to San Diego shortly after her death. Their trailer home was destroyed in the earthquake. They've been missing, presumed dead, ever since."

Brooke was convinced, but not comforted, by the information. The fact that Nash had been a prisoner of war sent a chill down her spine. He'd probably killed Wyatt's mother. He was physically and mentally abusive with Wyatt. He could survive in harsh conditions and blend into his environment. "Is the rescue crew ready?"

"They're en route," the older officer said. He walked away from Brooke's bed, maybe to share their findings with his superior.

"We can't let rescuers enter a potentially deadly situation," the younger officer said. "They need support from law enforcement."

Brooke pictured a SWAT team creeping through the forest. "Will they shoot Wyatt? If he tries to defend himself, I mean?"

The officer seemed puzzled by her concern.

"He's not like his dad," she said. "He's not a killer."

"He opened fire on your stepbrother."

"He was forced to. I don't think he'd hurt anyone by choice."

The officer nodded, acknowledging her statement. He didn't say he would pass it on to the team.

A crime scene photographer joined them a few minutes later. He took photos of her, paying special attention to the rope burns on her wrists and ankles. Then the police officers asked for her clothing. She changed into a hospital gown behind the curtain.

They put her clothes in an evidence bag and thanked her for her cooperation.

After they left again, Brooke waited for word about Leo. She finally approached the nurses' station and inquired about his condition. The nurse said he was still in surgery. Even though his injuries were minor, it took time to remove the metal debris and flush the wounds. Brooke used a landline at the nurse's desk to call her dad's cell phone. He didn't answer; it was past midnight. She left a message on his voice mail.

Her aunt Ella picked up on the first ring. "Hello?"

When Brooke heard her voice, she sank into an empty chair. Her legs wouldn't hold her weight anymore. "It's me."

"Brookie? What's wrong?"

The story poured out of her, along with an overflowing of tears. She hated replaying the events in her mind, but it was a lot easier to tell someone she loved. Her aunt believed in her without question.

"I'm coming right now," Ella promised. "Paul's getting a bag ready and we're going to drive straight there."

"Okay," Brooke said, sniffling.

"I'll see you in the morning."

Brooke said goodbye and hung up, wiping her cheeks. In the public restroom, she washed her hands and face, scrubbing at every stray fleck of mud. The antibacterial liquid soap irritated her skin. Taking a deep breath, she braced her hands on the sink and studied her reflection. Her hair was a mess and her eyes were puffy from crying. She looked insane.

Brooke had never obsessed over her appearance, like her mother. She'd never cared about nice clothes or perfect hair. But she experienced a sudden flash of intuition over her mother's personal habits. The divorce had torn her world apart. Then the earthquake had almost killed them. She'd felt powerless. Weak. Her focus on outer beauty wasn't a shallow conceit. It was an attempt to project calm and stay in control.

Brooke knew she'd been targeted because she was convenient and female. That man, Gary Nash, had tried to take away her power. He would have kept her locked up for his sick amusement and treated her like an object. A pretty toy to destroy. Even though she'd escaped, she wasn't unscathed. She didn't feel the same inside.

She wanted to be herself again, to put on a strong facade. This weepy, damaged girl in the mirror wasn't her.

When she came out, the nurse gave her a hand-me-down outfit and told her she could wait for Leo in his private room. She used the shower and pulled on the ill-fitting clothes. Leo returned from surgery, groggy but awake. He was wearing a hospital gown. A male nurse helped him move from the wheelchair to the bed.

After the nurse left, Brooke curled up next to him on the mattress. It was a narrow space, but they made it work. "Is this okay?"

He put his arm around her, unperturbed. "Sure."

"I don't want to hurt your leg."

"Where's my dad?"

"Not here yet."

"I should call my mom," he mumbled.

"I left her a message."

"Thanks."

She closed her eyes and just drank him in. They must have let him shower before surgery, because he smelled good. Not familiar-good, like the laundry detergent Lydia's maid used, but nicer than mud and sweat. "I love you, Leo," she whispered.

Maybe he was asleep, because he didn't answer.

ABBY PULLED HER HAND away from Nathan, horrified.

There were flashlights on the path leading to the hot springs. She grabbed her tank top to cover her breasts and sank into the water. He barely had time to drag his boxer shorts up his hips before a pair of strange men burst onto the scene. They wore raincoats and had shotguns strapped to their backs.

Abby was too mortified to speak to their rescuers. The fact that they'd interrupted an intimate moment couldn't have been more obvious. Her panties were floating on the surface of the water. Nathan looked particularly unhappy about the intrusion. Help had arrived a few seconds too soon.

She'd been caught giving a man a hand job, hours after her daughter had been kidnapped. It was the most embarrassing moment of her life.

The men with the flashlights said that Brooke and Leo were safe. They had ATVs ready to take Nathan and Abby to civilization. Abby thanked them profusely, clutching her tank top to her chest. When

Nathan asked the men for some privacy, they left the immediate area, seeming as chagrined as Abby.

Nathan climbed from the pool, wearing the ghost of a grin. "I'll get your backpack and bring you some dry clothes."

"I can't believe you think this is funny."

He dragged on his wet pants. "It's either laugh or cry."

She found herself smiling back at him. His lack of shame wasn't surprising; his bad-boy reputation wouldn't suffer. But she also realized that the opinion of strangers didn't matter. They hadn't done anything wrong.

He returned with both backpacks a few minutes later. She found a pair of leggings and pulled them on, along with a T-shirt and a light rain jacket. As soon as they were ready, their rescuers led them toward the ATVs. They'd parked as close to the camp as possible, carefully skirting the kidnappers' fortress.

The ride was uneventful. They doubled up on the ATVs and took it slow. No rifle fire or underground traps awaited them. It was dawn by the time they reached the forest service road, where they met a group of law officers.

A member of the rescue crew wrapped up Abby's ankle. Nathan needed first aid for the cut on his arm. They were both given pain relievers.

Once they were comfortable, Nathan and Abby were asked for very specific descriptions of the kidnappers' dwelling. Using topography maps and GPS imagery, Nathan pointed out its exact location. They spent the next few hours at the sheriff's station in Monarch. One of the deputies passed them photographs of an army lieutenant and a ten-year-old boy.

"This is the father," Abby said, studying the older man. He was younger, and clean-shaven, but she recognized his dead eyes. "I'm not sure about the boy."

Nathan couldn't identify either. "I'm sorry," he said, shaking his head.

At the conclusion of the interview, the deputy gave them an update on the search for the kidnappers. "Our team of investigators found the dugout you described, but it was empty. Both suspects are still at large."

Abby and Nathan exchanged a worried glance. "What if you don't catch them?"

"I'm confident that we will. Forest rangers are combing the woods, and they have bloodhounds. I have to ask you not to leave the area until they're taken into custody."

"Of course," Nathan said. "We're happy to cooperate."

The deputy drove them to the hospital in Bishop. Before he left, he suggested they stay in a local hotel rather than returning to the remote cabin. Abby nodded her agreement. Her ankle felt better, but she was exhausted from the sleepless night.

They met Leo and Brooke in a private room. Leo was eating breakfast. Brooke sat in a chair at his bedside. Abby's throat closed up at the sight. With a sound of surprise, Brooke stood, rushing toward her with open arms. Abby had never felt anything so emotionally fulfilling as her daughter's strong embrace.

When they broke apart, Abby studied Brooke's face. Her blue eyes were clear and lucid. She was crying happy tears.

"I was so worried about you!" Brooke said.

Abby turned to Leo and Nathan, who were both more reserved about showing affection. Nathan squeezed Leo's shoulder in greeting. The tray on Leo's lap would have gotten in the way of a hug. It was part male stupidity, part logistics.

A few minutes later, Ella and Paul arrived. Abby had never been happier to see her sister. After a round of introductions, they decided to walk across the street to the hotel. Nathan stayed with Leo to sign the release forms. He said goodbye to Abby, promising to catch up with her later. His dark gaze indicated that he remembered their unfinished business. Her stomach fluttered in anticipation.

Abby didn't have her credit cards or ID, so Ella paid for two rooms at the hotel. Paul stayed in the downstairs café, claiming he had to work on lesson plans. He probably just wanted to let them talk. Ella ordered breakfast while Abby took a long shower. When she came out, clean and refreshed, they sat down to eat.

Brooke tackled a stack of pancakes with her usual good appetite. She also gave a chilling but somewhat detached account of the abduction and the near assault. It seemed that Wyatt had made a positive impression on her. She felt certain he was a captive or a reluctant accessory to his father's crimes. He'd tried to help her.

Abby hugged Brooke again, disturbed by her ordeal. She thanked her lucky stars that Brooke hadn't been seriously harmed.

"I'm going to take a bath," Brooke said, drawing away from her. "Will you brush my hair when I get out?"

"Of course," Abby said, touched by the request.

When they were alone, Ella asked for Abby's side of the story. She shared every detail from searching for Brooke in the morning to losing her grip on reality last night. Ella didn't appear surprised by the blackout; Abby had experienced similar anxiety attacks before.

"I woke up in the hot springs," she said.

"How did you get there?"

"He carried me."

"Wow."

"Yeah."

"Did he take off your clothes?"

"No," she said, flushing. He'd taken off her panties, but that was…later.

Ella arched a brow. "I know something happened between you."

"How?"

"The way you look right now. And the way he looked at you in the lobby. It was part protective, part hungry."

Abby wasn't sure what to say. She didn't want to talk about Nathan. Giving voice to her feelings might make them more real. It was easier to believe that their encounter had been a dreamy fantasy, or temporary insanity.

Brooke emerged from the bath with a towel wrapped around her slender body. Like Abby, she had red marks on her wrists and tangles in her hair. Abby used a comb to work through the snarls. Brooke's hair was beautiful, shiny and strong. It had been so fine and pale when she was a baby.

"You used to cry every time I brushed your hair," Abby said.

"I did?"

"Even when you were little, you couldn't be bothered with braids or bows." She'd kept Brooke's hair trimmed in a pageboy style to make it easier. Brooke hadn't been interested in growing long hair until she got older.

Brooke fell silent for a moment, seeming drowsy. "Did my mom tell you she hooked up with Leo's dad?"

Ella's eyes widened with delight. "No!"

"I saw them kissing in the hot springs."

"Do tell," Ella cooed.

Abby set the comb aside. "It didn't mean anything."

"Why not?" Brooke asked.

Abby hesitated. It seemed foolish to speculate on Nathan's intentions toward her. She didn't want to give Brooke and Ella the wrong idea. More importantly, she was afraid to give *herself* the wrong idea.

She was so caught up in him already. If he didn't return the sentiment, she'd be crushed.

"You never looked half as flustered over Jeremy," Ella said.

"That's because they were just fuck-buddies," Brooke said.

Ella nodded at this frank assessment, agreeing.

Abby sometimes wished she hadn't encouraged Brooke to be so outspoken. "Have you talked to your father?"

"Yes. He's driving up from L.A. with Lydia."

Abby rubbed her temples, where a tension headache was forming. Ray would probably demand a sitdown meeting with law enforcement and try to throw his weight around. He might be rude to Nathan and Leo. This was the reason she didn't get emotionally involved with men: she didn't need the extra stress.

When Brooke climbed under the blankets, Abby stretched out beside her, stroking her damp hair until she drifted off. There was nothing she wouldn't do for her daughter. It felt good to be here for her, but also bittersweet. Brooke would leave for college again soon. She'd grown more independent every year.

Abby rose from the bed to finish her conversation with Ella. Like Brooke, Abby craved the company and closeness of loved ones. Talking with Ella always comforted her. They tiptoed outside to sit in lounge chairs on the outdoor balcony.

"Did you call Mom?" Abby asked.

"No."

"Good." Their mother tended to worry too much,

like Abby. If she knew what happened she'd want to drive up here and join them. There was no need to upset her at this point. Abby would tell her when they got home.

"So what's the deal with Nathan?"

Abby groaned, clapping a hand over her forehead. "I don't know."

"Come on. I told you about Paul."

Ella had slept with Paul the first night they met, when they were stranded on San Miguel Island. Abby had high-fived her for the bold behavior. She knew Ella wouldn't judge, so she confessed about their interrupted encounter.

Ella sputtered with laughter as she pictured the scene. "You can't leave things like this! Give the poor guy a happy ending."

Abby's pulse accelerated at the thought. She'd love to be with him in a mutually satisfying way, but she was concerned about the long-term implications. Sex would mark a beginning, rather than a resolution.

"He's hot," Ella said.

"Hot isn't everything."

"It's a good start."

"He's not a…fuck-buddy," she said, repeating Brooke's crude term.

Her sister didn't comment. Ella had already shared her opinion of Jeremy. She'd accused Abby of using him to avoid commitment.

"Ray's cheating again," Abby said.

"How do you know?"

"Leo told us. Lydia wants a divorce."

Ella's mouth twisted with displeasure. "Why are you presenting this as if it's evidence that all relationships are doomed?"

Abby glanced away, reluctant to acknowledge her fears. Ella was newly engaged and madly in love. Of course she believed in happy-ever-afters. Their mother had found a great guy the second time around. Why couldn't Abby?

"You deserve more than a fuck-buddy," Ella said.

"I'm afraid to get involved with him."

"Why? Is he a player?"

"No. He gave up drinking and sleeping around a few years ago."

"Then what's the problem?"

Abby had to spell it out for her. "He'll break my heart."

"Do you think he's worried about you breaking his heart?"

She hadn't considered that before, but it sounded reasonable. "Maybe."

"You're equally likely to get hurt, the way I see it. He has as much to lose as you do. You've both been burned before. You both have to take a risk. The real question you should ask is if he's worth your time."

"What do you mean?"

"Is he good enough for you?"

Abby smiled at the sisterly question. "Yes."

"Are you afraid to date him because he's untrustworthy, or because he's exciting?"

Abby tapped a fingertip to her lips, mulling it over. Nathan was well worth pursuing. The thought of letting him go made her chest hurt. He was exciting *and* trustworthy. But was she capable of trusting?

"If you can walk away without getting upset, why bother?"

"I can't."

"Then don't."

Abby had an important decision to make. Later, after she'd gotten some sleep. "I think Brooke has a crush on Leo."

"I don't blame her."

"What do you know about them?"

"She told me he kissed her over winter break. She'd just broken up with her boyfriend. Leo was comforting her."

"That's as far as it went?"

"He wouldn't take it any farther."

Abby ran the comb through her tangled hair, contemplative. Brooke was free to choose her own path. Make her own mistakes. Abby couldn't protect her from every danger. She could only hope that Brooke would be able to move on from the kidnapping, and not choose the wrong boys to fill the hole her father had left.

"Get some rest," Ella said. "I'll handle everything."

"You're a good sister," Abby said, her throat tight.

"I know."

"I'm happy for you and Paul."

Her eyes watered with tears.

"Don't," Abby said, looking away.

"I'll cry if I want to."

She laughed at Ella's petulant tone, her heart aching. They exchanged a long hug, and Abby went back inside, climbing into bed next to Brooke. Ella's questions fizzed like soda bubbles in her tired mind.

Was Nathan worth it?

When she looked back on her life with Ray, she had few regrets. They'd made a beautiful child together. But her overwhelming feeling about their relationship was sorrow. She couldn't bear the thought of going through another divorce.

She knew she'd made some bad choices. She'd married too young. She'd been too dependent on Ray. She didn't blame herself for his cheating—that was totally on him—but she had to take responsibility for her reaction. It wasn't healthy to be so guarded with men. Ray's betrayal hadn't broken her. She was twice as strong at thirty-six as she'd been at eighteen. She had a career and an identity. Her anxiety was manageable, for the most part. Nathan hadn't seemed horrified by her recent breakdown, and she'd recovered quickly.

She didn't have to live in fear.

But it was hard for her to climb these mental boulders, let alone jump off. What concerned her most was the intensity of their connection. She'd never been this drawn to a man. Maybe she was reaching her sexual peak, because she hadn't been half as responsive or uninhibited with Ray. Her powerful attraction to Nathan promised more than fleeting pleasure. She anticipated ups and downs. Fireworks and emotional tumult. She wasn't sure she could handle the fallout. She *didn't* trust him not to hurt her.

How did she feel about letting him go?

That was the kicker, because she couldn't imagine walking away. Not now, not like this. He might not be the best match for her. They might crash and burn. She'd never know if she didn't take the plunge.

Failing wasn't the true measure of weakness. Giving up without trying was.

CHAPTER TWENTY-TWO

NATHAN WOKE TO the sound of a razor being tapped against the edge of the sink.

He rolled over in bed and squinted through the open bathroom door. Leo was shaving. Nathan adjusted the sheets around his waist to make sure he was covered. Then he settled back to watch his son perform a task that was both foreign and familiar.

Leo used basic soap and a safety razor, like him. He wasn't experienced enough to be good at it. He did a few quick swipes over his chin that made Nathan wince. It was clear that no one had taught him how to shave properly. His movements were an unconscious imitation of Nathan.

"You have to go with the grain," Nathan said. "Especially on your neck."

Leo tapped the razor again and rinsed it under the faucet. He turned his head to one side. "It grows in all different directions."

"Try shaving away from your Adam's apple."

Leo took this advice, his brow furrowed in concentration. The end result was passable. Nathan would have gone slower and been more careful, but that was him. Leo didn't appear to give a damn about precision. His shaggy, uneven haircut was another expression of his individuality.

Someone must have delivered their personal belongings. Leo was wearing ragged cargo shorts with a studded leather belt. His backpack was open on top of the other bed. "Who brought your stuff?"

"Mom," he said, leaning over the sink to splash his face. "She's here with Ray."

Nathan noticed his own overnight bag sitting on a table by the door, along with his cell phone. He hadn't heard anyone knock. After taking a shower this morning, he'd fallen into bed and passed out from exhaustion.

"We're having dinner in a few minutes, if you want to come."

Nathan would prefer to avoid Ray's company. His first instinct was to decline, but Leo hadn't invited him to anything in years. "Who's going to be there?"

"Brooke and her family. Abby."

Well, that sold it. "Okay."

Leo left the bathroom, limping a little. He grabbed Nathan's bag from the table and launched it toward him.

"How's your leg?"

"Pretty good," Leo said. "The painkillers are dope."

Nathan ignored this provocation in favor of keeping the peace. He pulled on a pair of jeans and padded to the bathroom, barefoot. Although he still looked tired, he felt much better. His shoulder was a bit stiff from overuse. He combed his hair and brushed his teeth, not bothering to shave. It was hardly a formal occasion.

"Any word from the cops?" he asked when he came out.

"They found a body," Leo said.

"Was it the kid?"

"I don't know. We're supposed to go to the station tomorrow to identify him."

Nathan pictured the boy's scared face, now pale and lifeless. "Gunshot wound?"

"An arrow to the neck."

"Shit," he said under his breath.

"It's fucked-up," Leo agreed. "They said they're investigating connections to local unsolved cases and missing person reports. The FBI got called in. I think they're looking for the bodies of the other victims."

Nathan was glad Leo and Brooke weren't among them. He didn't know how to express his relief without getting emotional, so he said nothing. And it felt okay. It wasn't necessary to treat every moment like a bonding opportunity. His quest to reconnect with Leo didn't have to be all-consuming. They'd get there. It was a marathon, not a race.

Nathan put on his shoes and a T-shirt. He brought his wallet, but left his cell phone. Before they walked out the door, he handed Leo his crutches.

"Thanks," Leo said, securing them under his arms. He was wearing a Godzilla T-shirt with Japanese lettering. As they crossed the courtyard together, Nathan acknowledged that there were some things he'd never understand about Leo.

They had dinner reservations at the hotel café. Ray and Lydia were already seated at a table on the outdoor patio. When she rose to greet him, Nathan noticed that her eyes were a bit puffy, and there were tension lines around her mouth. But she looked gorgeous, as always. Her dark hair was trapped in a sleek ponytail. She wore a gauzy blouse and fitted skirt. Judging by her designer high heels, her ankle was fine.

Nathan nodded hello to Ray, who didn't bother to get up. He hadn't aged as well as Lydia, but he was fit and well-dressed. They never shook hands anymore. Years ago, Nathan had surrendered to the urge to crush Ray's elegant surgeon fingers in his stronger grip.

Lydia kissed Leo's cheek and hugged him close. When she released him to study his face, there were tears in her eyes. He said something in Portuguese that made her laugh. She'd always had a better relationship with Leo than Nathan, but he didn't feel any envy or resentment toward her. It just wasn't in him to begrudge their easy affection. She was the only person in the world who loved Leo as much as he did.

Abby and her family joined them a moment later. Someone must have brought her belongings from the cabin as well, because she was wearing a soft purple dress with short sleeves. Her legs were long and bare, her lips shimmery. Her hair was caught up in a loose knot at the nape of her neck. She looked pretty and put-together.

His heart thumped hard, like a fist knocking on his

sternum. She was lovely, with or without makeup. He couldn't decide if he preferred her all dolled up or au naturel. An image of her wet, naked body popped into his mind. He saw her with her thighs spread and her lips around his thumb, sucking gently as she stroked his cock. The memory had inspired him to use his own hand in the shower this morning.

Damn. She was hot.

He shelved his inappropriate thoughts and stammered a hello. Ella smiled at him in a way that suggested she knew exactly what he was thinking, because Abby had told her all about their erotic interlude.

To his credit, Ray stood to greet his ex-wife and hug his daughter. Lydia kissed Abby's cheek and wrapped her slender arms around Brooke. "I'm so glad you're not hurt," she said, stroking Brooke's hair.

The waitstaff had pushed several tables together to accommodate their large party. Ray had already commandeered the space at the end. Brooke pulled out a chair at the opposite end. Abby, Ella and Paul sat down on one side of the table. Nathan took a seat across from them, between Leo and Lydia.

The meal itself was pleasant. No one asked Abby or Brooke about the abduction. They didn't discuss the macabre task of identifying a dead body tomorrow. Leo told them about the ATV getting stuck in the pouring rain, but he made it sound like a funny anecdote instead of a struggle for survival. Brooke held his hand under the table.

Ella shared the story of the previous year's camping trip. She'd been stranded overnight on a deserted island with Paul.

"How did the two of you stay warm again?" Brooke asked, teasing her.

"I built a fire," Paul said, which made everyone laugh.

Nathan liked Abby's sister and her fiancé. Paul hit it off with Leo immediately. They'd surfed some of the same areas in Northern California.

Nathan couldn't believe he was sitting at a table with Ray Dwyer—and actually enjoying himself. Ray didn't appear as comfortable as Nathan in the setting. It was clear that Ella thought he was a jerk. She hardly glanced at him. When he complained to the waiter about the wine selection in a pretentious manner, Paul did a double take. Ray checked his cell phone repeatedly, commenting that the local police were inept.

"Put that away," Lydia murmured.

Ray stashed his phone and removed an envelope from his pocket. "I have an early birthday present for you," he said to Brooke.

She accepted the envelope with interest. "What is it?"

"Look inside."

Tearing it open, she shook out what appeared to be two plane tickets. "Where are we going?"

Ray moistened his lips, seeming nervous. "The tickets are for anywhere in the world in the next year. I thought you could take a friend to Europe, or your mother to the Bahamas. You can go wherever you want and stay as long as you like. You can have a nice vacation to make up for this…debacle."

She stared at the tickets instead of looking at him. Nathan could read the disappointment on her face. Ray had canceled this trip at the last minute, perhaps due to a tiff with Lydia. In his absence, Brooke had been kidnapped and traumatized. Instead of offering to spend more time with her, he'd bought an expensive gift.

"Can I take Leo with me?" Brooke asked.

A hush fell over the table. Ray recoiled at the suggestion, as if Leo wasn't worthy of her company. Over the course of the meal, Ray had been distracted and distant, ignoring the fact that Leo had risked his life for her.

"I don't think he'll make it past customs," Ray said.

"What's that supposed to mean?" Leo asked.

Lydia shot Ray a quelling look. "Not now, Ray."

"I spoke with the sheriff's office this afternoon," Ray said. "The deputies who collected the camping equipment seized a bag of premium-quality marijuana."

"Well, damn," Leo said. "Are they planning to smoke it, or give it back?"

Paul coughed into his fist, covering a laugh.

"Don't be a smart-ass," Ray said.

Even though Nathan had made similar comments to Leo in the past, he wouldn't stand for this kind of criticism right now. Not from Ray. Not twenty-four hours after Leo had been shot trying to save Brooke from a psychopath. Not while Nathan was sitting right there between them. "Lay off him."

"Lay off him?" Ray repeated, incredulous.

"That's what I said."

"He's lucky I didn't have him arrested!"

Leo leaned across the table. "You're lucky I didn't kick your ass for disrespecting my mother."

Ray's neck turned red. "How dare you."

"Go fuck yourself," Leo said, spoiling for a fight.

Nathan braced his palm on Leo's chest to hold him back. He didn't take his eyes away from Ray, who appeared on the verge of exploding. If Ray attempted to lay hands on his son, Nathan would make him regret it.

"Calm down, Ray," Lydia said.

"He just told me to fuck myself!"

"Maybe you should leave," Nathan said.

Ray glanced around the table and found no sympathizers. Brooke didn't ask him to stay. Someone had to be the rational adult, and it wasn't going to be Leo. Cursing under his breath, Ray shoved to his feet. After a short silence, Lydia excused herself to follow him.

"I'm sorry," Nathan said to Brooke.

"It's okay," she said, blinking the tears from her eyes. "He was being rude."

Abby rubbed Brooke's arm to comfort her.

Leo turned around to watch Ray argue with Lydia. When she tried to retreat, Ray gripped her elbow and refused to let go. "That's it," Leo said, fumbling for his crutches. "I'm going to kill him."

"Stop," Nathan said. "I'll handle it."

"I'll help," Paul offered.

Nathan rose to his feet and pointed at Leo. Paul got the message. His job was to make sure Leo didn't get up. Nathan walked across the courtyard, his heart racing. Ray wasn't a violent type. Nathan doubted he would try to get physical. If Ray did lash out, it wouldn't go well for him. Nathan hoped they could squash this without causing a scene. Brooke had suffered enough.

As Nathan got closer, Lydia jerked out of Ray's grasp and wrenched the diamond ring from her finger. "I never want to see you again," she cried, throwing it at his chest. The ring bounced off his shirtfront and rolled under a table.

Ray didn't go fetch. "This doesn't concern you, Strom."

Nathan stepped between them. "Let's go for a walk," he said, squeezing Ray's shoulder in a way that was more casual than menacing. Ray had the choice to join Nathan for a friendly chat or resist and suffer the consequences. When Nathan directed him away from Lydia, Ray came along without a struggle. They passed through the gated entrance at the side of the courtyard and stood at the front of the hotel.

It was a beautiful night, cool and clear. The sky was full of stars. Nathan released Ray's shoulder and took a deep breath, unsure what to say. Ray's relationship with Lydia was none of his business. Nathan didn't want to see her manhandled, especially in front of his son, but he couldn't get involved in their disputes.

"Do you care about Leo?" Nathan asked, searching for common ground.

"Of course," Ray said. "Why do you think I took his car away?"

Nathan accepted this answer. Ray was a selfish workaholic, but he must have some redeeming qualities. Lydia had fallen for him. So had Abby, once upon a time. "I know you care about Brooke. I'm glad she's okay."

Ray had to grace to look guilty. "Thanks for helping her."

"You're welcome."

"I thanked Leo earlier."

"Good," Nathan said, moving on. "I was upset with him for bringing pot on the trip. We discussed it already."

Ray squinted at him. "Are you saying that I should drop it?"

"Just give him some space. He's got a right to be angry. You cheated on his mother."

"That was a mistake," Ray admitted.

Nathan didn't want to hear about it. Getting too hammered to work the next day was a mistake. Doing it over and over again was a pattern of behavior. Ray's philandering fell into the second category.

"I still love her," Ray said.

Nathan felt nothing for him, not even pity. "I think you should stay somewhere else tonight."

Ray's mouth twisted with anger. He looked from

the manicured hotel lawns to the lighted hospital windows across the street. "You know what? I liked you better when you weren't a sanctimonious prick."

Nathan wasn't sure what *sanctimonious* meant. Sober? "It must have been easier for you to feel superior when I was drunk."

Ray stared at him for a few seconds, one eye twitching. Then he turned and left. Stomping over the damp grass, he got into his Bentley and drove off.

Nathan headed back to the courtyard. He spotted Abby, crouched under a table. She'd bent down to retrieve the ring Lydia had thrown at Ray. She straightened, handing it to Nathan for safekeeping.

"Thanks," he said, tucking it into his pocket.

"Did he leave?"

"Yes."

"Lydia went to the bathroom. Brooke's with her."

He nodded, catching Leo's gaze.

"It was nice of you to stand up for him," Abby said.

His chest swelled with emotion. He owed a lot to Abby. It felt good to be on Leo's side instead of fighting against him. "I learned from the best."

She laughed, tucking a stray hair behind her ear. The scrape on her cheek was disguised with makeup, but still noticeable to him. He glanced down at her feet. She was wearing those sexy leather sandals again. It was ironic that she'd ended up with the same injury Lydia had claimed to have.

"How's your ankle?" he asked.

"It's fine," she said, fiddling with the hem of her skirt. "Just bruised."

Nathan realized she was embarrassed. Maybe she regretted what they'd done in the hot springs. He might have been a little too eager, at first. He'd had to force himself to slow down and stop pawing her like an animal. "Did you get some rest?"

"I slept all day."

"Me, too."

When a flush blossomed across her chest, he wanted to peel off her dress and devour her. Every inch of skin. Under bright lights. In the hotel bed, in the shower, against the door. Out on the front lawn.

"Come to my room," he said, lowering his voice.

She nibbled her lip. "I should stay with Brooke."

He tore his gaze away from her, taking a deep breath. He was thinking with his dick. "Right," he said. "Sorry."

"Don't be sorry. I like it."

She liked it. Christ.

Her sister was watching them from across the room, so he tried to blank his expression. Ella gave Abby a thumbs-up, as if approving him as a suitor. Nathan laughed, rubbing a hand over his mouth.

"She's worse than Brooke about matchmaking," Abby said.

"She wants you to be happy."

"She wants me to get laid."

"I'm here to help."

"You're a saint," she said, smiling.

The waiter dropped off the check. Nathan wanted to take care of the expense, but Paul beat him to the punch.

"It's on me," Paul said.

"Are you sure?"

"Yep."

Nathan didn't argue with him. He made a mental note to send them a nice wedding gift. After Lydia and Brooke came back to the table, they called it a night. Nathan returned to his room with Leo.

Nathan started watching a baseball game, but he was too distracted to pay attention. His thoughts were on Abby.

Leo's phone rang a few minutes later. He took the call, his gaze sliding to Nathan. "Okay. I'll be right there." Tucking the phone into his pocket, he rose to check his hair in the mirror, causing more disarray with his fingertips.

"Where are you going?" Nathan asked.

"To hang out with Brooke."

"In her room?"

"Yeah. Don't wait up."

Nathan wondered if that meant Abby would come to him. He turned off the TV and rose from the bed, his pulse jumping. Even though he'd invited her, he wasn't prepared for her visit. He cleared his throat, uncertain if he should ask his son for help.

"What?" Leo asked.

"Do you have any condoms?"

Leo smirked at the question. He rifled through his backpack and found a couple of square packages, tossing them to Nathan. They were the ultra-thin kind, regular size. Nathan checked the expiration date and thanked him.

"I'm glad you're being responsible," Leo said.

"Same to you," Nathan said, helping Leo with the door. Nathan considered cautioning Leo about taking advantage of Brooke's fragile emotional state, but decided against it. They were both adults.

Leo made his way down the hall, using only one of his crutches. After he left, Nathan tidied up the room, his blood rushing with anticipation. He'd just finished straightening the comforter when someone knocked.

He opened the door to greet…Lydia.

"Can I come in?" she asked, her voice breaking.

After a short hesitation, Nathan stepped aside to let her pass through. He didn't really want her in his room, but it was hard to deny a crying woman. She was the mother of his child, and they'd been married for thirteen years. He'd always care about her. When her shoulders trembled with emotion, he put his arm around her.

"That was really sweet, what you did for Leo," she said, sniffling. She looked up at him. "What you did for me."

Warning bells sounded in Nathan's head. Her blouse was unbuttoned to the lacy border of her bra, revealing the upper curves of her breasts. She'd sought him out for comfort…and maybe something more.

"I've missed you," she said, catching the direction of his gaze.

Nathan didn't know how to react. He'd imagined this moment many times. Even after his stint in rehab, he'd tortured himself with fantasies of winning her back. He'd dreamed about cuckolding Ray.

Now he had the chance—and it was all wrong.

His feelings for Lydia were complicated. When things had been good between them, they'd been really good. If Abby wasn't in the picture, he might have taken Lydia straight to bed. But he wouldn't have fooled himself into believing they were getting back together. They couldn't erase the past. Her betrayal had devastated him.

Nathan released her carefully. "Ray's still in love with you."

"Is that what he said?"

"Yes."

Her eyes filled with tears again. She sat down on the bed. "I made a mistake."

"What do you mean?"

"You know how much I wanted another child."

He nodded, remembering how hard she'd taken the miscarriage. She'd been trying to get pregnant for years.

"I've been looking into adopting a little girl from Brazil. Ray doesn't want to be a parent again because he knows he's bad at it. I told him I'd forget about it, but I started the proceedings anyway. When he found out, he turned to another woman."

"That's why he cheated? Because he was mad at you?"

"It's a stupid reason. He's awful."

Nathan sat down beside her, passing her a tissue.

She crushed the tissue in her fist. "Maybe you can help me get over it."

"I'm here for you, but—"

"I miss you," she said, pressing her lips to his. Her palm slid up his thigh. "I miss *this*."

He removed her hand. "No. I can't."

She gaped at him in disbelief. Then she began to cry in earnest. Real, ugly tears that marred her makeup. "You're screwing Abby, aren't you?"

Nathan didn't answer. It was none of her business who he was sleeping with. She was married to someone else. Even though he took responsibility for their failed relationship, he didn't like the way things had ended. Lydia could have told him she wanted a divorce *before* she started seeing Ray.

"You've changed," she said, blotting her eyes with the tissue.

She was right; he had. And her surprise over this confirmed the irreconcilable differences between them. Lydia relied on fate, putting her life in the hands of a higher power. Abby controlled her own destiny. She believed that people could change for the better. She'd helped Nathan change the way he interacted with Leo. Getting sober was only half the journey. Meeting Abby was the other half. She'd given him hope for the future. He wouldn't throw that away for anything.

"Do you think Ray can change?" Lydia asked.

"I don't know."

She fell silent, lost in thought.

"Here," he said, pulling the ring from his pocket.

It was probably worth fifty grand. "Abby picked it up for you."

She accepted it with reluctance. "What did you do with the one I gave back to you?"

"I threw it off the Coronado Bridge."

"Really?"

"Yes."

"That's sad," she said, tearing up again. Now she was crying for him. For them. For the life they'd shared.

Water under the bridge.

When she rose to her feet, he followed her to the door, opening it for her. "I'm sorry," he said, kissing her forehead.

"I'm sorry, too."

"Take care of yourself."

"I always have," she said.

CHAPTER TWENTY-THREE

ABBY LEFT BROOKE and Leo alone in the hotel room.

Brooke claimed they were going to watch a *Teen Wolf* marathon. Abby didn't care what they did, as long as they were safe. She was glad to give Brooke the space she needed. It meant she could sneak away to see Nathan.

Hurrying down the hall, Abby rapped on the door to Ella's room.

Ella greeted her with an expectant look. "What's up?"

"Brooke and Leo are hanging out in my room."

"Oh," Ella said, stepping aside. "Come on in. I'll tell Paul to put on a shirt."

Abby glanced through the doorway, waving at Paul. It would be a shame to make him cover up. "That's okay. I'm going to Nathan's room."

Ella's eyes widened with delight. "For sex?"

Abby laughed, not answering.

"Abby's going to sleep with Nathan," Ella told Paul.

"Great," he said, scribbling in a notebook.

"I'm so proud of you," Ella said.

Abby said good-night to Ella and continued on her

way, giddy with anticipation. Nathan's room was on the other end of the building. As she rounded the corner, she saw Lydia standing outside his door.

And her world came to a grinding halt.

Abby faltered, almost stumbling on her sore ankle. She hadn't called first, so Nathan wasn't expecting her. Was he expecting Lydia? While she watched, rooted to the spot, he opened the door and let her in.

Son of a bitch.

It felt like a slap in the face. Like the shock of cold water after a long fall. She'd drummed up the courage to climb the boulder and jump off. For this. For nothing but an icy impact and a soundless dunk.

She braced her hand on the wall, dizzy. Her pulse rate climbed. She flashed back to the moment she'd walked in on Ray and Lydia. Abby hadn't even been aware that Ray was unhappy in their marriage. He'd always worked too much. The weeks before she'd caught the couple in his office hadn't been unusual.

She'd had no idea.

It was almost criminal how naive she'd been. Her initial reaction to the sight of them was confusion, not anger. Lydia was topless, with her skirt raked up. Her full, natural breasts bounced with every thrust. Abby had interrupted her husband with his pants down and his penis inside another woman, but her first thought had been: *this is a strange consultation.* Lydia clearly didn't need implants or liposuction.

When Abby imagined the same scene with Nathan standing in for Ray, her stomach churned with nausea. She closed her eyes and took steady breaths, praying she wouldn't black out or throw up.

After a moment of visualizing gentle waves lapping at the beach, she relaxed a little. Logic kicked in. Nathan wasn't Ray. He wasn't a womanizer. He'd let Lydia inside his room. That didn't mean they were having sex right now.

Abby couldn't dismiss the possibility, however. She'd seen the way Lydia had reacted to Nathan's defense of Leo. When Nathan had taken Ray aside to talk, she'd stared after them like a woman who realized she'd made a terrible mistake. Nathan considered their divorce his fault. He'd loved her "desperately." Nathan was ten times the man Ray was. It was only natural for Lydia to want him back.

Trying to stay calm, Abby considered her next move. If Nathan and Lydia were going to work things out, she couldn't interfere. They had a son together. She wouldn't knock on the door to interrupt them. But she couldn't just walk away, either. While she waited, she reminded herself that Nathan hadn't made her any promises.

So why did she feel so devastated?

After about fifteen minutes, the door opened again. Nathan kissed Lydia on the forehead. Her makeup was mussed. Her blouse appeared to have been hastily buttoned. Anyone would assume they were having an affair.

Abby's chest tightened with dismay. It was too late. She'd already taken the plunge. She was in love with him.

Instead of watching Lydia walk down the hall, he glanced at Abby. He frowned as if he could read her thoughts. The only thing worse than falling for a man she couldn't have was facing him. She'd rather run away than see pity in his eyes. She left in a panic, fleeing the scene as fast as her bruised ankle could take her.

"Abby," he called out, coming after her.

She didn't know where to hide. If she returned to her room, he'd find her. Pulse racing, she went the opposite direction. There was an ice machine at the end of the hall. She crouched down behind it, praying he'd gone the other way.

Five seconds ticked by before he found her. He leaned his forearm against the top of the machine, seeming amused by her strange behavior.

Well, fuck *him*. Her personality quirks weren't fodder for his entertainment any more than her feelings were his playthings. She jumped to her feet and shoved past him, tears streaming down her cheeks.

"It's not what you think," he said.

The pool area was just ahead, surrounded by an iron fence. It was dark and empty at this late hour. She fumbled for her key card to open the gate. When she slipped inside and closed the gate behind her, she felt safer.

He gripped the iron bars, looking in. "I didn't sleep with Lydia."

"I saw you kiss her."

"It wasn't like that. She needed a shoulder to cry on."

"That's all she needed?"

After a short hesitation, he nodded.

"Don't lie to me," she said, reading the deception. He wasn't smooth, like Ray. "Don't ever lie to me."

"She wanted to get back at Ray for cheating," he admitted.

"By having sex with you?"

"I didn't touch her."

"Were you tempted?"

A muscle in his jaw flexed. "Yes."

Bastard. "Why didn't you do it?"

"Why do you think?"

"I have no idea."

"Because I want *you*."

"You've already had her."

He squinted through the bars, seeming insulted by this statement. "Come on, Abby. That's not why I said no."

Abby brushed the tears from her cheeks. "Do you know how I felt when I saw your ex-wife go into your hotel room?"

"Tell me."

"Like I was dying."

His lips curved into a smile.

"Why is that funny?"

"It's not," he said, sobering.

"You think I'm crazy."

"No."

"You're laughing at me!"

"I'm not laughing at you," he said, his throat working with agitation. "I'm smiling because it feels good to know you care. I can't believe how fucking lucky I am."

"What do you mean?"

"You're brave and smart and hot as hell."

"I'm not brave," she whispered. "I'm afraid of everything."

"You might be afraid, but it doesn't stop you from taking risks or fighting back. Underneath that beauty is the heart of a lion."

She flushed at the compliment, unable to look away.

"I love that you came to my room to be with me," he continued, holding her gaze. "I love the way you speak your mind and put yourself out there. From the first moment we met, I thought there was something between us. Something special. Something real. But I didn't know you felt the same way until now."

She closed her eyes, overwhelmed with emotion. It was too much. She was too invested. "You're scaring me."

"I don't want to scare you. I want to take you to bed."

The reminder of physical pleasure settled her nerves. She could handle sex. It was the reason she'd sought him out.

Taking a deep breath, she opened the gate and joined him on the other side. He didn't crowd her, but he didn't give her a polite amount of space, either. She felt the tension in his muscles, the heat between them.

"No more pretty words," she said in his ear. "Just fuck me."

He didn't smile at this command. Maybe he was
done smiling for the night. She thought he might press
her back against the metal gate and take her right
there. He glanced around, as if to make sure they
were still alone. Instead of ravaging her in the deserted pool area, he grasped her hand and guided her
toward his room. That was probably for the best. She
didn't want to get interrupted again.

As they passed the ice machine, he pulled her into
her hiding place and pinned her against the wall. His
mouth descended on hers, hot and demanding. She
returned the kiss with fervor, wrapping her arms
around his neck.

He broke the contact, breathing hard.

She gasped as he sank to his knees before her. His
hands slid up her dress, gliding along the outsides of
her thighs. Anyone who happened by could see her.
Depending on the angle, they could see him. When
his fingertips found her lace panties, he tugged gently,
stripping the fabric down her hips.

"What—what are you doing?" she asked, flatten-
ing her palms on the wall behind her.

His answer was to push up her skirt. He touched
his tongue to her, kissing the closed lips of her sex.

Abby studied the empty hallway, her pulse racing. She didn't think she could respond in such a
high-pressure situation, but her body softened to his
warm, wet licks. She moaned, widening her stance a
little. He let go of her dress and took her panties all
the way off, careful with her bruised ankle. Then he

rose to his feet. His erection strained the fly of his jeans as he kissed her mouth again, sharing her taste.

"I thought you wanted me in your bed," she murmured.

"I want you anywhere."

"How about…behind a closed door?"

He tucked her panties into his pocket and took her straight to his room. As soon as they arrived, he pushed her back to the door. They kissed hungrily, hands groping, tongues entwined. He cupped her naked buttocks with a groan, grinding his erection against her cleft. She broke the kiss to help him get his shirt off. He pulled her dress over her head. While she fumbled with the clasp of her bra, he unbuttoned the fly of his jeans. Her breasts tumbled free. Moistening his lips, he reached into his pocket for a condom.

She realized he'd taken her request seriously. He was going to fuck her right here against the door.

It sounded hot, and she didn't doubt she'd enjoy every second. But after his teasing licks by the ice machine, and the steamy encounter at the hot springs, she longed to explore his body. Falling to her knees, she snatched the condom from his palm and tossed it on the bed. Then she tugged his jeans down his hips and lowered the waistband of his boxers. His cock jutted forth, thick and rock-hard. She wanted it in her mouth.

Looking up at him, she stroked his heated flesh in her hand. He was bigger than average. She didn't know how much of him she could swallow. Directing him toward her lips, she swirled her tongue around the tip, using her saliva to get him really wet. Then she stretched her mouth around him and sucked.

He didn't try to gag her or guide her head, the way some men did, but he wasn't shy about penetrating her mouth. Bracing his hands on the door, he watched her parted lips slide up and down on him. When she demonstrated the depth she was comfortable with, he thrust inside to that point, maybe a half inch beyond it. She moaned, digging her fingernails into his taut buttocks as he filled her mouth. The nubby carpet dug into her knees. She found herself taking him deeper, enjoying the minor discomfort and submissive pose.

"Fuck," he said, pulling away from her.

"You don't have to stop."

"I want to be inside you."

She wasn't going to argue. The performance and sensations had turned her on. When she straightened, he took her in his arms again, urging her toward the bed. They fell across the mattress together, his erection sliding along the cleft of her sex.

"I thought of you this morning," he said, rubbing his thumb across her cheek. "Your sweet mouth…"

"Please," she murmured.

"I like this," he said, moving his hand between her legs. She was wet and slippery. His blunt fingertip plunged in and out, making slick sounds. Writhing with arousal, she spread her thighs wider.

"Oh God," she said.

"Are you ready?"

As if he didn't know. He toyed with her stiff nipples, pinching and sucking them for so long she wanted to scream. Then he kissed his way down her body, pressing his lips to her quivering belly. He removed her sandals, very gently, before settling his mouth between her legs. Once there, he teased her with soft nibbles and light flicks of his tongue.

Desperate for release, she shoved him off her and crawled across the bed, searching for the condom. When she found it, she tore the package open and rolled the latex on him. Then she pushed him down on the mattress and climbed astride.

"Easy," he said, gripping her hips to steady her. Even as wet as she was, she struggled to accommodate his thickness. She leaned forward to adjust the angle. He gritted his teeth as she enveloped him inch by inch.

"Ooh," she said when he was all the way in. She closed her eyes, relishing the sensation. For several seconds, they stayed like that, connected and motionless. When she started to move, he helped lift her up and down. Back and forth. His shaft grew slick with her moisture and her breasts jiggled with each thrust.

"I can't last much longer," he groaned.

She braced her hands on his chest and covered his mouth with hers, biting his lower lip. "Touch me."

When she straightened, he looked down at where their bodies were joined. He licked the pad of his thumb and placed it over her clit. Her breath hitched as he moved in slow circles. She arched her spine, lost in sensation. When the orgasm broke over her, she threw her head back and sobbed his name, bucking like a wild woman.

She was still shivering with ecstasy when he rolled on top of her. Wrapping his fists in her hair, he slammed his body into hers, pounding her against the mattress. Once, twice, three times. His last thrust penetrated to the hilt. He came with a hoarse shout, his shoulders quaking from the power of his release.

When it was over, she clung to his neck, in no hurry to push him away. His penis pulsed inside her. He was hot and sweaty, his chest hair rough against her breasts. His heart thumped in time with hers. Finally he withdrew from her and rose to dispose of the condom. Then he joined her in bed again, pulling her close.

It wasn't just sex. If she didn't need more, she would get up and leave. Staying with him, sleeping beside him…that was relationship stuff.

"I forgot how much I used to hate Lydia," she said, stroking his hair.

"You hated her?"

"I hated them both."

She still hated Ray sometimes for hurting Brooke. The plane ticket stunt had been typical. Ray wasn't always a terrible father, and he sincerely loved Brooke. He just didn't seem capable of giving her his complete attention. Expensive gifts and infrequent visits were the extent of his parenting commitment. He'd become more driven each year, more selfish.

"What changed?" Nathan asked.

"Remember how I said I felt out of place at my dad's house?"

"Yes."

"My stepmom treated me like a guest. But Lydia treated Brooke like her own daughter. That meant a lot to me."

"She had a miscarriage."

"When?"

"Years ago."

"I didn't know," Abby said.

"She always wanted a girl."

"Do you think that's why she's been so good to Brooke?"

"Maybe. Brooke is easy to get along with, too."

Abby contemplated that for a moment. In many ways, Lydia had been a better parent to Brooke than Ray. It was one of the positive outcomes of their divorce. "I can't hate someone who loves my child."

He lifted his head to study her. "I know what you mean."

"Do you hate Ray?"

"I'll never like him."

Abby turned off the lights and pulled a sheet over their naked bodies. Then she curled up next to him, savoring his warmth. What a strange turn of events. She would never have imagined having an affair with Nathan Strom, or feeling sorry for Ray and Lydia.

A week ago, she hadn't believed she could fall in love again.

CHAPTER TWENTY-FOUR

Brooke wasn't paying attention to *Teen Wolf.*

Her mind kept straying to Wyatt and his father. She knew the police had found a body in the woods. She wasn't looking forward to seeing it up close. Her skin crawled whenever she pictured that poor boy in the cold, dark morgue. What kind of father killed his own son? Her dad was no prize, but at least he wasn't a homicidal maniac.

Although she relished Leo's company, she felt restless. Now that they were in a safe place, she had time to second-guess her behavior over the past few days.

They'd sort of hooked up at Mavericks this winter. She'd twined her arms around his neck and pressed her lips to his. After a short hesitation, he'd responded. He'd kissed her like a boyfriend, putting his hands on her body and his tongue in her mouth. Then he'd stopped and pushed her away, as if remembering who she was. Instead of talking to her about it, he'd turned on the engine and driven out of the parking lot. He'd gone straight to her dorm at Berkeley, getting rid of her as soon as possible.

Since then, they'd only seen each other a few times. They still hung out and cuddled. Her play-

ful attempts to instigate another make-out session
had failed. He'd made it clear that he wasn't going to
kiss her again, let alone have sex with her. He'd told
her to get herself off, as if that would lessen her desire for him.

Maybe she'd pursued Leo because she felt more
comfortable with him than with anyone else. She
didn't trust other boys as much. Alex had claimed
she wasn't feminine or relaxed enough to come. Leo
had said that wasn't true, but he'd also seemed annoyed with her for touching him. It was confusing.
Nice girls weren't supposed to get horny or be aggressive. They were demure and undemanding, frolicking
in meadows with butterflies.

It troubled her to think that she'd done something
to draw Gary Nash's attention. That he'd targeted her
because she'd been too friendly to him on the trail.
Her bikini was too small, her shorts too short. Her
manner was too provocative. She was too desperate,
too needy. Too energetic in her affections. Even her
mother thought so.

She studied Leo from beneath lowered lashes.
He was sitting beside her on the bed, his injured leg
propped up on pillows. His jet-black hair was casually disheveled. If she leaned in to smell him, he'd
smell good. He was smooth and clean and handsome.
When she thought of Wyatt's less-attractive features,
slack with death, her heart twisted in her chest. She
and Leo were lucky in so many ways.

Leo muted the TV. "What's wrong?"

"Nothing."

"You're acting weird."

"How?"

He gestured to the distance between them. That was unusual. Nine times out of ten, she was plastered against him.

"My mom told me to stop hanging all over you."

"She did?"

Brooke hugged a pillow to her chest, shrugging.

He looked hurt. "I thought she liked me."

She smiled at the misunderstanding. "She does like you. She thinks I'm bothering you. Throwing myself at you."

"You're not bothering me."

To her dismay, tears filled her eyes.

"Why are you crying?"

She brushed the tears away, embarrassed. "You told me to find someone else to…"

"Fuck?"

For the first time in years, she couldn't bring herself to repeat a vulgar term.

"Forget what I said. I was being an asshole."

"You meant it."

"Actually, I didn't."

She wasn't sure she believed him. "I know you get mad when I touch you. When I try to make you want me."

"You don't have to try."

"I don't?"

"I'd want you even if you didn't touch me. And I'm not mad at you. I'm mad at the situation. I'm mad because I can't have you."

Brooke studied him for a moment, her heart racing. "Why not?"

He glanced away, as if reluctant to elaborate.

"Because of my dad?"

"Because of a lot of things."

"Like what?"

He didn't answer.

She shoved the pillow aside and rose from the bed. All of the hurt and frustration and fear she'd experienced over the past few days seemed to well up inside her. "If you're not interested, just say so. I can handle it. I'd rather get rejected than strung along because you don't have the balls to tell me the truth."

His mouth thinned with anger. "You want the truth?"

"Yes."

"You remember that photo of us at the pool party?"

She flushed at the memory, nodding. It was right after graduation. She'd had her first taste of alcohol, gotten tipsy and fallen into the pool in a yellow sundress. When she came out of the water, the fabric clung to every curve. One of her friends had taken a photo of Leo carrying her into the house. She'd been trying to kiss him. He'd been trying to keep her decently covered, without success. That image had been uploaded to Facebook, but removed at Brooke's request. "You saw it?"

"Not only did I see it, your dad saw it."

"You're kidding."

"No."

"How?"

"He was snooping around my room, and I had it saved on my computer. With other assorted images."

It took her a few seconds to understand his meaning. The photo had showed a lot of skin, including half her ass. He'd been wearing low-slung board shorts. They'd both been dripping wet. "You were looking at it for…"

"Yes," he said, not meeting her gaze.

She couldn't believe he'd used that picture for sexual gratification when there was explicit porn all over the internet. The idea gave her hot flashes. "Did my dad ask why it was on your computer?"

"He's a guy. He didn't have to ask."

"What did he say?"

"That he'd call the cops on me if I touched you. He threatened to plant a bag of pot in my car and have me arrested. He also said he'd cut off my balls, but I assume that was an exaggeration."

Brooke curled her hands into fists. "If he ever did anything to hurt you, I'd never speak to him again."

"It doesn't matter."

"Of course it matters! It's not fair."

"He's right about us, though. You and me…it's not a good idea."

She flinched as if he'd struck her. "How can you say that?"

"Because it would change things between us. I care about you too much to fuck up our relationship. I get frustrated when we wrestle around, but I like touching you. You shouldn't feel bad about touching me."

"Why would you fuck it up?"

"I'd drag you down, Brooke."

"That's not true."

"It is, and you know it is. You're going somewhere. I'm just…getting high."

She sat next to him on the bed again. His drug habit concerned her, but she wouldn't scold him. "Don't listen to my dad. He might be rich and successful, but he's barely human. Instead of judging you, he should look at himself."

"He won't."

"We don't have to tell him."

He shook his head, denying her. "Maybe after you finish school. For now, you should have fun. Date other people."

"Is that what you want to do?"

"Yes," he said, looking her in the eye.

She supposed it would be more reasonable to take a rain check. They were enrolled in different colleges. He was planning to spend a semester abroad. Their parents might get a divorce. They should wait for a better time instead of starting a furtive, long-distance relationship. But patience wasn't one of her virtues. Leo's confession about the pool-party photo had turned her on. He wanted her. She wanted him. They were alone in a hotel room. Why shouldn't they do what felt natural?

"We can still be together," she said. "Just this once."

His eyes darkened at the suggestion. "Just this once?"

She wrapped her arms around his neck, toying

with the leather cord he wore. It was attached to an antique Japanese coin, which lay at the hollow of his throat. She'd given him the pendant for his birthday last year. "I want the closeness you talked about, just for tonight. You don't have to be my boyfriend."

Although he hesitated, he didn't say no outright. His pulse throbbed beneath her fingertips. When she moistened her lips, his gaze lingered there for a few seconds. Then he opened his mouth, as if to try to dissuade her again.

She shut him up with a kiss.

That was the end of his resistance. He kissed her back with enthusiasm, exploring her mouth in silky strokes. He tasted hot and minty and eager. She'd wanted to do this for so long. The last time, in his car, she'd been drowsy and uncertain, lost in a marijuana haze. Now she was fully awake, fully aware. She straddled his lap and pressed closer, threading her fingers through his dark hair.

He was already aroused, throbbing against her, but he didn't rush anything. They kissed until she felt drenched in him, her mouth melded to his. She took it to the next level by tugging off his shirt and staring, lust-struck, at his beautiful chest. When she pulled her top over her head and released the clasp on her bra, he groaned.

She cupped her hands over her breasts, suddenly shy again.

He frowned at her in confusion. "What are you doing?"

"I'm…small."

"So what?"

"If you had a small dick, wouldn't you be embarrassed?"

His gaze lowered to the apex of her thighs. She'd been rubbing on his erection for at least thirty minutes. "Your tits are sexy," he said, digging his fingernails into her hips.

She relaxed her hands a little. "They are?"

"Fuck, yeah."

Her nipples jutted forth, demanding attention. He was watching her intently. She stroked the sensitive tips, wiggling back and forth on his lap. This action sparked a stronger reaction than she'd anticipated. With a low growl, he flipped her onto her back and yanked off her shorts. Her panties came down with them. Then she was completely naked, breathless with excitement. He kissed her mouth again, his hands roving over her body. He squeezed her bottom and swirled his tongue around her stiff nipples. By the time he worked up to touching her between the legs, she was slick with desire.

That seemed to please him. His nostrils flared as he slid one finger inside her, very gently. Then he withdrew, using that fingertip to stimulate her in slow circles. She moaned at the sensation, biting down on her lower lip.

He studied her face, seeming enthralled. "Is this good?"

"Yes."

"Should I go slower?"

She didn't know how to tell him what she wanted, so she covered his hand with hers and showed him. He adjusted his rhythm easily, increasing pressure. She realized that Alex had never bothered to learn her body. After a token effort to arouse her, he'd declared her ready and climbed on top of her.

Leo was more attentive, more imaginative. He paused to dip his fingers inside her and resumed strumming at a steady pace. He also sucked on her earlobe in a manner that was blatantly suggestive of oral sex.

"Oh, yes," she said, gripping his wrist.

His breath fanned her ear. "Like this?"

She came with a sharp cry, exploding in pleasure. The climax hit her like a freight train and went on forever. He kept stroking her tingling flesh, gentling his motions but not stopping until she quieted.

"Wow," she said, feeling boneless.

"I told you there was nothing wrong with you."

"I guess you were right."

He made no move to unbuckle his belt, so she did it for him, pressing her palm to the front of his shorts.

"We don't have to—"

"I want to."

She thought his injured leg might get in the way, but it didn't seem to bother him. He put on a condom and positioned himself over her. When he slid into her, it felt so much better than she'd expected. Hotter, slicker, sweeter. She wrapped her legs around his waist, transported. He kissed her as if her lips were honey. Although he rode her slow, it was over fast. Burying his face in her neck, he found his release with a low groan.

Somehow, she managed not to whisper *I love you*.

Afterward, they got dressed and watched TV. She clung to him, wondering if they'd ever cuddle like this again. Maybe it would be awkward to see him on Thanksgiving break, hoping he didn't have a girl-friend.

He was right—sex changed everything. Their relationship would never be the same. She'd risked losing him for a few minutes of pleasure. Mind-blowing, toe-curling pleasure, but still. Now that it was over, she felt greedy and selfish.

She didn't voice those concerns, although they weighed heavily on her. Leo had given her one of the best nights she'd ever had. He'd also warned her of the consequences before he touched her. Instead of listening, she'd kissed away his protests. What would he say now, besides I told you so? He'd been an active participant, but she was the clear aggressor. She had to take the lion's share of the blame.

Leo didn't seem to want to talk, either. He took a pain pill—*now* his leg was hurting—and turned off the TV. Brooke dimmed the lights, snuggling closer to him. His breaths grew steady and even with sleep.

Her cell phone rattled about an hour later, startling her awake. She sat up and grabbed it. There was a short text from her father:

pleas come to cabin i hurt my back

Rubbing her eyes, she tried to call him. He didn't pick up, so she texted a quick reply, asking if he was okay. Again, no answer.

Damn it.

Her father wasn't a tough guy about injuries. He was a board certified surgeon. He'd send for an ambulance if he needed one. It was unusual for him to make this kind of request from her, but who else could he ask? Lydia had thrown her ring at him. He was hundreds of miles from his friends and family. His current paramour couldn't help him.

The text itself was odd, too. He made abbreviations on occasion, but rarely misspelled words or ignored capitalization rules. Maybe his batteries were dying and he had to text fast. That would explain his lack of response.

She rose from the bed, careful not to wake Leo. Shoving her feet into flip-flops, she put on her Baja hoodie. Ella and Paul had gone to the cabin to retrieve their belongings earlier today. Ella had driven her mom's SUV back. The keys were sitting on the table.

Brooke scrawled a quick note to Leo and slipped out the door. As she walked down the hall, she considered waking up Paul and Ella. She didn't want to bother them, so she decided against it. There was no way she'd interrupt her mother and Nathan.

She could handle this. She needed to talk to her father anyway. He'd reached a new level of callousness with his latest gift. Those tickets were like a precancelation of their next trip. He was no longer available for vacations with her.

It would serve him right if she let him suffer at the cabin all night. One of her mother's favorite jokes was to take a picture of Brooke flipping him the bird. She'd pretend to send the image and they'd laugh.

Brooke relished the thought of replying to his text with a middle finger. Or this message: Sorry, Dad. I'm not available to be your daughter anymore. I hired a replacement daughter with some of the money you gave me. She'll be handling all of our future interactions. Frowny face.

Her mom's SUV was in the parking lot. Brooke opened the door and climbed behind the wheel. The whole way to the cabin, she alternated between regretting what she'd done with Leo and reliving every moment in graphic detail. No wonder her friends liked sex, if it was that good even a fraction of the time.

She was *definitely* not a lesbian.

When she arrived at the cabin, she parked beside her father's Bentley. The front door was unlocked. She opened it and stepped inside, glancing around. The living room was dark, but the lights in one of the bedrooms were on.

"Dad?" she called out, walking down the hallway.

Before she reached the light, someone grabbed her from behind and clapped his hand over her mouth.

CHAPTER TWENTY-FIVE

BROOKE'S SCREAM WAS muffled by a sweaty palm.

When her attacker locked his arm around her waist, she kicked out with both legs, trying to knock him off balance. Her head rocked back against his chin. He stumbled and went down to the carpet with her, grunting in pain.

His grip loosened. He lacked either the strength or the determination to hold on to her. His body felt skinny beneath hers, not physically imposing. She could get away from him if she struck now. Before she could elbow him in the gut, he shoved her aside and got up. Even though the hallway was dim, she recognized him.

"Wyatt," she breathed. "You're alive."

A crease formed between his brows, as if he didn't expect her to be pleased. But she was sincerely happy to see him instead of his father. He grabbed a shotgun from the corner of the hall and slung it over his shoulder, saying nothing. The gesture spoke volumes. As did his attempt to grab her, however halfhearted.

"Where's my dad?" she asked, swallowing hard.

"He's in one of the bedrooms."

"Is he hurt?"

"I thought you didn't like him."

Chills traveled along her spine. Maybe Wyatt wasn't the harmless, homely boy she thought he was. He'd drummed up the nerve to kill his own father. Had he done something terrible to hers?

"I don't like him," she said, her voice quaking. "I love him, though. I can't help it."

Wyatt seemed to understand this sentiment. His expression softened a little. "He's bound and gagged, but he's okay."

"Can I see him?"

He didn't answer. "Stand up and walk to the last bedroom."

She scrambled to her feet, heading toward the open door at the end of the hall.

"Go slow."

Heart pounding, she approached the lighted room with careful steps. It was one of the guest bedrooms, not the master suite. Her father wasn't inside.

"Get on the bed," Wyatt said.

Fear rushed through her blood, making her dizzy. Was he going to rape her? Should she fight now, before it was too late?

"See that notebook? I want you to write for me."

There was a yellow legal pad and a pen on the corner of the mattress. The items seemed incongruent with a murder plot or sexual assault attempt. She moved forward to pick them up with shaking hands.

Wyatt locked the door behind them and pulled up a chair. He looked pale and exhausted, with dark circles under his eyes. The bones in his face were more prominent than ever, as if he hadn't eaten in days. She didn't know how he'd managed to get here. He must have hiked for twenty-four hours without stopping.

His hair was wet and matted. He appeared to have showered and changed clothes. The ribbed undershirt and expensive trousers he was wearing probably belonged to her father. He'd tucked the pants into his own beat-up army boots.

Brooke sat down on the bed and opened the notebook, her pen poised like a receptionist waiting for dictation.

"I need you to write down everything I tell you."

She studied him for a moment, afraid to ask why he couldn't do this without her help. "Can you write?"

"I can read and write, but I'm slow. It would take me days to fill up a page."

She nodded her understanding.

"You write what I say, word for word, and I'll sign my name when we're done. Then I'm going to kill someone."

His casual threat made her flinch. He was planning to kill her—or her father. She gripped the pen tight, trying not to tremble. "Why me?"

"What do you mean?"

"My father can write fast."

He shifted in his chair, uncomfortable. "You're easier to talk to. Prettier to look at. You're also the only one who escaped."

Her eyes filled with tears. She wanted to beg him not to kill anyone, but she couldn't form the words. So she stared at the yellow paper and waited. He began in clipped sentences. The things he told her were horrific. He gave detailed accounts of his father abducting and torturing young women. He knew the victims' names. He remembered their identifying characteristics and what they'd been wearing. There were four, not including her.

The most difficult part for her to write was about the third victim's capture. This woman had been taken on a hiking trail with her dog. The protective animal had bitten the hell out of his father's arm. Nash broke its neck, but a nasty infection ensued.

"I could have killed him then," Wyatt said. "I could have let him die or helped the girl. Instead I nursed him back to health."

"How old were you?"

"Thirteen."

Brooke wiped the tears from her eyes and kept writing. Wyatt described the atrocities the victim had endured under his father's hands. She'd been the most combative captive and suffered the most abuse. A year later, she used a rope to hang herself.

Wyatt had been deeply disturbed by this experience, like any normal human being. He'd found the courage to help the fourth victim escape. His father had hunted her down and shot her. Wyatt had spent three days with her dead body in a stone pit.

Brooke's handwriting was smeared and shaky. She turned another page, scribbling about the fifth victim— her. They'd used a remote-operated deer call to mimic the sound of a woman screaming by Echo Lake. Wyatt had left a trail of wool threads for her family to follow. She owed him her life.

His voice grew hoarse as he continued. Nash had become furious with Wyatt during the search for Leo and Nathan. He'd turned and pointed his rifle at Wyatt's chest. Wyatt raised his crossbow and pulled the trigger.

His father missed. Wyatt didn't.

When they were finished, he signed the paper and handed her a map with four X marks. They were burial sites, she realized.

"Why did you come to this cabin?" she asked.

He returned to his chair and sat down. "When we searched through your backpacks, I saw a note with the address."

"You memorized it?"

"I'm better with numbers than letters," he said. Taking the shotgun strap off his shoulder, he held it over his lap. "You can leave the room now."

Her stomach dropped as she realized who Wyatt was going to kill: himself.

"No," she said, dismayed. "Don't do this."

Over the past few hours, he'd recounted the entire story. There was no indication that Wyatt had ever participated in rape, torture or murder. He'd assisted in the kidnappings against his will and done his best to thwart them. He'd shot his father in self-defense. He'd helped Brooke the only way he could.

At worst, he was a victim. At best, a hero.

"It wasn't your fault," she said.

He shook his head. "I can't live with what I've done. What I've seen."

"Your father was a monster, not you."

"I'm a monster, too. I feel worse about killing him than kidnapping you."

"You saved me."

"Did you mean it when you said you'd run away with me?"

Her breath caught in her throat. She couldn't run away with him, but she had to stop him. How could she stop him? "You need to eat something," she said, putting the pen and paper aside. "I'll make you a sandwich and you can sleep for a few hours. I'll stay right here with you. In the morning, you'll feel better."

His eyes watered with emotion. "Go on. Get out."

"I'm not leaving this room."

"Please," he rasped. "I can't do it in front of you."

"Then don't do it. Let's just talk."

He tightened his grip on the shotgun. "I'm done talking."

Brooke stared back at him, overwhelmed with despair. He seemed determined to follow through on his plans. She thought about approaching his chair, but he might be able to raise the barrel to his mouth and pull the trigger before she reached him. She had to find another way to connect with him. To convince him.

"Do you have any family?" she asked, tentative.

"Not anymore."

"Where would we go, if we ran away?"

His lips twisted with regret. "Forget it."

"I'll drive you anywhere you want to go. Mexico, Canada…"

"No. It was a stupid idea. I know you'd never—"

He broke off, shaking his head. "I know I'm not fit company."

"That's not true. I like you."

He made a sound of disbelief.

She didn't like him the same way she liked Leo, of course. She wasn't sure if Wyatt really liked her that way, either. Maybe she'd become a symbol to him. The girl who'd escaped, when he couldn't. He might have gotten out of the woods, but he'd never escape the trauma of a horrific childhood. His father had committed atrocities. Wyatt had killed him. That kind of baggage wasn't easy to leave behind.

"I like you," she repeated, twisting her hands in her lap.

His gaze grew dull. "You don't have to lie. Just go."

"I'm not going."

"Then you'll see how ugly I can be."

She didn't know what else to say. He wasn't going to listen to her, anyway. She had to take drastic action.

He cocked the shotgun. "Last chance, pretty girl."

She bit down on the edge of her fist to smother a cry of distress. Then she got an idea. He was a sixteen-year-old boy with a crush. He thought she was pretty. Maybe she could use that against him. On impulse, she tugged the striped hoodie over her head. When he studied the front of her thin tank top, she felt a surge of hope.

"What are you doing?" he asked.

"Do you want me?"

"I want to die," he said in a strangled voice.

Her heart broke for him. He might have given up

on himself, but she wasn't going to give up on him. So she continued the clumsy striptease, removing her tank top and bra. He stared at her naked breasts, his jaw slack. Suicidal or not, he seemed tempted.

It felt strange to expose herself again so soon after her last encounter. Sleeping with Leo had changed the way she felt about her sexuality. His praise had boosted her self-confidence. Before Leo, it wouldn't have occurred to her that she could distract Wyatt this way. She hadn't considered her breasts worthy of interest, much less life-saving mechanisms.

She circled her soft nipples with her fingertips until they stiffened. "Would you like to touch me, Wyatt?"

"Yes."

"Come here."

He rose from the chair, as if driven by an irresistible force. Although he brought the shotgun with him, he set it at the foot of the bed. Then he sat down next to her. When she brought his hand to her breast, he closed his eyes and shuddered.

He wasn't handsome, but he was sweet. He'd endured too much in his young life. Assuaging his pain was no hardship. She leaned forward and pressed her mouth to his, pretending he was Leo.

ABBY AWOKE WITH a start.

Her cell phone was blinking on the nightstand. Nathan's arm was draped over her waist, his heavy thigh sandwiched between hers. With another man, she might have felt trapped or smothered. When he pressed his lips to the nape of her neck, she shivered with pleasure. Ignoring her phone, she reached back to thread her fingers through his hair. He lifted his hands to her breasts. His shaft swelled against her buttocks, nudging her sex.

She wanted him like this, from behind. They'd kissed and talked for hours, but they hadn't made love again. Her body still felt primed for action. He was obviously ready to go. "Nathan," she murmured, arching her spine.

He slid into her, just an inch. "Fuck."

"Yes."

"I should put on a condom."

He really should, but he didn't. She shivered with pleasure as he brushed his thumbs over her nipples and kissed her neck. Instead of withdrawing completely, he teased her with the tip of his cock, barely penetrating her.

Then someone pounded on the door of the hotel room. "Dad! Let me in."

Nathan cursed under his breath, pulling away from her. Abby clutched the sheet to her chest, watching as he rose from the bed and wrapped a towel around his waist. He went to the door and opened it.

Leo shoved his way inside. He looked frantic, and he didn't have his crutches. "I think something happened to Brooke," he said in a rush. "She left after midnight and she's not answering her phone."

Nathan closed the door behind him, glancing at Abby.

Abby grabbed her phone to read her messages.

There was a short text from Brooke at 12:47 a.m., saying she'd borrowed the SUV to check on Ray at the cabin. Abby tried to call her, but she didn't pick up. Neither did Ray. When she dialed the landline number for the cabin, she got a disconnected signal.

Okay. Now it was time to panic.

"She drove to the cabin," Leo said. "We have to go there."

"Give us a minute," Nathan said, retrieving Abby's lingerie from the floor.

Leo flushed and went back outside. While she scrambled into her clothes, Nathan tugged on a pair of pants.

"Do you have your car?" she asked.

He nodded, putting on his shirt and shoes. "Lydia brought it."

Abby gathered her purse and sandals, dialing 911 on their way out. The responding officer didn't know if a disconnected line was cause for concern, but he said he'd send the next available patrol car.

Nathan drove like a NASCAR racer, passing the few other vehicles on the road. Leo urged him to go faster. Abby wanted to get there alive, so she stayed silent. The idea of Brooke being in danger again was almost inconceivable to her.

When would this nightmare end?

She hoped they were worrying over nothing. Maybe Ray was fine, and Brooke had turned off her phone for some reason. It wasn't like her to be so irresponsible, however. She was reckless and impulsive, but thoughtful. After she went on risky adventures, she sent dutiful text messages to let Abby know she was okay.

"How are you doing?" Nathan asked Abby. "Hanging in there?"

"By a thread," she said.

He didn't tell her everything would be fine, or that he'd protect her and Brooke. They had no control over this situation. It was out of their hands. Abby's cell phone rang before they reached the cabin. She didn't recognize the number.

"Hello?"

"This is Deputy Clegg with the Monarch Sheriff's Station."

"Are you at the cabin?"

"Not yet. I'll be there in about ten minutes. I just wanted to give you some information pertaining to the case."

"What is it?"

"We've identified the body as belonging to Gary Nash."

"Gary Nash," she repeated. "Not his son, Wyatt?"

"That's right. Wyatt Nash is currently unaccounted for."

"And Gary Nash is dead."

"Yes, ma'am."

Abby looked sideways at Nathan, somewhat relieved by this news.

"You can still visit the morgue for a viewing," the deputy said. "Some victims think it helps give them closure."

Being referred to as a victim unsettled her. She

wasn't one. She was a survivor. But she couldn't say she hadn't been traumatized by this experience. What she'd seen in those tunnels. The horrors she'd imagined. More nightmares and panic attacks loomed on the horizon. She wanted to see Nash on the table and make sure he was never getting up.

"Thank you," she said, ending the call. "Gary Nash is dead."

"Good," Nathan said. "He can burn in hell."

"His son is still missing."

Although Brooke had seemed very sympathetic toward Wyatt, Abby felt uneasy. The kid had put an arrow through his father's neck. He'd lived in a torture chamber with a psychopath. He was no Boy Scout.

At the cabin, Nathan parked behind Abby's SUV and they all got out. The front door was open. Nathan and Leo checked the bedrooms while Abby shouted for Brooke, her heart stuttering in her chest. They found Ray bound and gagged in the master bedroom. He was alive, so they didn't pause to help him. Brooke was their main priority.

The last bedroom was locked. Abby rattled the doorknob. "Brooke?"

"Don't come in," Brooke cried out. "He has a gun."

Nathan gestured for her to step aside. He broke through the door in two hard kicks. Brooke was in front of the bed with Wyatt Nash. They were wrestling for control of a shotgun like kids fighting over a toy on the playground.

She was also topless.

The sight of her in distress seemed to trigger a feral response in Leo. He lowered his shoulder and charged, tackling Wyatt. They rolled across the bed and fell over. The shotgun landed on the other side, out of reach. Brooke stumbled backward with a sharp cry. Abby rushed to her daughter's side, putting her arms around her.

Leo gripped the front of Wyatt's shirt and started wailing on him. He punched Wyatt three or four times in a row. Although Wyatt was skinny, he had a surprising speed and agility. Maybe his father had taught him some combat techniques. He evaded Leo's next punch and drove the heel of his hand into Leo's nose.

Nathan broke them apart by grabbing Wyatt and hauling him to his feet. Leo got up and kept swinging, driving his fist into Wyatt's stomach.

"Stop it," Brooke screamed, pulling away from Abby. She gripped Leo's right arm to prevent him from hitting Wyatt again. "Stop hurting him!"

Nathan had Wyatt's arms wrenched behind his back, motionless. Blood dripped from a cut above the boy's eye, streaking down the side of his face. He was breathing hard, his mouth set in a grim line, but he wasn't struggling.

Leo wiped his nose, which was also bleeding, and looked at Brooke. "He was trying to force himself on you."

"No, he wasn't."

He gaped at her in disbelief. His gaze dropped to her breasts, as if her nudity was proof of Wyatt's guilt.

Brooke let go of his arm to cover her chest, flushing. Abby found Brooke's discarded clothing items and brought them to her. She didn't know what to think. The scene was too chaotic to process.

"Get me something to tie him up with," Nathan said to Abby.

Ray's overnight bag was sitting in the corner, its contents spilling out across the floor. She grabbed an expensive silk tie and handed it to Leo, who secured Wyatt's thin wrists. The boy didn't resist or speak. Nathan sat him down on the bed, keeping a firm grip on him. Leo stood guard near the shotgun.

They had the situation under control, so Abby and Brooke left the room. Brooke put on her bra and tank top in the hall, her shoulders trembling. When her face crumpled with emotion, Abby drew Brooke into her arms. "Shh. It's okay now."

A moment later, sheriff's deputies entered the house. They handcuffed Wyatt and took him away in the back of a squad car. They also freed Ray, who was bound and gagged in one of the guest rooms.

More law enforcement officers came to interview Brooke, including a pair of FBI agents assigned to the case. She showed them the five pages of notes she'd written at Wyatt's request.

According to Brooke, the boy had planned to commit suicide, and she was trying to stop him. She didn't mention her state of undress. Neither did Nathan or Leo. Abby stayed by her side the whole time to support her.

Ella and Paul brought everyone breakfast. Lydia

came also, hugging Leo and even Ray. The mood at the cabin was somber.

They were all safe. The ordeal was over.

After the law enforcement officers left, Nathan drove Abby and Brooke to the morgue. Leo came along for the ride. Abby had seen her share of dead bodies, mostly beloved residents. Some not-so-beloved. The sight of Nash didn't affect her as deeply as she'd feared. He looked like a corpse, not a monster.

They retrieved their belongings from the hotel and headed back to the cabin. Nathan reached across the console to hold her hand while Leo and Brooke sat on opposite sides of the backseat, staring out their respective windows.

CHAPTER TWENTY-SIX

BROOKE HADN'T DONE anything wrong. Leo knew that.

Wyatt Nash had attacked her father. He'd lured her to the cabin and made her write his sick sob story at gunpoint. Then he'd traumatized her further by threatening to blow his head off. She hadn't wanted him. She'd wanted to avoid seeing his brains splattered on the ceiling. Leo understood what happened. Even so, his gut reaction wasn't sympathy. It was jealous rage, as if she'd cheated on him.

They weren't dating. He wasn't her boyfriend. Okay, yeah—he'd fucked her. That had been an incredibly stupid decision, fueled by years of pent-up longing. She'd needed comfort and he'd given it to her. But he had no ownership over her. He had no hold on her, no right to tell her what to do with her body.

He thought they had a special connection, though. They'd been through a lot together. Last night had been…intense. He knew she'd enjoyed herself. She'd responded to him. He'd made her come. They'd both agreed not to start a relationship, but he'd sort of assumed she would pine over him, just a little. Daydream and fantasize about him, the way he daydreamed and fantasized about her. He was in no hurry to hook up with other girls. He didn't even want to wash her scent off his hands.

It had been a shock to find her half-naked with Wyatt Nash, hours after leaving Leo's bed. Leo thought he'd been rescuing her, defending her honor. But no. She'd let that freak touch her. She'd begged Leo not to hurt him.

Every way he looked at it, he felt rejected. Cast aside. Maybe the best night of his life hadn't meant that much to her.

He hated himself for feeling this way. He should be comforting Brooke, not sulking like a kid who'd lost his favorite plaything. His dad was holding Abby's hand across the console. Leo could do that with Brooke. Taking a deep breath, he hazarded another glance at her. She was staring out the window, toying with the plastic hospital bracelet that was still around her wrist. He remembered the sounds she'd made when she came. Her mouth had formed a soft O of pleasure when he slid into her.

Leo tore his gaze away. Instead of offering his hand to her, he clenched it into a fist. His knuckles were scraped and swollen from Wyatt's ugly face. Their fight hadn't done his injured leg any favors, either. He wanted a pain pill. Better yet, a few hits of weed. He needed to mellow out before he exploded.

As soon as they arrived at the cabin, he got out of the backseat and hobbled inside. He had a joint stashed in his iPod case. It would make everything better. Ray's insults, his mother's tears, the disturbing memories of violence, his dark fury. All of that bad shit would fade. So would the good shit, like Brooke's pretty face at the moment of orgasm. But that was a price he'd have to pay.

He retreated into one of the bedrooms with his backpack. Before he could find his iPod case, his mother knocked on the door. "Leo?"

"Yeah."

She came inside and sat down on the bed. Her eyes looked red, as if she'd been up all night crying. "I need to talk to you about Ray."

"I don't want to talk about Ray."

"He's sorry."

Leo made a sound of skepticism.

"He's grateful to you for saving Brooke."

"I didn't save Brooke."

"He said you could have your car back."

"What about you?" he asked, annoyed. "What's he going to do for you, besides work all the time and sleep around?"

She moistened her lips, hesitant.

"Don't tell me you've forgiven him."

"We both made mistakes," she said, looking away. "Just like me and your father."

Resentment welled up inside him, festering beneath the surface. Even if his dad had been 90 percent at fault, Leo wished she'd been honest with him about the reasons they'd split. "I know you cheated on Dad."

"He told you?"

"Brooke told me."

Tears filled her eyes. "I didn't want you to find out."

"Why?"

"I thought…you wouldn't love me anymore."

"That's dumb, Mom. I could never not love you."

"You mean the world to me," she said in Portuguese.

He knew that. His dad had been gone a lot, and Ray was even more absent. It had always been just the two of them. She did his laundry and cooked his favorite meals and doted on him. "You're a great mom."

Her chin wobbled with emotion. When he put his arm around her, she pressed her face to his shoulder and cried. "I want you and Ray to get along."

"I want him to treat you better."

"We're going to start counseling."

Leo wasn't optimistic about her chances of patching things up with Ray. She should kick him to the curb and move on with a guy who was capable of loving someone other than himself. She deserved to be happy.

They discussed Leo's plans for the rest of the summer, which were flexible. He would hang around the house as much as possible for the next few weeks in case she needed him. As far as Leo was concerned, Ray was the one on probation.

"How are things with your father?" she asked.

"Okay," he said, shrugging.

She smiled at his guarded response. "It's good to see the two of you talking again."

He thought about the surfing lesson he hadn't agreed to. She'd be disappointed in him for saying no, so he didn't mention it.

"We're leaving now if you want to come with us."

"I'll go with Dad," he said. He'd rather ride his bike, but that wasn't an option with his injured leg.

"I can bring you back for your motorcycle next week."

He stood up to hug her goodbye. She seemed so much smaller now, so slight in his arms. "I'll be home tonight, I guess."

"Be sweet to Brooke," she said, touching his face. "She has such a crush on you."

"Did she tell you that?"

"She didn't have to."

He felt a stab of guilt for crossing the line with her. That wasn't the kind of sweet his mother would approve of. He was ashamed of what he'd done and how he felt. "She's affectionate with everyone. It doesn't mean anything."

Maybe he'd protested too much, because her gaze sharpened as she released him. "She's a lovely girl. I'm sure you've noticed."

He'd done a lot more than notice—and there was no way he'd discuss it with his mother. If Ray had told her about his computer files, she'd never mentioned it. Leo still had the pool party photo saved in a secret folder.

Ray interrupted their conversation by coming in to shake his hand and thank him. Leo accepted the peacemaking gesture for his mother's sake, but his tense grip and narrow eyes conveyed the following message: I'm watching you, buddy.

After they left, Leo found the joint he'd stashed.

He turned it around and around in his fingers, struck by a strange ambivalence. Maybe he should wait until later. The urgency he'd felt to get high had slipped away, leaving an empty space inside him. A hard surf session or a fast ride might fill it, but he couldn't do either until his leg healed. He put the joint in his pocket, remembering his last motorcycle ride with Brooke. He could still feel her arms around his waist and her breasts pressed against his back, her taut thighs squeezing his.

He had to get out of here.

Grabbing his belongings, he left the room. His dad was out front, probably ready to go. Brooke was sitting at the kitchen counter with a glass of orange juice. He couldn't leave the cabin without saying goodbye to her.

Their eyes locked over the rim of her glass. A private conversation would be better, so he inclined his head toward the side door. She got up and followed him to the patio. It was a small space with a round table and a couple of cushy lounge chairs. He squinted at the glare of sunlight on the table's beveled glass surface.

Brooke was unusually grim. She didn't smile or flirt or tease. All of the playfulness had been sucked out of their relationship. "Are you heading back to L.A.?"

He nodded. "You?"

"San Diego."

"When do your classes start?"

"Three weeks."

"Same for me."

They were both silent for a moment.

"I think I'll give those open plane tickets to Ella and Paul for their honeymoon," she said. "Unless you want to use them."

He'd forgotten her offer to take him jet-setting. That was ruined, too. "No."

She raked a hand through her hair. It was damp from the shower. She'd changed into cutoffs and a thin T-shirt with no bra. He tore his gaze from her chest, his heart thumping. If he didn't get away from her, he was going to do something he'd regret.

"I'm sorry," she said.

"Don't be."

"I didn't mean to hurt you."

"I know."

She seemed to expect a different response, or a better explanation, but he couldn't give her one. He was too emotional right now, too confused. Seeing her with Wyatt *had* hurt him. Sleeping with her had been a mistake.

The best thing to do was walk away. Make a clean break.

They could repair their relationship and be close again. In a few months, he'd be able to restrain himself. They could talk and cuddle without tearing each other's clothes off. At this point, he just couldn't do it. He couldn't even stand next to her without picturing her naked and aching to touch her.

"I'll call you," he said.

She flinched at his obvious attempt to end the conversation. "Okay," she said, giving him a quick hug. "Take care."

"I will."

They often said *I love you* before parting ways. He knew she meant it as a friend or a sister. Today, she didn't say it.

Neither did he.

NATHAN LOADED UP his belongings, preparing to leave.

Ray had rented the cabin for the entire week, but no one wanted to stay. Too many bad things had happened here. By midafternoon, only the original four remained. Leo came outside with his backpack, looking miserable. Nathan assumed Brooke was the reason. Leo's fury over Wyatt went beyond big-brother protectiveness.

"You ready to go?"

Leo leaned against the passenger door of Nathan's car, nodding.

"Okay, give me a minute."

Before Nathan could walk back in, Abby and Brooke stepped out. They were all hitting the road at the same time, it seemed.

"Do you need to get something?" Abby asked.

"I was just going to say goodbye."

She hid a smile, tucking a flyaway strand of hair behind her ear before she turned to lock the front door. Brooke surprised him with a full-body embrace. He was touched by the gesture. Over the past few days, he'd grown attached to Brooke. She released him and stepped away to give them some privacy.

Abby was still wearing the soft purple dress from the previous night. She'd reapplied her makeup and braided her hair. A pair of sunglasses perched on top of her head. Her face was more relaxed than it had been during the camping trip. There were still issues to sort through and problems to worry about, but the situation no longer seemed dire. They were alive. The kidnappers were accounted for.

Nathan was eager to pick up where he and Abby left off in his hotel room. He couldn't wait to take her home. With a start, he realized that he wanted her by his side…permanently. He was in love with her.

The epiphany didn't unsettle him as much as it should have. He hadn't fallen for her at first sight, but they'd clicked immediately. They had similar backgrounds and life experiences. She'd become his partner in survival. It seemed as if he'd known her forever because they'd been through so much together.

Nathan had always been goal-oriented and up for a challenge. Now that he'd recognized his feelings, he could focus on winning Abby over. He'd have to go slow. She might share her body without reservations, but she wasn't as free and easy with her affections. Earning her trust wouldn't be a simple task.

"I want to see you again," he said.

A flush crept up her slender throat. "Okay."

"This weekend?"

She glanced at Brooke, her top priority. "I'll have to check my schedule."

Brooke crossed her arms over her chest, sighing heavily.

"It doesn't have to be just the two of us," Nathan said.

Instead of answering, Abby took out her cell phone and requested his number. After he gave her the digits, she sent him a quick text. He glanced at his screen to read it. Call me. Satisfied, he put his phone away. He wanted to kiss her, but he restrained himself. She might not be comfortable with a possessive display.

Abby gave Leo the keys to the cabin so he could return for his motorcycle. She thanked him for everything he'd done for Brooke. He nodded, avoiding Brooke's gaze. Brooke kept her distance, for once.

After they left, Nathan climbed behind the wheel and started the engine. He was glad this vacation from hell was over. In addition to multiple life-or-death situations, there had been enough family drama to "choke a goat," as his father used to say. But he'd also found Abby and reconnected with Leo.

Things were looking up.

Leo shook a tablet out of his prescription bottle and popped it into his mouth, taking a swig of his energy drink. Nathan didn't think the pills were as awesome as Leo claimed, because they seemed to have a very mild effect. Leo hadn't been sluggish during the fight with Wyatt earlier this morning.

"What did your mother say?"

"She's not leaving Ray. He agreed to marriage counseling."

Nathan didn't criticize the decision. Therapy had saved his life. "Maybe everything will work out."

"Only if he gets a personality transplant."

"You don't have to live with them, you know. My door's always open."

"I'm nineteen," he said, scowling. "I can move out on my own."

Nathan had a pretty good idea why he hadn't done that. Daredevil surfer or not, Leo was a real mama's boy. It was one of his most endearing qualities. "I noticed some tension between you and Brooke."

Leo stared at the tree-lined road, his eyes narrow.

"Do you want to talk about it?"

"Let's talk about you and Abby instead. Did you put those condoms to good use?"

Nathan tightened his hands on the steering wheel. Leo's quick temper and cutting remarks weren't so endearing. He seemed upset with Brooke, maybe for taking off her top. Nathan wasn't sure if Leo understood that Brooke had disrobed out of fear and desperation, not by choice. Wyatt had been wrong to put her in that situation, and to force her to write his disturbing life story.

"You know it wasn't her fault," Nathan said.

"Yes."

"She didn't ask for it."

"Jesus, Dad."

"What?"

"No one *asks* to get terrorized at gunpoint."

"I'm sure they don't, but some people think girls

who wear tight clothes or drink too much are asking for an attack."

"Only assholes think that."

Nathan was glad Leo wasn't among them. He focused on the road, deciding not to pry. Leo's feelings for Brooke were none of his business.

"I slept with her," Leo said, scrubbing a hand down his face.

"You didn't."

"I did."

Nathan shouldn't have been thrown for a loop by this news. He'd seen them together. Brooke was beautiful. They were both hormonal teenagers. The real shock was that Leo had managed to keep his hands off her until this point.

"You don't have to lecture me," Leo said.

"I wasn't going to."

"It won't happen again."

No wonder he looked unhappy. "Okay."

"I didn't twist her arm, either."

"I believe you."

He stared out the window. "I should have said no."

"It was her choice, too. Why are you taking all of the responsibility?"

"Because I have the penis?"

Nathan laughed, knowing exactly what he meant. Sometimes it seemed like the center of the universe, the nexus of all bad decisions.

"I don't want to lose her," Leo said, growing serious.

"Give it time, and be there for her. She's been through a lot."

Maybe this advice resonated with Leo, because he didn't appear as melancholy. He fell silent for a few minutes before he spoke again. "I have to get my leg rechecked in a week. I should be able to go surfing after that."

Nathan straightened in his seat. "Yeah?"

"I guess I could give you lesson."

A smile broke across Nathan's face. "I can drive up to L.A. next weekend."

"Nah, I'll come to your house. Mom says I can have my car back, and I know of a nice beginner spot in La Jolla."

Nathan's chest swelled with emotion. He couldn't believe they were making plans to spend time together. A week ago, Leo hadn't even accepted his calls. Now he was the one offering to visit. "I'd like that."

"I'll bring you a longboard," Leo said generously. "It's what old guys ride."

CHAPTER TWENTY-SEVEN

IT WAS A LONG DRIVE to San Diego.

Abby was concerned about Brooke, who slept most of the way home. After they arrived, she stayed up late, staring at the TV but not really watching anything. The next day, she started crying at breakfast and didn't stop.

Abby hugged her and comforted her as much as possible. Brooke had always been emotional. She was demonstrative and dramatic, prone to short outbursts. It wasn't typical for her to mope around in silence or dwell on negative things, but this wasn't a typical situation. She'd survived a harrowing experience. Instead of trying to cheer her up, Abby encouraged her to talk about her feelings.

Ray used his connections to get her an appointment with the best psychologist in the area. Brooke went willingly and seemed to find the session helpful. Abby bought her a healthy lunch at her favorite juice bar. When they returned home, there was a delivery truck in the driveway. Someone had sent a simple sunflower bouquet.

The flowers were from Leo. Brooke read the card and burst into tears. Abby picked up the note to see what had upset her. It was a short message: "Hope you're okay." Frowning, she followed Brooke to her bedroom.

"Can I come in?"

"Yes."

She opened the door and stepped inside. Brooke was sprawled across the bed, her face buried in pillows. Abby hadn't changed the decor since Brooke had left for college. It was a colorful space, and fairly girly. Brooke had never been interested in frilly dresses or boy bands, but she liked stuffed animals and feminine colors. She'd gone through a unicorn phase when she was seven or eight. The figurines were still on her shelves.

Abby waited for Brooke's smothered sobs to quiet. "I've been thinking about turning this room into an office."

Brooke lifted her head. "What?"

"I'm kidding."

She looked around at her belongings, almost as if she didn't recognize them. "You can redecorate. It's not a shrine."

Abby wasn't in a hurry to change things. They already had a spare bedroom that could double as an office. She didn't want Brooke to feel like she couldn't come back after college. She would always be welcome. "The flowers are nice."

Brooke's lower lip trembled.

Abby was beginning to suspect that some—maybe even most—of these tears were for Leo. Brooke wasn't just traumatized, she was heartbroken. Abby sat down on the bed. "If you want to talk about it, I'm here for you."

The whole story spilled out. Brooke sobbed about begging Leo to sleep with her even though she knew he wanted to be just friends. Then he'd acted cold to her. She felt confused and guilty for kissing Wyatt.

Abby stroked her back, murmuring words of comfort.

"I'm so stupid," Brooke wailed. "I thought I could make him love me."

"You're not stupid."

"Now it's going to be awkward between us and he'll hate me forever."

"He doesn't hate you. He sent you flowers."

She made a muffled sound of despair.

"Have you talked to him?"

"I've been avoiding his calls."

Abby understood why she would do that. She was hurt and embarrassed and...weepy. "He cares about you, Brooke. When boys don't care, they don't call."

"Did Leo's dad call you?"

"Yes," Abby said after a pause.

Brooke rolled over, tucking one arm beneath her head. "Are you going out with him?"

"We haven't made plans yet."

"Why not?"

Abby was reluctant to leave Brooke alone at a time like this, and it would be insensitive to invite Nathan over. "He can wait."

Brooke wiped her cheeks. "I want you to be happy, even when I'm not."

Abby didn't tell her that was impossible.

Instead of calling Nathan or Leo, they treated themselves to a girls' afternoon out. They went to a matinee, strolled along the beach and visited the nail salon. After they came home, Brooke made plans for the weekend. She would spend Friday with her best friend, and then ride the train to Ella's house on Saturday morning. Ray had promised to take her to a baseball game on Sunday afternoon.

"Are you sure you're up to it?" Abby asked.

"Yes," she said firmly. "I want to hang out with friends and do normal things."

Abby didn't argue, although her first instinct was to keep Brooke home and hold her close. Being a caretaker was Abby's default position, the easiest role for her to slip into. She was nervous about the prospect of seeing Nathan again. What if their chemistry had been fueled by adrenaline? What if her feelings weren't real?

She spent the next few days agonizing over him, torn between fever dreams and anxious thoughts. They made a date for Friday night. The retirement center was only a few miles from his house, so she promised to meet him at a restaurant in his neighborhood. He sounded pleased, and the low pitch of his voice made her shiver with anticipation. She had to hang up before she blurted out an offer for phone sex.

The chemistry was still there, apparently.

On Friday afternoon, she got ready to leave the house. Although she'd planned to take the whole week off, there was some paperwork she wanted to take care of before the Monday rush. She fussed over her appearance, choosing a sleeveless summer dress with buttons down the front and high-heeled sandals. After a long deliberation, she pinned up her hair and added red lipstick. The sophisticated look would draw attention at the retirement center, but so what? Having a date after work wasn't a crime.

She found a purse that matched her shoes and slipped the lipstick inside, along with a few essentials. Then she turned away from the mirror before she could decide to change again. Brooke and her friend were in the kitchen, making chocolate chip cookies. It was her favorite comfort treat.

"How do I look?" Abby asked them.

"Hot," Stephanie said.

"Like a classy prostitute," Brooke said.

Abby's stomach fluttered with unease. "Is it too much?"

"No," Brooke said. "It's perfect."

"I have to stop by work first," she said, grabbing a light sweater. "I'm not sure when I'll be home."

"Tomorrow, if you're lucky."

Abby said goodbye to the girls and headed out the door. Her "fancy" outfit sparked a few compliments from coworkers and at least one wolf whistle from a male resident. She hid in her office and tried to concentrate on the pile of paperwork. Thoughts of Nathan kept creeping in. About twenty minutes before she had to leave, she abandoned the task in favor of strolling the corridors. She enjoyed interacting with residents and making sure their needs were met. To her surprise, Nathan walked in the front door.

It was almost like seeing him for the first time. She was struck anew by his height and lean physique. He was ridiculously good-looking. Everything about him dazzled her, from his clean-shaven jaw and precise haircut to his casual clothes and strong forearms. He was holding a bouquet of flowers.

Like father, like son?

She came forward on unsteady legs, her heart hammering in her chest. When he caught sight of her, his eyes darkened. After a few seconds of studying her face, he skimmed her body with approval.

"You look nice," he said, clearing his throat.

"Are those for me?" she asked.

He glanced at the flowers, as if he'd forgotten he had them. "Yes."

"Thanks," she said, accepting the bouquet. "My office is right here."

He followed her in, watching while she put the flowers in a vase on her desk. It was a basic, no-frills space. She had a few small paintings on the walls and a photograph of Brooke winning a track medal.

"I thought we were meeting at the restaurant," she said.

"I wanted to see where you work."

Deviations from the plan usually made her anxious. Maybe he *was* a calming influence, because she didn't mind. He'd taken a risk in coming here, and she was flattered by his interest. "I'll show you around."

They went on a brief tour of the facilities. She introduced him to some of the residents they passed along the way. When he met Mr. Papadakis, Nathan smiled and said, "I've heard a lot about you," before shaking his hand.

Mr. Papadakis squinted at him. "Do I know you?"

"He's a famous athlete," Abby said. "Guess who?"

"Arnold Palmer," Mr. Papadakis said.

Nathan laughed at this answer, not bothering to correct him. "Can you name my favorite drink?"

His rheumy eyes lit up. "Iced tea and lemonade."

"You got it."

Smiling, she guided Nathan down the hall and back to her office. She grabbed her purse, walking outside with him.

"Should I drive?" he asked.

"Sure."

She didn't care if her SUV stayed in the parking lot all night. He led her to his car and opened the passenger door for her. It was an expensive vehicle, but not flashy. He got behind the wheel and headed toward the coast. They were having dinner at a restaurant in Mission Bay. Traffic on the freeway was heavy, as usual.

"How's Brooke doing?" he asked.

"Not too bad," she said, giving a summary of the past few days. She didn't mention Leo out of respect for Brooke's privacy.

"And you?"

"No panic attacks, but I've had a few nightmares."

"Of what?"

"Him," she said, meaning Gary Nash. "His eyes."

The federal agents she'd been in contact with had updated her on the case. Human remains had been found in one of the graves Wyatt had marked on the map. They were still looking for the other bodies. When all of the victims were located and identified, Gary Nash would be revealed as a serial killer, and the media would have a field day.

Abby was anxious about the aftermath. She didn't want reporters hounding Brooke for an interview or coming to the house. Ray had said he would do everything in his power to keep her name out of the papers. He'd hired an attorney who specialized in victims' rights. Abby wasn't sure it was possible to prevent Brooke's personal information from getting out, but she could always refuse to speak with the press.

Nathan reached across the console to hold her hand. The feel of his warm skin against hers was electric. She flushed at the memory of drawing his thumb into her mouth. Among other things. Dinner was going to be…interesting.

"The authorities haven't been able to locate Wyatt's relatives in Florida," she said, releasing his hand. "He's been placed in a group home for now. Brooke talked to him on the phone yesterday."

Nathan changed lanes, glancing in his rearview mirror. "Really."

"Do you think he's dangerous?"

"I don't know."

"He left the trail of threads," she reminded him.

"Why is she talking to him?"

Abby wasn't sure. Brooke liked to live on the edge,

and she thought Wyatt was sweet. She also might be feeling rejected by Leo. "She wants to be his friend, I guess. They're both survivors. He doesn't have anyone else."

Nathan didn't say anything more, though his concern for Brooke was clear. Abby appreciated the sentiment. She knew she worried too much. It was a relief to share some of the burden with him.

"How's Leo?" she asked.

"Good," he said, relaxing a little. "He's coming to visit next weekend. I asked him to give me a surfing lesson."

He looked so pleased with the prospect that her chest expanded with happiness for him. "That's wonderful, Nathan."

He smiled at her. "You and Brooke should join us."

"No," she said, reluctant to intrude.

"We could have lunch after, then."

Again, she hesitated to accept. Brooke had called Leo to thank him for the flowers, and she seemed a lot less upset about their relationship. Even so, she might prefer taking a break from him to let her heart heal.

"You don't want to make future plans?" he asked.

"That's not it."

"Good, because I'm ready to pencil you in for every spare moment."

His tone was teasing, but the words made her giddy. Her desire for him had grown over the past few days. Their connection felt stronger than ever. She wouldn't mind skipping dinner and driving straight to his place.

"What are you doing tomorrow?" he asked.

"I'm free all weekend," she said. "I don't have to go home tonight."

His dark gaze cut to hers before returning to the road. "If you decide to stay, I'll make it worth your while."

She'd already decided, but she didn't say so. Not that it was much of a secret. He'd encountered very little resistance from her so far. He knew he could have her again. What he didn't seem sure of was where they were headed, beyond his bedroom. His attempts to pin her down for another date before this one had even started indicated that he wanted more than a night of uninterrupted sex.

They arrived at the restaurant and were seated on the outdoor patio, where they could watch sleek boats sail into the sunset over Mission Bay. Abby wasn't too nervous to eat, and the food was delicious. She enjoyed Nathan's company. He spent a lot of time staring at her, instead of their gorgeous surroundings.

"Do you want more children?" he asked, startling her.

She had to take a sip of water before answering the question. "Is that what you've been thinking about, impregnating me?"

"No. Well, not specifically."

"Good."

"I've been thinking about giving you everything you want," he said in a lowered voice.

"You're serious."

"Yes."

Abby hadn't thought about babies in years. It hadn't seemed fair to bring a second child into the world when Ray wasn't even there for Brooke. Since the divorce, it hadn't been an issue. Casual relationships didn't warrant this kind of conversation. She was surprised Nathan had brought it up so soon, but this wasn't a typical first date. Their relationship was already serious. They'd been intimate. Maybe it was best to address the issue before she fell even more hopelessly in love with him.

"I've spent the past eighteen years taking care of Brooke," she said. "When she went off to college, it was really hard for me to let her go. I'm sure it will be just as hard when she leaves this month. But I finally feel like I'm adjusting to the transition. I'm actually looking forward to focusing on myself."

He rubbed a hand over his jaw, weighing her words.

"Is that a problem?" she asked, uneasy.

"Not at all."

"You're not ready to pencil in a second family?"

"No," he said, the corner of his mouth quirking. "I never thought I'd get remarried, let alone have more kids."

The way he said it suggested that he was open to a second marriage. Her pulse fluttered with a mild sort of panic.

"Now that I'm getting along with Leo again, I don't feel like such a failure as a parent," he continued. "But I still can't imagine starting over. It's such a huge responsibility." He studied the bay for a moment, contemplative. "There's something they teach you in therapy called living in the moment. Being present. That's what I want to do. Hang out with Leo when I can. Spend time with you and Brooke."

Her throat closed up with emotion, because she wanted exactly the same thing. "That sounds nice," she said, her voice hoarse.

They lingered over dessert and left well after dark. Then he paid the check and drove her to his posh downtown condo. It was a beautiful space with dark hardwood floors and modern geometric furnishings. Floor-to-ceiling windows showcased a spectacular view of the bay, which sparkled with lights.

"What do you think?" he asked, as if his multimillion-dollar home might not meet with her approval.

"Heights make me nervous," she said.

"I'll move."

She laughed. "You're eager to please."

"Very eager."

"Where's the bedroom?"

His gaze darkened. "This way," he said, leading her down a short hall. His room had the same large windows, but a touch of a button brought a privacy shade down. The bed was large and low to the ground, with simple white linens.

Abby ducked into the bathroom to freshen up. Her lipstick was worn off, but she didn't bother to reapply it. When she came out, he was sitting on the bed. He watched her walk across the room, his throat working with agitation. She unbuttoned the front of her dress and slipped off her shoes.

"I've been wondering what you were wearing under your dress all night."

She took it off, standing before him in a black lace bra and panties. The sheer fabric revealed more than it concealed. "Now you know."

He pulled her into his lap, skimming his hands along her curves. His touch caused shivers to ripple down her spine. Her skin broke out in goose bumps as he threaded his fingers through her hair, kissing her mouth again and again.

He made love to her as if the world might end tomorrow. She responded the same way, stripping his shirt off his shoulders and fumbling with his belt. He stroked every inch of her body and she explored his shamelessly. Her nipples jutted against the lacy cups of her bra, which were damp from his mouth. He spread her legs and licked her through the fabric of her panties, driving her crazy with need. She returned the favor, sucking him slow and wet and deep. By the time he entered her, she was desperate to come. He kept her on the edge of orgasm, circling her clitoris with his thumb and then easing off.

"Please," she sobbed, digging her nails into his shoulders.

He withdrew from her and kissed her intimately, using his tongue to bring her to orgasm. A few hot licks had her exploding into a thousand pieces, crying out his name. She was still shuddering when he removed the condom, pumping his cock with one hand. He spurted across her quivering belly, his jaw tight in ecstasy. When he was finished, he fell back on the bed, spent.

"Sorry," he said, breathing hard. "I'll get you a towel."

Abby didn't mind. He seemed to relish giving her pleasure as well as taking his own. His lack of inhibitions excited her. She felt cherished and well-used, her body slick with passion. She'd never been like this with anyone else.

He brought her a damp washcloth, rubbing the fabric over her still-tingling flesh with tender care.

"I think I'm reaching my sexual peak," she said.

He laughed, kissing her relaxed mouth. "You have excellent timing." After he discarded the washcloth, he tugged on his boxer shorts and stood by the window. He seemed troubled, as if he wanted to say something.

"Should I get dressed?"

"No," he said, perusing her naked body. "I love you like that."

The words stunned her. He didn't mean *I love you*. It was just careless phrasing. Even so, her heart leaped into her throat.

He raked a hand through his hair, cursing.

Feeling vulnerable, she sat up and brought a pillow to her chest. "It's okay. You don't have to—"

"I love you," he said.

She frowned at him in confusion.

"I'm in love with you." He moved to stand between her and the door, as if he expected her to bolt. "I'm sure this comes as a shock, and I hope it doesn't scare you away. I had this plan to win you over slowly."

She hugged the pillow tighter.

"I just can't wait. Maybe it's because I've been alone too long. Maybe it's because I know how it feels to lose everything. Now that I've found you, I want to keep you close. I want to wake up next to you every morning and sleep with you every night."

It dawned on her that he was telling the truth. Although the situation made her anxious, she couldn't resist him. He was so earnest. So handsome. The hot body didn't hurt, either. She was ready to take the leap and trust him with her heart.

"I'm in love with you, too."

His jaw went slack. "What?"

"I love you," she said, smiling.

"You do?"

She tossed the pillow aside and rose from the bed, twining her arms around his neck. "I really do."

"Are you sure?"

She nodded.

"Say it again," he demanded.

"I love you."

He kissed her breathless, falling back onto the mattress with her. They focused on living in the moment, enjoying the present and loving each other. She agreed to stay the night, and he definitely made it worth her while.

* * * * *

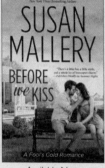

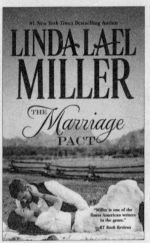

TERI WILSON

Ever since she was a little girl learning to make decadent truffles in her family's chocolate shop, Juliet Arabella has been aware of the bitter feud between the Arabellas and the Mezzanottes. With their rival chocolate boutiques on the same street in Napa Valley, these families *never* mix. Until one night, when Juliet anonymously attends the annual masquerade ball. In a moonlit vineyard, she finds herself falling for a gorgeous stranger, a man who reminds her what passion is like outside the kitchen. But her bliss is short-lived when she discovers her masked prince is actually Leo Mezzanotte, newly returned from Paris and the heir to her archenemy's confection dynasty.

With her mind in a whirl, Juliet leaves for Italy to represent the Arabellas in a prestigious chocolate competition. The prize money will help her family's struggling business, and Juliet figures it's a perfect opportunity to forget Leo…only to find him already there and gunning for victory. As they compete head-to-head, Leo and Juliet's fervent attraction boils over. But Juliet's not sure whether to trust her adversary, or give up on the sweetest love she's ever tasted….

Available now wherever books are sold!

Be sure to connect with us at:

Harlequin.com/Newsletters
Facebook.com/HarlequinBooks
Twitter.com/HarlequinBooks

PHTW875

REQUEST YOUR FREE BOOKS!

2 FREE NOVELS
FROM THE SUSPENSE COLLECTION
PLUS 2 FREE GIFTS!

YES! Please send me 2 FREE novels from the Suspense Collection and my 2 FREE gifts (gifts are worth about $10). After receiving them, if I don't wish to receive any more books, I can return the shipping statement marked "cancel." If I don't cancel, I will receive 4 brand-new novels every month and be billed just $6.24 per book in the U.S. or $6.74 per book in Canada. That's a savings of at least 22% off the cover price. It's quite a bargain! Shipping and handling is just 50¢ per book in the U.S. and 75¢ per book in Canada.* I understand that accepting the 2 free books and gifts places me under no obligation to buy anything. I can always return a shipment and cancel at any time. Even if I never buy another book, the two free books and gifts are mine to keep forever.

191/391 MDN F4XN

Name	(PLEASE PRINT)

Address		Apt. #

City	State/Prov.	Zip/Postal Code

Signature (if under 18, a parent or guardian must sign)

Mail to the Harlequin® Reader Service:
IN U.S.A.: P.O. Box 1867, Buffalo, NY 14240-1867
IN CANADA: P.O. Box 609, Fort Erie, Ontario L2A 5X3

Want to try two free books from another line?
Call 1-800-873-8635 or visit www.ReaderService.com.

* Terms and prices subject to change without notice. Prices do not include applicable taxes. Sales tax applicable in N.Y. Canadian residents will be charged applicable taxes. Offer not valid in Quebec. This offer is limited to one order per household. Not valid for current subscribers to the Suspense Collection or the Romance/Suspense Collection. All orders subject to credit approval. Credit or debit balances in a customer's account(s) may be offset by any other outstanding balance owed by or to the customer. Please allow 4 to 6 weeks for delivery. Offer available while quantities last.

Your Privacy—The Harlequin® Reader Service is committed to protecting your privacy. Our Privacy Policy is available online at www.ReaderService.com or upon request from the Harlequin Reader Service.

We make a portion of our mailing list available to reputable third parties that offer products we believe may interest you. If you prefer that we not exchange your name with third parties, or if you wish to clarify or modify your communication preferences, please visit us at www.ReaderService.com/consumerchoice or write to us at Harlequin Reader Service Preference Service, P.O. Box 9062, Buffalo, NY 14269. Include your complete name and address.

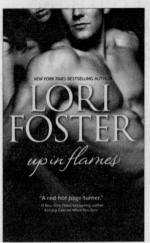